CAPTURED DESIRE

A MAFIA ROMANCE

RAYA MORRIS EDWARDS

Captured Desire by Raya Morris Edwards

Copyright © 2023 Morris Edwards Publishing
All rights reserved. No part of this publication may be reproduced, stored, or transmitted without prior permission of the publisher of this book.

This is a work of fiction. Names, characters, places, and incidents either are the product of the author's imagination or are used fictitiously. Any resemblance to actual, historical or fictional persons, living or dead, events, or locales is entirely coincidental.

FIRST EDITION

This book is for all the ladies who want spanked, fucked, and called a good girl by a morally gray man with a crooked smirk.

Author's Note

He might have the red flags of a book boyfriend, but I promise he doesn't fuck like one. Keep the red flags fictional and read this book instead.

TRIGGER WARNINGS

Kidnapping/drugging
Heavy themes of religious trauma (not kink related)
Religion related discussions of virginity
Loss of virginity/blood
Drugging/attempted rape (not by MMC)
Some mention and on page content regarding eating disorders
Murder, fighting & discussion of torture
Discussion and content concerning grief and parental loss
Discussion of domestic violence and sexual assault

SEXUAL CONTENT

Explicit sexual content throughout
PIV and oral sex acts
Dirty talk
Sex club scene with voyeurism
Spanking
Spit play
Loss of virginity/blood
Light public play

CHAPTER ONE

DURAN

I'd been sent on assignment to much worse places than a resort in Miami. It sat right on the shore, halfway built into the cliff. Looking out over the bluest water I'd ever seen. Ebbing and roaring, depending on the time of day and the weather. Last night the tide had been gentle, but this morning, it crashed angrily against the rocks.

I'd gotten in late this afternoon to find the last available room was the honeymoon suite. Feeling the full irony of the world's most stubbornly single bachelor in the city staying in a suite meant for honeymooners, I booked it. It wasn't like a I had another option.

My brother Lucien owned this resort. I recalled when he'd bought it last year and had it fully redone to match his uncommon tastes. I'd made a mental note to go there and check it out sometime, but I'd never had a chance.

Yesterday afternoon, he'd called me out of the blue. I was doing what I did best—trying to recover from a hangover after working the room at an exclusive party all night. I'd left with the information I needed around dawn, passed it on to Lucien, took a quick nap, and headed down to the coffee shop on the corner near my apartment.

When Lucien's name appeared on my phone, I couldn't help but roll my eyes.

"Yes, what?" I said, putting the phone to my ear.

"We have a target in Miami," he said. "We need to meet up with him."

I glanced up at the chalkboard even though I knew what I was going to order—four shots of espresso shaken with ice and a shot of white chocolate, topped with a half cup of dry foam. Lucien hated it when I ordered it around him. He only drank incredibly masculine cups of black coffee or straight, scorching hot espresso.

"Are we talking *the* target?"

"We are." Lucien's voice was curt.

"Okay," I said, catching the barista's eye. She wandered over and popped her gum, giving me the once-over. She was new, which meant I was going to have to either explain my drink or order something simpler. "How soon do you need me to leave?"

"Go pack your things and have my plane take you," said Lucien.

"Goddamn it," I sighed, leaning on the counter. I flashed the barista a smile and she arced a brow. "Can I have my usual? It's four shots, shaken with a shot of white chocolate and half a cup of dry foam."

3

"Jesus Christ," said Lucien in my ear.

She narrowed her eyes as she typed on the register. She scrawled on the cup and passed it to a second barista standing behind the espresso machine.

"It's Duran," I said, frowning.

"I know your name," she said, reaching behind the counter and lifting a tabloid magazine. I cringed at the blurry photo of me, shirtless and hanging over a balcony, in the upper right corner. I wasn't particularly surprised. A gossip columnist had done a scathing write up of me last month in one of the city's most popular trash magazines. I'd been recognized a few times since.

"Want me to sign it?" I said, taking my wallet out.

"No, thanks," she said, tossing it aside and swiping my card. "You fucked my friend, that's where I really know you from."

"I probably didn't," I said.

I probably had.

"Jesus," Lucien barked. "Having fun?"

The girl pivoted and I scooped my card up and moved to the back of the shop to wait on my coffee.

"Okay, where are you sending me," I said, trying to push the uncomfortable interaction out of my brain. It wasn't the first time something like that had happened, but it was the first time it had me rethinking some of my actions.

"The Aqua River Resort," said Lucien. "It's the one I bought last year."

"How long am I staying?" I said.

"A day or two," Lucien said. "Not sure yet."

The barista handed me my cup and I ducked from the shop, stepping out onto the hot pavement. I was halfway down the block when I noticed something on my cup. I lifted it and looked at the bottom and couldn't bite back a short laugh.

"What?" Lucien asked.

"The barista who just looked at me like I was something on her shoe wrote her number on my cup."

Lucien sighed and I heard him sink down into his desk chair. "Please just keep your pants zipped and get on a plane."

I drained the cup and tossed it into a trash can. "On my way."

After hastily packing, I'd landed in Miami around four with enough time for me to get checked into my suite. I'd put away my things and made a drink from the bar in the corner. The sun was just beginning to melt into gold a few inches over the horizon. The breeze smelled of clean salt and humidity.

Drink in hand, I pushed open the double doors to the balcony and they swung open to reveal a view of the resort. Tan exteriors glistening in the sun, glittering blue water spread out like a vast blanket to where it met the crystal clear sky. Down below were the rooftops of the resort cottages, linen curtains fluttering, bright red flowers waving gently beneath the harsh sun.

My phone chirruped in my pocket, reminding me what time it was. I absolutely couldn't miss my dinner meeting. But before I went, I needed to get some of this energy out either in the pool or at the gym. I could never think clearly until I'd had a good, thorough sweat and then a long shower.

I let my eyes skim over the rooftops and the figures moving across the beach. There were plenty of beautiful women here, but not many who were single. It was a romantic spot, which made it less suspicious for conducting mafia business, but that also meant that it wasn't an ideal spot for hooking up.

Maybe that was why Lucien had sent me here. He was always telling me I was reckless, even going so far as to make me sign NDAs with the women I slept with. I went along with it because he'd been badly burned in the past so I understood.

My eyes came to a sharp halt as they fell on a window just one level below me. The door was open and the table on the balcony had a glass of pink wine and a book, facedown with the spine bent. Just inside the door, slightly out of view of anyone looking directly in, was a young woman in a white lace sundress.

She was stunning. Her skin was tanned like she spent a lot of time laying in the sun and her dark blonde hair fell halfway down her back. I could tell the ends were dyed. She looked a little bit Italian, but it was hard to tell from this angle.

My eyes flitted lower, perusing her body with impunity. Her breasts were full and teardrop shaped with a natural droop that I liked. In fact, I'd go so far as to say she had my ideal shape. My mind wandered to what lay beneath the flimsy lace front of her dress.

She turned and her hand went up, untying the halter neck. The dress slipped down her body and my dick woke like a dragon in my pants. No hesitancy, just fully hard and ready to go at the sight of her body in those lace undergarments. She leaned over, giving me a flash of her round ass, and picked up her phone again.

She was taking pictures of herself. Something ugly twitched in my chest. I didn't even know this girl, but the thought that she was photographing her nearly naked body for some other man pissed me off.

I shook my head. Trying to clear it. She was a stranger standing on a distant balcony. She wasn't mine and I didn't want her to be. I was just taking advantage of the fact that she clearly didn't care if anyone saw her strip down to her lingerie. If she was going to give me a show, I was happy to enjoy it.

Her hips swiveled. She lifted the camera, one arm across her skimpy bra, and took a picture.

I cocked my head, watching as she pulled her strap up again and pushed the door open further. Her head turned left and right and she stepped out onto the balcony.

Her body went still, the phone slack in her hand. Her face tilted up as a cool breeze came off the ocean. Chasing away the afternoon heat for a second.

For the first time, I could see her face in clear view. She had a full mouth, a heart shaped face, and thick lashes smudged with dark makeup. Her nose had the lightest dusting of freckles across it and a hint of sunburn on the tip.

She looked like she was thriving and strong and I found that incredibly attractive. My eyes moved lower again, but this time they made it past her breasts to her curvy thighs, a line of muscle running down the sides.

Right then, I hoped she wasn't sending that picture to a boyfriend because if she was here alone, I was getting a taste before I left tomorrow.

She leaned on the railing and her back arced the tiniest bit. My mind went to the dirtiest place possible and my dick went even harder beneath my zipper. Begging to be let out. My hand drifted down and palmed the rise as I imagined what it would be like to feel her body push back against mine.

Was that crossing a line?

My mind tripped me up. I'd spent my entire life trying to be different than the man who'd raised me. He was an abuser, a womanizer, a coward. I might sleep around, but I never once had crossed the line into pushing myself onto anyone who didn't offer their consent on a platter. That was what made it fun, that was what made me not...him.

I loved sex, I loved the thrill of the hunt. But I didn't use women and I left them satisfied and warm with post-orgasm glow.

I looked down at my cock, pushing hungrily against my zipper. I could go in the shower and jerk myself off to the thought of this girl. I could use the mental image of her unwitting body to satisfy myself.

Or I could get dressed and have my work meeting, and then go find out if she was willing to let me satisfy us both.

I knew which one I wanted. Sighing, I left the balcony and turned on the shower. I thought I had my head in the right place when I stepped beneath the hot spray, but all it took was my hand brushing the overly sensitive head of my cock for me to fold.

My lids fluttered. Fuck, that felt good.

My hand wrapped around my length, jerking it lazily. Maybe this was better, maybe it would keep me from having an awkward moment downstairs. My eyes closed, water streaming down my face and chest. My mind spiraled, filling with a montage of erotic images of her that I had no license for.

Legs wrapped around my waist. Hips pumping as she bounced on my cock. Hair tumbling down her back, my fingers twisted in it. Full mouth parted, panting out her pleasure as her tits bounced before my eyes.

My balls tightened and heat shot down my spine. My palm hit the wall and my teeth gritted. Fuck. Me. That was embarrassingly fast.

Sighing, I straightened and reached for the shampoo. It wasn't what I'd intended, but it was harmless. The only problem—I was still hard. Frowning, I washed and tried to ignore the pressure downstairs as I dried. By the time I had my suit on and my hair slicked back, it had calmed down enough I could take myself downstairs and have a business meeting.

That was a relief. Having to explain to Lucien that I'd missed a meeting because I couldn't get my dick to calm down wasn't on my list of preferred pastimes.

I swiped my phone one more time. It was almost five and I needed to meet with the target and get my work done.

Then, it was time to play.

CHAPTER TWO

IRIS

It was my first time going on a trip alone outside the city.

My father had argued with me for weeks, but my mother had stood her ground and urged me to go. I was twenty-one, she reasoned with my father, old enough that going to a gated resort in a wealthy city would be safe.

That had made me feel guilty because I hadn't told her the truth about what I was really doing in Miami. She was under the impression this was a church related retreat, not a brand sponsored trip.

If she knew I'd spent the last few days in a bikini on the beach, she'd be livid. And if she'd known I was paying for it by modeling and creating sponsored content for a lingerie company as well as the resort, I would be disowned.

My parents were strict, but inattentive. It was easy for me to hide my social media accounts and brand trips from them. My mother spent her time distracted at church and the country club with her friends. My father was a bookkeeper for the Italian-American mafia outfit. He stayed out of the spotlight on purpose. He didn't like the morals of his peers and he justified his involvement by keeping to pushing papers.

My parents were very Catholic, not the kind that the upper classes of the outfit were. Those were all cultural Catholics who went to mass on Easter and Christmas with a long list of unconfessed sins stamped on their souls. They liked the traditions, but not the beliefs.

My parents really believed it. I followed the rules more out of fear than anything, but there was always a little bit of rebellion in me that I couldn't squash.

It was that rebellion that had led me to give my first boyfriend a blowjob in the back of the car outside St. Bede's Cathedral and then slink inside to confess what I'd done. It was fine, I told myself again and again. But the guilt was too overwhelming to risk doing it more than once.

At least I hadn't done anything really bad, like losing my virginity to him. I'd just sucked him off and that wasn't really sex…right?

I asked my cousin and she said it wasn't.

It was the same reasoning I used to justify the way I'd obtained my large social media presence. My parents didn't know that I had an Instagram account with over two million followers and they definitely didn't know that it was full of provocative pictures of myself. None of them were nudes. They were just sexy, so it wasn't like I was doing anything really wrong.

It was therapeutic. It let me explore my sexuality—without committing what my parents had taught me was a mortal sin—and having actual sex.

I'd spent my entire life finding loopholes, I was very good at it by age twenty-one.

Tonight, the resort was crowded. I put on a teal dress with a draping front and a short skirt and headed down to the dining room closest to my room. My heels clicked and my matching purse caught the light as I stepped up to the hostess's stand.

"Just one?" the tall woman asked, glancing up.

"Yep, just me," I said, offering a smile.

"Oh, you're the brand influencer, aren't you?" she said, pulling out a menu. "They said they were having you as a guest this week. Has everything been good for you?"

I followed her towards a booth in the back. "It's been amazing. This is one of the nicest places I've ever stayed."

"That's great," she said, setting my menu down and stepping back. "Can I start you off with anything to drink?"

I slid into the booth, adjusting my short skirt so it didn't ride up my thighs, and glanced toward the bar. "Could I get a water and a vodka soda, please?"

"I'll have your server bring it to you right away."

I thanked her and she disappeared across the room, leaving me alone once more. Feeling like I needed something to do with my hands while I waited, I pulled out my phone and opened Instagram and began scrolling mindlessly. Flipping past a picture of my closest childhood friend, Zita, looking conservative in a blouse and long skirt. My finger hovered over the like button for a moment before I pulled it back.

I bit my lip, setting down my phone. I'd gone to Catholic school and had a confusing experience there. It was strict and I'd spent most of my adolescence with a dry mouth, locked in the fear that everything might send me to eternal torment. At a certain point, unsure of the answers to anything, I'd stopped trying.

I was tired and confused.

And tired of being confused.

My friends slowly slipped away. After I started doing social media as a job, most of them blocked me online and stopped speaking to me altogether. Zita had kept in casual contact, but I knew she disapproved and that cast a shadow over our relationship.

Now, I didn't really have a lot of friends besides a few women I'd met online that I saw maybe once a year for work trips. I was an only child so my social circle consisted of my parents and their friends and they were all the more pious members of the organization. The ones who disapproved of what the upper classes did.

Being alone didn't bother me anymore.

I glanced up just as a pair of men passed by, their backs to me. One was around six feet and the other an inch or two taller. The one closest to me had light brown hair and he was older, maybe in his forties, and the other one had black hair and his face was turned away. I could tell by his muscled forearm, his coat draped over his elbow, that he was young.

They paused in the doorway, speaking quietly. The younger man turned eventually, giving me a view of his face. My brows shot up—he was gorgeous. He had a strong, handsome face with a short beard, dark hair swooped back over his head, tanned olive skin, and a blunt aquiline nose. Exactly my type.

They conversed quietly, standing there looking rich and handsome. I couldn't tear my eyes away. They seemed important and the younger man was a little familiar. Like I'd seen him online or plastered across a magazine. Maybe he was an actor or a model. The city was full of them.

"Vodka soda."

I shifted my attention to my waiter, a young man not much older than I, and smiled, accepting the drink. He flushed as we made eye contact and shifted his feet.

"Hey, I hope this isn't weird, but I follow you online," he said.

"Oh...thanks," I said, smiling. "I appreciate the follow."

I was never sure how to respond to that when people said it, luckily it didn't come up much. He dipped his head and fumbled in his pockets for his notepad.

"What can I get for you?" he said, his tone becoming formal. "There's a new dish we're featuring tonight that's barramundi with lemon and dill and a side salad with a raspberry vinaigrette."

I smiled up at him, snapping the menu shut. "That sounds divine. Thank you very much."

He dipped his head and disappeared, his face flushed again. As he moved out of my line of sight, the dark haired man appeared in it. Still in the doorway, but by himself this time, hand in his pocket. His eyes were fixed on me, clearly sizing me up.

My throat tightened and went dry and I jerked my eyes down to my vodka soda. It was ice cold and frosted with a hint of lime on the rim. I took a sip and glanced around the room. A group of young men had just appeared through the side entrance. They lined up along the bar and the tallest of them glanced over his shoulder. His brow rose and his eyes did a slow up and down perusal of my body.

Warmth flickered, coupled with discomfort. Perhaps I shouldn't have worn such a revealing dress.

I shifted back into the booth, trying to cover my bare legs. The tall man nudged his friend and they both looked over. His friend jerked his head at me, winking and flashing a smile.

Heat crept up my neck. Before I could stop myself, I fluttered my lashes back at him. They both glanced at each other and the tall one reached for his glass, like he was getting ready to head my way.

The dark haired man from the other end of the bar appeared, blocking their path. Confused, I shrank back. He exchanged a few words with them and the tall man lifted his hand, palm up. A gesture of defeat. The dark haired man jerked his head. Accepting it. Then he swiveled on his heel.

He was heading my way. Walking towards me with a faintly amused smirk on his mouth and a glitter in his eyes. Before I could react, he was right in front of me. Sliding into the booth across from me like it was his table.

"That seat isn't open," I said.

He leaned back, spreading his knees. "Not anymore it isn't."

I cocked my head, lifting an eyebrow. His face was comprised of perfect angles, a strong masculine jaw, and a mouth with a tantalizing curve. His eyes were big and almost black in the low lighting. He was pretty and he knew it, I saw his arrogance in the way he looked at me. Like he'd already seen me naked.

"Someone is meeting me," I said.

"No, they're not," he said. "I checked with the bartender and you're here alone."

I glanced sharply to the side. "They're not supposed to give out that kind of information."

He shrugged once, lifting a hand—wrist laden with an expensive watch—to the waiter. "My brother owns the resort."

I narrowed my eyes, leaning back and folding my arms.

"That doesn't impress me," I said. "Lots of people own resorts."

He cocked his head and the corner of his mouth tugged back in a crooked smirk, revealing white teeth. There was something uneven about them and it took me a moment to realize what it was. He had a blunt canine and a sharp one. I cocked my head, surprised that I found it sexy.

He folded his arms over his chest, mimicking me. I tried to be offended for a second, but, my God, he had a nice pair of muscled forearms. Tanned from the sun and speckled with black hairs.

"Fine, no one is meeting me here," I admitted. I leaned in and took a sip of my drink. "But you could have asked before you sat down."

"That's true," he said. "Let me skip that question and ask another. May I buy you dinner?"

I felt my jaw go slack, but before I could respond, the waiter had appeared. He looked crestfallen that I wasn't alone anymore. The man turned to face him and his hand tented, his fingertips resting on the table as he asked for the menu. I stared down at his hand as a slow warmth started in my lower belly.

It was lean and his fingers were long with square fingertips. He looked like he did some work with them, enough to give him faint callouses on the heels of his palms.

They looked capable, like he knew just what to do with them. He probably did, with a face like that surely he got a lot of practice.

"Did you already order?"

I shook myself, nodding before I realized I hadn't said yes to dinner. He smirked again, turning back to the waiter.

"I'll just have the same," he said. "What was it...the barramundi?"

"How...how did you know that?" I asked, my brows knitting.

The waiter disappeared and the man turned back to me, crossing his ankle over his knee. He had a casual way of sitting that belied a lot of arrogance and a little...darkness. Like he'd done things that contrasted sharply with his clean, handsome demeanor.

Was I out of my depth?

"They put specials on the board every night and I know they ask everyone if they want the special first," he said. "So just a lucky guess and a bit of process of elimination."

The first few sips of my vodka were hitting me, melting my social anxiety. "Oh okay," I said, matching his smirk. "I didn't know I was having dinner with Sherlock Holmes tonight."

"Hardly," he said. His eyes flicked down over my teal dress, lingering on my breasts. "I didn't know I was having dinner with Aphrodite tonight."

He knew that line was a miss and we both laughed, the atmosphere relaxing. I took a deep drink of my vodka soda and lifted my hand for the waiter to bring me another. When I turned back, he was watching me with that faintly amused expression.

"So what do you do?" I asked.

"I'm a hardened criminal," he said.

I choked, setting my drink down. "What?"

"But when I look at you in that dress, I'm just a hard criminal," he said.

Goddamn it, he was getting through to me. I clapped my hand over my mouth, trying not to laugh and failing miserably. His lips twitched at the corner and his chin jerked, like he knew he was breaking down my walls and he'd expected nothing less.

"So what are you doing in Miami?" he said, fixing those bottomless eyes on me. "All alone. On your own."

There was an undercurrent to those words that sent a shiver up my spine, but not of fear. More of...anticipation. Like being so far away from home, sitting across from a tall, dark, and sexy stranger, was about to open a forbidden door I'd been scared to unlock before.

My body went still as a realization hit me. I could sleep with this man if I wanted to. He was clearly interested in me, he'd bought me dinner and he was teasing me like he had one goal in mind.

Getting my panties down around my ankles.

My toes curled. If I wanted, I could let him. There was nothing holding me back anymore. Despite my parents best efforts, in my heart I no longer believed it was wrong.

The problem was…my head was still terrified of doing the wrong thing. And it liked to remind me of my fear, guilt, and shame on a regular basis.

I looked up, feeling like a deer in headlights. He smiled slightly, the corner of his mouth turned up in a sensual smirk. Like maybe he would eat me whole and I would enjoy every second of it.

The air between us went deliciously tense. He leaned back, clearly forgetting about his question as his eyes fell. Skimming over the draping front of my dress, over the soft rise of my cleavage, and back up to linger on my mouth.

"I'm here alone," I said.

Where had that come from? I swallowed, throat dry, and wished silently I could take it back. I set my empty glass down and the waiter replaced it in a flash, but I didn't reach for it. Maybe I wanted to be sober…maybe I wanted to see where he would take this.

A trickle of shame moved through my chest.

I pushed it away and focused on the stunning man sitting across from me. His throat bobbed and he lifted his glass to his lips, black eyes fixed to my face.

"Would you like to keep being alone?" His voice was husky, deep in his chest. "Or should I keep you company?"

"Company?" I whispered.

"You look like you're overthinking this," he murmured. "If you're lonely, I can keep your mind occupied. Maybe the rest of you too."

I opened my mouth, choked on my words, and cleared my throat.

"Maybe," I managed.

He sat back, but those eyes burned into me like live coals.

"I booked this resort last minute," he said. "The only room left was the honeymoon suite."

I lifted an eyebrow. "I'll bet it's nice."

"There's a lot of space," he said. "The bed is huge, looks out over the ocean. I'm only here for the night…it would be a pity to waste all that space when I could share it with a beautiful woman."

"Just any beautiful woman?" I whispered.

The gaze he dragged over my body felt like being undressed.

"No, specifically the most beautiful girl in this room," he said.

My heart hammered, but I ignored it. There was no way I was going to admit to this man, this gorgeous man, that I was a virgin and the furthest I'd gone was oral.

Correction...that I'd only ever *given* oral before. My ex-boyfriend had never offered to go down on me and I'd never had the courage to ask. Especially not after the guilt that followed blowing him.

The murmur of voices around us faded until there was nothing but those beautiful eyes on my face. Like a velvet dark sky without a single star. I took a quick breath, realizing that if I let myself, I could sink into those eyes like deep water. I could drown in him.

"You're beautiful," he said smoothly.

"Thank you," I whispered.

His gaze flicked lower. "You have a lovely mouth."

"I get lip injections," I said, before I could stop myself. "I mean, not that often, but sometimes I do."

He shrugged once. "Injections or not, I don't give a fuck, just take the compliment, princess."

Princess. The word broke down my last bit of flimsy resistance and I decided right then I was going to do something with him. Not sex, I wasn't ready for that, but we were going to go somewhere and I'd let him at least put his fingers between my thighs. Or take my top off and put that sensual mouth on my breasts, flick his tongue over my nipples. Suck on them...maybe work his fingers down below while he did.

Heat gathered in my lower belly, centering between my thighs. The thin, lace panties over my pussy felt damp and I could feel a slight throb in my clit. I shifted, my lids flickering as my thong pressed against my most sensitive point.

He saw the movement and he looked hungry. Like he'd been starving for weeks and I was his favorite meal.

"What are you going to do with all that space in your suite?" I asked softly.

"I was hoping you might help me find out," he murmured distractedly.

Daringly, I leaned forward, making sure he could see down the front of my dress.

"What would you do?" I whispered. "If you had me up in that bedroom?"

A twinge of guilt moved through my chest, but I shoved it aside. I was loose with vodka, feeling free of my former life back home, and honestly sick of carrying around the constant guilt. There was nothing shameful about having desires. I'd just had it ground into my head for twenty-one years that sex was a terrible thing. It was muscle memory at this point.

He cocked his head, black gaze flaring.

"You like having your pussy eaten, princess?" he said, a huskiness to his voice that made me want him more.

Flushing, I nodded just enough for him to make out the movement. In reality, I had no idea if I liked it or not, but it sounded nice. In fact, it sounded like heaven to just lie back and have a sexy, dark haired stranger put his mouth between my legs and use his tongue to spoil me.

He stood in one fluid movement and held out his hand, palm up. My eyes traced over the callouses, wondering how he got them. He looked wealthy, he had that casually rich look about him, but he also looked like he didn't mind getting his hands dirty.

I laid my fingers in his and stood. Without speaking, he set a hundred dollar bill down on the table even though we hadn't been served our food yet, and gently ushered me across the room.

"I'm a bit hungry," I murmured, as we stepped into the foyer.

He glanced back. "I'll order something up to my room."

We turned and began walking up the stone hallway to the highest level of the resort. The sun had set and the sky was crystal clear overhead. Stars dotted the velvet blue and the ocean washed back and forth against the pale sand. Everything felt still and peaceful except the pounding, wet heartbeat between my thighs.

"There's something," I said, hesitating. My teeth began gnawing at my lower lip.

He turned, his face gentle. "Are you okay?"

"I just wanted to...I'm not...I don't want to sleep with you," I managed.

His brows moved together, confusion flickering across his face. "Alright...can you clarify what you mean?"

I looked up at him and everything hit me at once. How tall he was, towering over me, how velvety and gorgeous his dark eyes were, how his hair—a little longer on top—had fallen over his forehead in the sexiest way. How he smelled faintly like sandalwood and how there was a single trickle of sweat down his neck to his collarbones.

To a thin chain draped around his neck.

A scapular? No...he was wearing a religious medal with a crucifix engraved into it. I stared at his chest, squinting to try and see through his white button up. His gaze traveled down.

"Are you Catholic?" I asked.

He shrugged. "I'm...it's a cultural thing. I'm Italian and everyone around me is, but clearly I prefer going down on my knees for other things, princess."

I barely heard him. Inside, my chest was a battle of shame and desire. My eyes kept bouncing back to that medal around his neck. The problem was, it was hanging against his firm chest, speckled with just the right amount of dark hair. I chewed my lip. Was it really so bad just to mess around?

I'd done it before. It wasn't like this was my first time.

My brain clung to that reasoning. The damage was already done when it came to using fingers and tongues. I'd already given a blowjob, I already had that mark on my record. So if I did somehow change my mind and regret it, I could go back to confession and it wouldn't be that embarrassing.

I was aware my reasoning was faulty. But I didn't care anymore.

"I don't want sex," I said quickly, my voice rushed. "But I want oral."

He cocked his head, the corner of his mouth tugging up. "Oh?" he said in that silky, deep voice.

He took a step closer and I took a step back and we were against the cold stone wall. Behind us the ocean rushed softly and a nightbird twittered. He bent and his mouth hovered an inch from mine. I could smell sandalwood, mixed with the salty breeze. The scent of vodka on his breath edged the air with giddy desire.

"I'll bet you taste like heaven," he murmured.

My hands clenched together behind my back. His black eyes were so close I was drowning in them. A pool of still water in the night, bottomless and beautiful. He leaned in and my lashes closed. Then his mouth was on mine and I couldn't stifle the moan that rose in my throat.

God, he tasted so good. Any resistance faded and I melted as his hands gripped my waist and bent me back. His hot tongue brushed mine, his mouth coaxing my lips apart. Fireworks went off in my brain. Warmth centered in my lower belly slid down my thighs and curled my toes.

He pulled back, eyes glittering. His chest heaved.

"Fuck," he breathed.

I nodded, mouth dry. I'd been kissed before, but not like this. That was breathtaking, worth any guilt or shame.

How much better would his mouth feel on my pussy?

"You're really good at that," I breathed.

His smile flashed. "So are you."

I couldn't break the moment. Our eyes were locked. Our hearts pattered—I swore I saw his lift his shirt. His fingers gripped my waist, holding me to his body. There was something hard and long digging into my lower belly and it was giving me a raw pulse between my legs.

"Should we go to the room?" he asked hoarsely.

I swallowed. "Yes, I think so."

He took my hand, leading me silently up to the door at the end of the hall.

"This is me," he said, halting and taking his key card out. He tapped it and the door swung open, revealing a luxurious suite.

I hesitated as he stepped inside. He was a stranger and I was about to go into his bedroom.

"You alright, princess?" he asked.

I bit my lip. "What's your name?"

The corner of his mouth tugged up, flashing that sharp canine. "Getting cold feet?"

I shook my head.

"Duran," he said.

"I'm Iris," I said.

"A beautiful name for an equally beautiful woman."

I laughed, shaking back my hair. "You're smooth, Mr. Duran."

"Duran is my first name," he said, taking my elbow and guiding me into the room. The door shut behind me and silence fell.

The bed sat on the far side of the room, beside the open balcony. Its presence was loud. Moonlight and a salty breeze swept through and fluttered the linen drapes over the bed. The stone floor was polished and everything smelled like him. Masculine, but comforting at the same time.

His hand rested on my hip. I whirled quickly to face him and collided with his firm body. His other hand came up and cupped my cheek and then his mouth was on mine. Kissing me again...so gently I felt like a flower opening up to his touch.

A delicate flower.

A crushed flower, breaking apart beneath his fingers.

No, not now.

I shoved my thoughts into a mental box and threw the box away. His lips parted and his tongue flicked through, contacting mine. Oh, he was sweet fire and his heat surged through my veins. A moan worked its way up my throat and I let myself sink into his hard chest as his other hand moved up to cup the nape of my neck.

He broke away, breathing hard. His gaze sucked me in, mesmerizing me. Without warning, he picked me up and tossed me onto the bed, flipping me on my stomach.

"Duran!" I gasped.

He yanked my zipper down and slid my dress off, leaving me naked except for my skimpy bra and panties.

"Goddamn," he breathed.

"Wh...what?"

He raked over me with his gaze, lust simmering. There was something animal in his face and the droop of his heavy lids. A delicious shiver moved down my spine.

"You're the sexiest fucking thing I've ever had in my bed," he said.

I laughed, heat creeping up my face. "I doubt that. You're not exactly hurting in the looks department."

He sank down beside me. His hand slid around and unhooked my bra, slipping it down. His gaze dropped and his throat bobbed. A faint sound came from his throat, almost a whimper as my breasts fell free.

"Jesus *fucking* Christ," he said hoarsely. "You are a goddess."

Part of me wanted to laugh, but the other part of me didn't dare because he was deadly serious. His lips were parted in distraction and his eyes were flitting up and down my body. Taking it all in, absorbing it.

His hand came up and I saw it move towards me in slow motion and then his calloused palm closed around the soft skin of my breast.

Oh my, that felt good...that felt right. Like his hands had been made to cup my breasts. A deep shudder moved down my stomach, all the way to the apex between my thighs.

The corner of his mouth tugged up. "You sound so sweet when you feel good."

My head sagged back. My eyes closed.

I had a feeling, he was going to be worth it.

CHAPTER THREE

DURAN

She was nervous, but her cheeks and nose were flushed with excitement. I hesitated, my hand still cupping her perfect breast. Perfect was an understatement. They were soft and warm, heavy with a little natural droop. There was just something about tits this shape that made the stupid part of my brain take over.

Why wasn't I diving in? She was on her back, waiting for me. Eyes big and pink lips parted.

I'd done this so many times. But something was different about her and it held me back.

"Are you okay?" she whispered.

I nodded, sinking down so I was on my hands and knees over her. Her thighs slid apart to reveal the strip of silk between them. My eyes lingered on the damp spot on her panties.

Fuck, that made me rock hard.

Her gaze dropped and I knew she could see the rise of my erection beneath my pants. My mouth twitched. She was staring at it like she'd never seen a man get hard before.

"You can touch," I said.

She bit her lip. Her hand lifted and grazed my stomach. Shockwaves moved down my thighs and my cock throbbed. Her fingertips slid down and she hesitated for a second before cupping me gently through my pants.

Oh God.

My jaw went tight and before I could stop myself, my hips thrust into her palm. Riding her hand. Her mouth fell open and her cheeks went dark pink, but she didn't pull back.

"It feels big," she whispered. "And hard."

I sank down over her, resting my groin against her pelvis. "I'll show you mine if you show me yours."

Her breasts heaved and I thought she was going to back out. But she just slid her thumbs under her panties and pushed them right down her thighs. I moved off her, surprised. She was a confusing person. One moment I thought she wanted to pull back, but the next she was all in.

"You're in luck," she whispered. "I just had a wax."

"I'd eat it regardless," I said. "But I do love when it's soft."

Her toes curled into the sheets. There was that hesitation again. I put my hands on her knees and stroked down her calves, sliding them under the arches of her feet. Her lids fluttered as I caressed her soft skin.

"Do you want to see it?" she whispered.

"Fuck, yes, I do," I said.

Her curvy thighs slid apart and my eyes dropped. Lightning shot down my spine and I felt the tip of my cock leak into my boxer briefs. I'd never seen a pussy as perfect as this woman's. My jaw went slack and my brain shorted.

"Are you okay?" she asked.

I didn't answer. Instead I bent between her thighs and dragged my tongue over soft, naked pussy. Her gasp rang in my ears and the taste of her cunt exploded in my mouth. Sweet, almost orange flavored, with a hint of musk. There was an element of pure pheromones and it made me want to push my face into her cunt and soak her scent into my skin.

I couldn't find the right words to describe it. My bigger head was turned off for the night.

"Oh God, your tongue," she gasped, her lower back arcing.

I lifted my head, swiping down her pussy with my finger and putting it in my mouth.

Her pupils blew and her breasts heaved.

"Feel good, princess?" I murmured.

I bent and licked in a slow circle around her clit, sliding my tongue down between her labia to the opening of her sex. She was soaked and her muscles clenched as I tongued it, rewarding me with another rush of wetness. My brain thrummed with intense satisfaction.

God, did this woman have witchcraft in her veins?

I pushed my mouth against her soft sex, flicking the tip of my tongue. Licking over the folds around her entrance. Dragging back up to her clit. It was swollen with arousal, peeking out from the hood. I gently took it in my mouth and sucked.

Her eyes rolled back and her hand shot out and buried in my hair.

"Oh…oh…that's not fair," she whispered.

I looked up. "Fair?"

"I don't know—it's just—that's the best thing I've ever felt," she said.

My pride shot to the ceiling. She was a perfect ten in my book and I was the best thing she'd ever felt. My ego was on cloud nine. She could have asked me for my entire net worth in this moment and I'd have written a check.

"If you change your mind about the sex, I'll make it even better," I murmured.

I regretted that right away. Her arousal stuttered and she chewed on her lip.

"I'm not on birth control," she said. "And I'm ovulating."

"I can wear a condom," I said.

She took a deep breath. Her brows scrunched together, furrowing her smooth forehead. Instinctively, I shifted up to cup her face, brushing her hair back.

"Hey, sorry I said anything. No sex tonight," I assured her. "Just mouths and tongues. Okay?"

Her shoulders relaxed. "Thank you," she breathed.

I wasn't sure what the fuck I was doing, but I bent and kissed her lips. She gave a soft moan and my whole body melted into hers. Our kiss started out hungry and turned ravenous. Oranges and pheromones aside, she tasted of something I hadn't expected.

Like the home I'd always wanted.

Happiness I'd chased, but never caught.

Shaken to my core, I pulled back. Her ocean eyes were hazy and her hips rode my thigh, sliding her slick, little pussy against my dress pants. I shook my head once—I was being stupid because my dick was hard and I had a naked woman in my bed. As soon as I finished, I'd get my clarity back.

Her hands came up, digging into my shirt. I slid off her and stripped it. My medal rustled and fell against my bare chest and I pivoted away to hide it. She'd shied away from it before, I should probably take it off.

Quickly, I removed it and balled it up in my shirt before turning back around. Her eyes followed me, huge and round, as I unbuckled my belt and slid my pants off. Not standing on ceremony, I shoved my boxer briefs down and straightened.

She clapped a hand over her mouth.

"What?" I asked, glancing down.

I was rock hard, but otherwise everything looked normal. He hands clenched into fists and rotated slowly.

"You have a huge dick," she said in a rush.

My ego purred. "Thank you."

"I don't know if I can fit that in my mouth."

"Oh, I'll bet you can, princess."

She got to her feet. Gliding naked toward me and sinking down to her knees. There was that hesitation on her face again. Was she nervous about my size? I knew I wasn't small, but I'd never had trouble getting it inside anyone with proper preparation before. If I'd planned on fucking her, I'd have gotten out the lube. But we were sticking to her mouth so she could go at her own pace.

Her soft hand gripped me and I pulsed, jerking in her grasp.

"You don't want to come first?" I said through gritted teeth.

She shook her head. "I want that in my mouth."

I twitched again and precum slipped down my length and dripped onto the carpet. Her pink tongue darted out and caught the underside.

My vision flashed and fireworks burst in my head. Fuck me, that hot tongue was lapping up to the head of my cock. My balls tightened.

"You dirty girl," I hissed, sliding my hand into her hair.

She licked her lips and popped the tip of my cock into her mouth. My head fell back and the ceiling swam overhead. I could feel her tongue lapping up the underside, sucking as she went. It was clear to me right away she wasn't very experienced, but I didn't give a fuck. I liked that she hadn't done this for a lot of other men.

If that made me a dick, so be it.

I looked down, cradling her head with one hand. My hips began pumping gently, thrusting over her tongue. Her soft lips were wrapped around the middle of my cock and her eyes were hazy, fixed on me. Her lashes were wet, makeup smudged on her cheeks.

I stroked her cheek. "Pretty little slut," I praised. "You're doing so well."

She moaned and I felt it vibrate through my groin. Pushing me closer to the edge. Her lashes fluttered. She liked being praised. Her cunt was probably dripping on the carpet.

"Are you going to swallow for me, princess?" I asked.

She nodded enthusiastically, turning her eyes up. Our gazes locked and she pushed her soft lips down further on my cock and sucked hard. Moaning and twisting her hips as she did.

Pleasure shot down my spine and my grip clenched in her hair as I came hard. So hard my vision flashed. Her tongue kept lapping at the underside of my cock and her throat convulsed. Fuck me, she was swallowing every bit of my cum.

"That's my girl," I managed, loosening my fingers so I could stroke them down to the nape of her neck. "Swallow it for me, princess."

Her throat constricted. My orgasm ebbed, leaving me shaken. No one had ever sucked me off like that in my life. Or maybe it was just something about this girl that made it feel like the first blowjob I'd ever received.

She pulled back and my cock popped from her lips, still rock hard. I thought I saw a flicker of that strange look in her eyes. Like she was unsure if what she'd done was alright. I pulled her up and tossed her back against the bed, climbing between her thighs on my hands and knees.

"That was amazing," I breathed, kissing up her stomach. "Has anyone ever told you you're the fucking prettiest girl in the world?"

She froze and I hesitated, unsure why I'd said that. I ran my eyes over her—I wasn't wrong. She was one of the most beautiful women I'd ever seen. But that was a weird thing to tell a hookup.

I distracted her by dipping my head and swiping my tongue over her soaked pussy. Fuck me, she'd loved giving that blowjob. Her pussy was dripping down the inside of her thigh and her clit was swollen and pink. I slid my mouth over it and settled between her thighs, one arm locked under her lower back to keep her elevated.

"Oh," she gasped. "Oh…right there."

I lapped over her clit, keeping pressure on either side with two fingers. Beneath my palm, her entrance pulsed hot. Twitching every time my tongue dragged over her sensitive, little bud. My hips worked against the bed, my cock still rock hard and ready for more.

I felt her fingers brush my cheek and I glanced up. They were slender with unpainted, manicured nails. Each finger had a little gold ring on it, except her actual ring finger. It looked startlingly naked in contrast.

She pushed her grip into my hair, holding my head down over her pussy. I liked that little bit of assertiveness. Paired with her strange blend of hesitation and enthusiasm, it was sexy.

Her hips went stiff. Excitement tore through me, but there was no fucking way I was messing this up so I forced myself to keep still. My tongue moved in slow, short strokes over the side of her clit. Working it with the tip while her pussy tightened under my palm.

Her lower back arced.

Her breath sucked in.

A shudder moved through her rounded thighs and arched feet.

Her eyes flew open.

"Oh God," she whimpered hoarsely.

Her orgasm rolled through her like a slow wave that just kept building until she cried out. I gripped her hips, holding her down as she shook. She writhed so hard I couldn't keep my tongue in place. Instead I pushed my mouth against her clit and just let her grind on it.

She whimpered her way through her pleasure and I only surfaced for air when she was limp on her back. The air filled with our panting. I knew she was so sensitive, but I still held her thighs in place and bent to clean her off with my tongue.

"No, please," she moaned, batting at my head.

"I earned this, princess," I said, brushing her hands away.

She relented, too weak to fight me off, and I gently circled her pussy with my tongue. I knew she had to be so wet inside. With one hand, I pressed her thighs apart and with the other, I spread her open with two fingers.

What the fuck?

She still had her hymen. I glanced up, but she was staring vacantly at the ceiling. All flushed and pretty from pleasure. So was that why she'd wavered between unease and enthusiasm? Clearly she had some sexual experience, but she definitely still had her virginity, so not very much. I frowned.

She should have just told me that. I would have understood, but I definitely wouldn't have taken her to my room if I'd known.

Clearly that's why she hadn't told me.

I took a beat to clear my head. No, I was overthinking this. We'd never agreed to have sex—in fact that was firmly off the table. So it didn't really matter for our purposes that she still had her hymen. We were sticking strictly to mouths and tongues.

"You okay?" she breathed.

I kissed the inside of her thigh. "Just hard and thinking about your mouth, princess."

She propped herself up on her elbows. Her dark blonde hair fell over her shoulders and flushed face.

"Should we just take turns until we fall asleep?" she said, her voice husky.

I moved up her body and bent to kiss her soft mouth. She moaned and her nipples rubbed up against my chest. I broke away and took her chin in my fingers. A little smile crossed her lips.

"Sit on my face," I said. "Ride it and if you're a good girl, I'll come in your mouth again."

"Oh? Is that my reward?"

"You were begging for it earlier," I said, dragging my thumb over her lower lip. "Come for me and then let's see what this perfect mouth can do."

CHAPTER FOUR

IRIS

I woke, unsure where I was or why I was so sore beneath the blanket. My eyes felt sticky, but my body was heavy, like I'd taken a sleeping pill before bed. Pushing myself up on my hands and knees, I straightened slowly and sat back on my heels. A soft breeze fluttered the curtains across the room.

No, no, no.

What had I done?

Oh God, I was in a stranger's bed. Not just any stranger, but the sexiest one I'd ever met. I was naked and there were little pink marks on my hips where he'd gripped me, holding me still while he ate me out.

A wave of guilt so intense it cramped my stomach crashed over me.

I needed to go now.

I whirled, searching for something to cover myself with. My clothes were nowhere to be seen, but his white button up from the night before was draped over the bed. Hesitantly, I picked it up and brought it to my face.

Crisp, pleasant sandalwood and a hint of an intoxicating masculine scent. A shiver moved down my spine to the soles of my bare feet on the cold stone. I slipped the shirt on and buttoned it. My hands shook and shame hit me like a wall of bricks.

I was a whore.

I could hear the quiet whisper of judgement in the back of my mind.

It was a sin. That's what I'd had ground into my head for years. Even without sex, I'd done something terrible.

My head spun—I needed some water to settle my stomach. We hadn't ended up eating last night and I was lightheaded.

Arms wrapped around my body and stomach fluttering, I began padding around the room in search of a drinking glass. The honeymoon suite was big, but there were only two other rooms. A door that led to a bathroom and a door on the far wall.

I ducked into the bathroom and gathered my hair, bending over to drink from the tap. The cool water broke me out of my panic. I hadn't realized how thirsty I'd been all night.

I gulped the cold water down until I had to resurface for a breath. Thirst quenched, I wiped the makeup from my face, washing it as well as I could with hand soap, and went back out into the main room.

Had he left? Or was he in the locked room.

Could I just leave?

Maybe he was on the other side of the door. I glanced over my shoulder, even though I knew the main area was empty, and knocked. So quietly it barely made a sound. Taking a quick breath, I knocked harder.

Silence. I tried the knob.

It wasn't locked. The deadbolt was turned, like it had been secured in a hurry, but not turned all the way. Mouth dry, I reached out and grasped the knob and jiggled. It swiveled and the door pushed open to reveal an office. The window was open, curtain fluttering, and on the desk in the center of the room was an open laptop.

My curiosity was getting the better of me. Far stronger even than the shame in my stomach.

I knew better than to look, but somehow my feet carried me across the room. I just wanted a quick peak, just to get some indication who this man was, and then I'd leave for good.

Using my elbow, I bumped the computer mouse and the screen lit up. My eyes skimmed over the screen, expecting it to be regular business paperwork. And my heart stopped.

This was in inventory, a detailed list of weaponry, bought and sold. Legal and illegal.

My stomach churned and heat crept up under my collar. Under the collar of *his* shirt. Revulsion rose in the back of my throat and I whirled and charged back into the main room and slammed the door.

"What the fuck are you doing?"

My head snapped up. He stood in the doorway, holding a tray of Turkish coffee and a plate of olives, cucumbers, sweet pastries, and bread drenched in honey. Even in my terrified state, my stomach growled. Eyes glued to me, brows drawn together, he set the tray down. Slowly, his gaze narrowed.

I backed against the door, suddenly painfully aware that I was almost naked and he was fully dressed in pants and a linen shirt. His dark hair was mussed, like he'd rolled out of bed and run his hands through it. Last night he had looked so powerfully attractive, but today, looking at me like this, he was terrifying.

His black eyes burned and his face was etched like stone. Silently, he strode across the room until he was inches away. Heat and sandalwood filled my senses as he bent down until he was eye level with me. I bit my lip, trying hard not to whimper as I scrunched back against the door.

"I didn't see anything," I whispered.

"Who the fuck *are* you?" he hissed.

"Just Iris," I managed. "I really didn't mean to snoop, I promise. I just woke...and...and you weren't there and so I went looking for you."

He picked me up easily, hard hands on my waist, and moved me to the side. With a flick of his wrist, he opened the door, and his long legs took him across the room to the computer in a flash. His brow lifted as he saw the computer screen, still on, with his documents sitting there in plain sight.

Mouth dry, I began backing up. I was so fucking sorry that I'd decided to go back to his room with him. Maybe this was my divine punishment for what I'd let him do.

Quick as a flash, his arm moved, ripping something from the drawer. A pistol trained on me. It looked brutal against the soft backdrop of the office, but not against the rage simmering in his eyes.

My hands came up, clapping over my mouth. The scream was muffled, but it split the room. Ice rushed through my body and glued my feet to the floor.

"Who the fuck are you?" he said, his voice deadly. "Who sent you?"

I shook my head, too petrified to speak.

He took a step closer, never taking his eyes or the gun from me. "You seduced me and got into my room, didn't you?"

Tears welled up, burning hot as they dragged down my cheeks. I hiccuped, peeling my hands from my face, and ran my wrist beneath my nose. I was pathetic, shaking, my nose dripping and my body shuddering. He didn't care. He was nothing but hard, cold rage.

"I'm sorry," I whispered. "I'm nobody, I just did something stupid. Just let me go and I swear...you'll never see me again."

He laughed, a short, soft sound. "You're good."

"No," I begged. "I swear, I'm not a spy."

He cocked his head. "Who said you were a spy?"

"I didn't!"

"Oh, yes, you just did."

He surged forward and his hand gripped my upper arm, spinning me around and pinning me against his body. I heard him push his gun into his belt, but that barely lessened my fear. He didn't need a gun to hurt me, he was brutally strong and almost a foot taller.

He bent me over the bed, pushing me onto my stomach. Fear ripped through my body and I bucked hard against him. My vision flashed red as his hand came up to the back of my neck, brushing my hair aside, and gripping the back of my skull. Holding me in place.

"Relax," he snapped. "The last thing I want is to touch you like that."

There was a sharp pricking sensation in the side of my neck and cold flooded through my body. Roaring started in my ears and I cried out, trying to scream for someone. Hoping a passing maid or concierge would hear me.

He slid his fingers over my mouth and I pulled my lips back and bit hard into his palm. His body startled. His stomach tensed against my back and he ripped his hand away, swearing from between his teeth

A little surge of triumph moved through me. Then my vision flashed and began darkening at the edges.

He'd drugged me and I couldn't fight that off. Whatever he'd injected me with was seeping through me like poison. Dragging me into a darkness deeper than those eyes I'd once thought were beautiful.

CHAPTER FIVE

IRIS

I woke on a wave of nausea. My stomach roiled and the side of my throat ached. Beneath me, the world rocked, and in the distance I could make out the faint cry of gulls. I peeled my burning eyes open. What had he injected me with?

My throat was so dry I could barely swallow. I pushed myself onto my side and my stomach rebelled, threatening to evacuate everything.

I pushed myself up onto my elbows. I was on a boat, I could tell that much, in the lower cabin. There was a small window to my left that showed a patch of blue sky, dotted with fluffy cream clouds. Beside the narrow bed sat a tray with a silver bowl, a glass of ice water, and a bottle of painkillers.

At least my captor had some sense of decency.

I grabbed the bowl just in time and everything in my stomach came up noisily, filling my senses with an acrid taste. Flashes of heat and ice moved through my body and I gagged, trying to push bile up from my stomach. There was nothing left. It had been ages since I'd eaten anything.

My hand shook so much I could barely set the bowl aside and bring the glass of water to my lips. Ice cold relief spread over my tongue, soothing the pulsing heat in my temples.

Oh God, that was so much better.

I wiped my damp forehead and rinsed out my mouth, spitting into the bowl. Something trickled down my neck, a bit of sweat, and slid between my breasts. I looked down, realizing I was still in one of his shirts, this time a light blue one.

Anger bubbled. How dare he put his fucking shirt on me.

The doorknob turned and I scrambled back against the wall as it pushed open. For a second no one entered and then the sound of rapid French wafted through. Whoever it was, they were having a conversation just outside. Furtively, I glanced around the room, searching fruitlessly for an escape route.

There was none. The room was tiny.

My heart thudded. My ears rang.

The door pushed open and he stood there. Duran whoever-he-was, the man who had drugged and kidnapped me. My stomach warmed unexpectedly, confusion whirling through my foggy head. He wore a white shirt, halfway unbuttoned, and dress pants. On his feet were a pair of expensive shoes. He looked far too good to be so terrifying.

"Rise and shine, princess," he said, dragging a chair after him into the room and shutting the door.

He locked it and the sound triggered a wave of panic in my chest.

"Where am I?" I whispered, voice cracking.

"On a boat," he said.

He placed the chair in the middle of the room and sat in it, leaning back to spread his knees wide. A sudden memory of myself with the thick length of his cock in my mouth flashed through my mind.

Whore.

Wincing, I pulled his shirt tighter around my body, trying to disappear into the wall behind me. He cocked his head, eyes narrowing. He studied me and it felt like being raked over hot coals.

"So," he said. "What should I do with you?"

I swallowed, the taste of vomit rising in my throat. "Are you going to kill me?"

He laughed quietly and shook his head. "No, I'm not. Unless you give me a good reason to."

"I didn't do anything," I said firmly, gathering my courage. "I wasn't lying to you."

He shifted, cracking his neck. "See...here's why I don't believe you, princess. You are a single female at a very expensive resort and yet, you said you were there for work. What kind of work do you do that could pay for a stay like that?"

I bristled, despite being at a complete disadvantage.

"I'm an influencer," I said, drawing myself up.

His jaw, covered in a trimmed beard, flexed. "So you're an Instagram model?"

I nodded. "Kind of. I just take pictures of myself and sometimes brands pay me to try out products or go to places and advertise them. The resort paid me to stay for a week and then I had a brand deal with a lingerie company. It's not a big deal, but it is my income."

He reached into his pocket and took out my phone. The sight of it in his hand made my blood boil and I lurched forward, making a grab for it. Quick as a flash, he jerked it away and snatched my wrist.

"Sit back," he ordered.

Cowed, I obeyed, but I pushed my lower lip out to let him know I was pissed. He gazed down at me for a moment and slid back, lifting the phone and swiping the screen.

"How did you get into my phone?" I snapped.

"I used your thumb and then I changed the passcode," he said. "It's not rocket science."

"That's violating," I said, drawing myself up and folding my arms over my chest. His shirt rode up, exposing my bare thighs, and his gaze ghosted over them. A flicker of something passed through his eyes before he pulled them back to the phone.

"You post some very interesting photos, Miss Scavo," he said, setting the phone aside. "Does your father know you do this?"

I shook my head. What was the point of lying?

"I don't need his permission," I said firmly.

"I know who you are and I know who your father is," he said. "He's a bookkeeper for the outfit. I don't see him much, so I'm not familiar with your family, but it's my understanding...they're a bit traditional."

My jaw went slack. "How...how did you find that out?"

He sighed. "Esposito."

"What?"

"My last name is Esposito," he said. "Duran Esposito."

My whole body froze and my fingers curled in the sheets. I knew the Esposito family...everyone did. The Esposito brothers had taken the city by storm after the death of their father, carving a name for themselves in just a few short years.

Lucien Esposito, the older of the two had a reputation as a ruthless businessman and an even deadlier underboss in the mafia. He worked under Carlo Romano, the head of the organization, and some argued he held an even greater sway over the city. His younger brother Duran...well, he had a reputation for being an magnetic playboy.

I stared up at him and some of my fear ebbed. He was in the outfit, and technically I was by proxy even if I was a no-name, so he wouldn't kill me. That would cause too much of a stir.

He saw the gears in my head turning and he narrowed those obsidian eyes. Pinning me to the wall with his gaze.

"Oh," I croaked. "Okay, so you know I wasn't a spy then."

"No, I fucking don't," he snapped. "Just because your father works for my brother doesn't mean you wouldn't betray us. In fact, it makes it even likelier. Having someone on the inside, someone who isn't going to attract a lot of attention, would be a decent plan for getting to me."

"You're fucking paranoid," I mumbled.

He leaned in. "It's my job. And I'm not paranoid, I'm careful. And I'm going to be very, very careful with you, princess, until I find out just how dangerous you are."

CHAPTER SIX

DURAN

I left her sitting in her cabin, balled up with fury on the bed. I'd gotten myself into a fucking mess taking her on a whim like that. She was the daughter of one of Lucien's men and it would be a problem when her parents realized she was missing.

Lucien would be furious, in his own ice cold way. My brother was stoic, rarely letting his emotions show beyond a flicker of disdain behind his hazel eyes. But I knew the twitch in his jaw muscle would be out of control when this got out, especially if she ended up not being a spy.

My hand drifted down to my phone. Maybe I should just call him and explain what had happened.

I didn't have the patience for the verbal backlash I'd get from him.

"I fucking told you so," he'd snap. "This is exactly why I don't fuck around the way you do."

No, I was going to handle this on my own. It was my business, I was my own man with an international network that spanned across the globe. I could broker deals, buy and sell weaponry without batting an eye. The least I could do was find out if this irritating girl was dangerous or just in the wrong place at the wrong time.

I went up to the empty upper deck. No one else could come on this assignment with me because the meeting last night had been strictly between myself, Lucien, and our target. My closest friend, Ahmed, had been on the boat this morning, but he'd left before we'd arrived to fly across the country with his girlfriend. It was his boat, but luckily he hadn't minded me taking it so long as it was just out to the private island.

The ocean spray peppered the front of my shirt and pants as I leaned on the railing. As far as I could see was roiling blue, but at the center of my vision, a faint gray blotch appeared.

I narrowed my eyes as the island appeared and moved closer at a snail's pace. Why hadn't I been able to get her off my mind for the last two days? From the moment I'd looked down and caught sight of her on her balcony, she'd nagged me like a splinter under my skin.

Maybe because she was too perfect. She looked like the kind of fantasy I'd make up in my head while I got myself off in the shower.

Perhaps because I *had* fantasized about her while getting off in the shower.

Annoyed, I stalked downstairs to my cabin and locked the door. The video monitor for her room was set up on my desk. I tapped the screen and sank down as a grayscale image flickered to life.

She was sitting on the bed, arms still wrapped around her knees. She wasn't crying, but her eyes looked puffy. Shifting, I adjusted myself and tried to ignore the half-boner beneath my zipper.

It wasn't her, it was purely physical.

She was gorgeous. Taller than I liked usually, maybe five-five, with a lean frame, big, heavy tits, and just enough ass to squeeze in my hand. But even those things paled in comparison to her full mouth and big, blue eyes. Her messy hair was golden at the end and got darker the further it went up.

It was probably all fake, I thought dismissively.

But...I didn't care. Fake or not, she was annoyingly perfect and it made me want to go down there and dump her over the side of the boat and make her swim home.

On the screen, she got up and began circling the room until she found the bathroom. She took the bowl of vomit and disappeared into the tiny room for a moment. When she reappeared, she was cleaned up and the bowl was washed out.

She began pacing again. Running her fingers through her hair and knotting it at the nape of her neck. She had all these bohemian style rings on her fingers, tipped with square, natural nails. I wasn't usually into that style, but on her body...fuck me.

All she wore was my button up shirt. It came down to the middle of her thighs, revealing her legs. Fucking beautiful, curvy legs. I scowled, glancing down at the front of my pants. My sudden half-boner had disappeared, but I could feel the pressure, just waiting for its next opportunity.

There was a sharp knocking on the door. Grateful for the distraction, I got to my feet.

"Come in," I called.

One of the crew members, a tall young man, appeared in the doorway. "We're here, sir. We have the boat set up to take you to shore."

I turned the security monitor off. "Alright, I'll get the girl."

He nodded, stepping aside to let me walk by. I strode down the hallway, so narrow I had to angle my body, and walked right into her room without knocking. She whirled, giving a little gasp, and stared up at me with her mouth hanging open.

I could see a flash of her pink tongue past her teeth. The same tongue that had licked the underside of my cock like it was the best thing she'd ever tasted.

Fuck.

I cleared my throat. "Are you going to come quietly, princess, or do I need to put you over my shoulder?"

There was a short silence.

"At least…come quieter than you did the first time," I said, unable to bite my tongue hard enough to keep the words in.

She bristled and hurried to conceal it, but I caught a glitter of defiance, deep in her eyes. Finally she gave a barely perceptible nod and wrapped her arms around her body. Covering the outline of her nipples visible through my shirt.

"Fine," she said flatly.

She looked so afraid, so defeated, that it roused something in my chest. Without thinking, I reached out and took hold of her chin and forced her to look up at me. Her breasts heaved, her body tensed, but she refused to meet my eyes.

"Look at me," I ordered.

She shook her head once.

I felt my brow arc and I slid my hand beneath her jaw and forced her to turn her face up to mine. Her eyes narrowed, pure hatred passing through them in a wave. Then she spat at me, missing by a mile.

She fucking *spat* at me.

For a second, I just stood there, too shocked to comprehend. Being the brother of one of the most powerful men in the city gave me a lot of privilege. Women tripped over themselves for my attention, they did exactly what I wanted. They did not spit on me unless I asked for it.

There wasn't a single shred of regret in her eyes. No, her jaw was jutted into my palm and her gaze was narrowed on me. Crackling with fire.

"If I were you, I'd treat me with a little more respect," I said coolly. "Considering how disadvantaged you are as my prisoner on an island that no one else knows about."

Some of the fight drained. "An...island?" she whispered.

"Yes," I said. "We're about to head to my private island where I can finish my work and decide what I want to do with you. I was thinking I might just keep you for myself, but I like good girls and you are a wildcat who bites and spits. I don't have use for that kind of behavior."

"Oh, so you just like women who do exactly what you like?" she spat, the fire returning. "Should I just roll over and open my legs for you and you'll give me a treat for being so good?"

She had a lot of attitude for someone without options. I closed my hand around her wrist and pulled her out of the room. "I'm not particularly interested in your cunt. One and done for someone like you."

We entered the hall and I pushed her in front of me, tucking her hands behind her back. I could tell she hated having her wrists restrained, but she didn't fight it.

"Really?" she asked, glancing back. "You almost blew your load just from eating it."

"You are an insufferable brat," I said, keeping my cool because I knew it pissed her off.

"Thanks, it takes one to know one."

"I'm going to dump you in the water and let the sharks deal with you," I said grimly, spinning her as we turned the corner to face the stairs.

"Go ahead. I'd prefer that to being here with you," she snapped. "Still a better experience than letting you go down on me last night."

My patience snapped and I took her upper arm and pushed her up against the wall. Her eyes widened slightly and her breathing picked up. I could smell her when we were close like this, our bodies fitted together in the narrow hallway, and the scent made my head spin.

"Really?" I said quietly.

"What?" Her full mouth parted.

"You came on my tongue, princess," I reminded her. "You rode your orgasm out on my mouth like you were riding my cock. You had your thighs locked around my head so hard I almost passed out. I can still fucking smell your cunt on my face, so don't pretend I didn't make you see God."

Her stomach tensed, I felt it against my forearm. Her lids flickered up to my eyes and down to my mouth. Then she swallowed and looked away.

"Let me go," she whispered.

"No," I said.

"I'll shut up," she said in a rush. "I'll shut up until we get to the island. I promise. Just get off me."

I shifted, realizing abruptly what was making her so willing to negotiate. My cock was rock hard, digging into her lower belly. I withdrew abruptly, peeling her off the wall and shoving her up the stairs without another word.

CHAPTER SEVEN

IRIS

He tied my hands behind my back and put me on the rowboat like I was cargo. Burning with anger and feeling incredibly sorry for myself that he'd kidnapped me, I sat in silence beside him as we moved closer to the island.

The sun was scorching overhead and my knees were getting burnt, propped in front of me. I was completely naked beneath his shirt so I had to sit with my thighs squeezed together so I wouldn't flash the two crew members.

It was a long, uncomfortable ride to the shallow water.

He stepped into the water in his shoes and dress pants and held out his hand to me. The boat rocked as I stood and I wavered, fear bolting through my chest. His hand shot out and gripped my hip, shifting me so I fell against his chest and into his arms.

He was solid, lean with muscle. One arm slid beneath my knees and the other supported my back below my shoulder blades. I couldn't move, I couldn't properly squirm with my hands tied behind my back. My stomach turned. Being this helpless was the worst feeling in the world.

And yet...the warmth of his chest against my arm was sending confusing signals. Did I hate it or was it responsible for the tingling between my legs.

"Please," I muttered, completely humiliated.

"What is it, princess?" he said. "I'm not letting you walk."

"No," I said, cheeks flushing. "My shirt is riding up."

I could feel the breeze fluttering the edge of the shirt, feeling unusually cool over my sex. It took a second for me to realize what that meant. At some point I'd gotten wet and I hadn't noticed until now. My cheeks went even hotter than they already were.

"I won't let anyone see your pussy," he said. "Me, I've already seen it, so what can it hurt?"

I opened my mouth to retort and shut it because my body was a traitor. My nipples ached, painfully aware of how close our bodies were. I turned my head, watching a trickle of sweat move from his dark hair and disappear beneath his collar.

A compound towered over us just beyond the beach. A huge, square building with two stories and a wrap-around balcony. It was surrounded by a thick, tropical garden, with a fountain bubbling by the large front door. If I hadn't been forced here against my will, it would have been a luxurious vacation spot.

He carried me across the sand and set me down on the stone porch. I stumbled and he caught my elbow, holding me while he punched a number into the keypad. The doors whirred and he turned the knob, pushing them in.

A blast of air conditioning hit me as he pushed me inside, cooling my sunburnt skin. I hadn't realized how thirsty and tired I was from the boat ride until now.

He strode inside and locked the door, hitting the button to lower the shades in the front window. We stepped into an open living room and kitchen. Still holding my wrist, he crossed the room to the fridge and yanked it open.

"I'll give you something to eat up in your room," he said. "And then I expect you to have dinner with me. If you refuse, I will cuff you to the chair and feed you myself."

"You're disgusting," I snapped, before I could stop myself.

He ignored me, pulling open the fridge. "Would the princess like water infused with cucumber or berries?"

I drew myself up. "Cucumber, thank you very much."

He laughed, taking a glass bottle with cucumber slices in it out and pulling three Uncrustables from the freezer. He put them into a bag along with a granola bar like he was packing me a school lunch. Then he pushed it into my hands.

His hard fingers wrapped around my elbow. I winced and followed him up the wide, stone stairway to the upstairs level. There was a short hallway and a foyer that looked out onto the balcony. The walls were smooth, white wood with brightly colored, block paintings of flowers and tropical leaves. The floor underneath was cool stone.

He steered me to the left and pushed open a door, guided me into a bedroom. I pushed out my lower lip and wriggled my bound arms. His mouth thinned and he unfastened the binding. The blood surged back down my arms and I rubbed my wrists, my hands tingling.

"You can stay up here while I sort out some things," he said.

I turned, sending him a venomous glare. "So that's your plan? Just lock me up with a few snacks?"

He looked me up and down with uncomfortable slowness. I wasn't sure why I cared. He'd seen me naked, he'd put his mouth on the most intimate parts of my body. He'd watched me writhe and beg for him. That was ten times more humiliating than anything he was doing right now.

But still...I hated how vulnerable I felt under his hot, dark eyes.

"That's my plan," he said finally.

"Okay," I said, taken aback by his honesty. "Can I get some real clothes?"

He gestured towards the open bathroom door, a stone tub visible just beyond. "I had housekeeping bring some clothes up for you. Tomorrow I'll take you somewhere and buy you more."

I glanced back and forth, between him and the bathroom. "You're a weird kidnapper."

"How so?" he said, stepping back into the hall.

I put my hands on my hips. "Well, you gave me snacks and cucumber water. Now you're going to take me out shopping."

His brow arched and his lips parted, a flash of canine showing. A little shudder went through me.

"Now that you're here, I'm sure I can make you useful," he drawled. "I don't trust you for a fucking second, but I need arm candy while I handle some business. You'll look good on a yacht, hanging off my arm like a good girl."

I gaped, heat moving over me in a rush. "I will not be your arm candy."

He shifted, his untucked shirt falling back and revealing the butt of his gun. I stepped back, fear bolting through my chest. Had he shown it to me on purpose?

"You will do as I say," he said softly.

He shut the door and I heard the lock whir. Anger overtook the panic and I darted forward, turning the handle and tugging on it fruitlessly. My fists came down on the hard surface, pain splintering up my forearms as I beat on it.

"Hey," I screamed. "Fuck you, let me out, you fucking asshole!"

I heard his soft laughter coupled with the sharp sound of his footfalls disappear down the hall. Frustrated, I turned and began pacing the room, checking the perimeters of my cage.

The room was made of the same sleek, white stone and white wood paneling. The large windows were locked with a bolt, like they'd intended on using this room as a prison, but I could still see through the thick glass to the tropical garden below and the ocean beyond.

The cool stone floor was partially covered in a soft, white rug that matched the fluffy comforter on the bed. The bamboo table beside it had a lamp and an alarm clock and that was it. It was comfortable, the kind of luxurious I didn't really understand because it was so sterile.

My chest tightened. Back at home, my room looked out over the front lawn. I had a big bed stuffed with blue and white pillows and walls lined with bookshelves and paintings. In the summertime, I kept my windows open and my box fans on full blast.

Automatically, I reached for my phone and remembered he had it.

Fuck him.

Furious, heart aching, and dizzy with homesickness, I stalked into the bathroom. It was much more to my taste with sleek marble countertop decorated with silver and gold, a large stone tub, and a huge circular mirror. On the sink was a vase of fresh flowers and a little zip pouch. Beside it sat a bag with folded clothes inside.

I filled the tub and peeled off his shirt. Stained and crusted with salt. Feeling rebellious, I dumped it in the trash. Too bad for him if he wanted it back.

It was a small victory, but it gave me a tiny sense of control back.

When the bubbles were at the top, I sank with a sigh into the hot water. I caught my own gaze in the mirror over the tub. I didn't look like I'd just been kidnapped. I looked like I'd gotten a little suntanned on vacation and now I was relaxing in a spa tub. My brows scrunched together.

He really wasn't a very good kidnapper. I made a mental note to tell him that again.

It was an hour later when I finally scrubbed myself raw and washed my hair. Swaddled on the bed, I sipped my water and nibbled on my defrosted sandwiches. Through the window, the sun sank lower over the ocean.

I gritted my teeth. I'd rather walk over hot coals than eat dinner with him, but I was pretty sure I didn't have a choice.

I went to get ready, although I wasn't sure why I wanted to look good. In the pouch was some generic makeup and skin care. I rubbed serum into my face to make it glow and dabbed on some lip balm. There was a mini bottle of mascara for my lashes and brows, but that was it.

The clothes were clearly for a shorter woman. I pulled on the linen shorts and tied the drawstring, turning and tugging them to cover my ass. The bra didn't fit, but there was a bikini top that covered enough. I tied it on and pulled a white tank top over it. The sandals were too small so I opted to go barefoot.

I pivoted in the mirror, knowing I looked good. Especially considering I'd been drugged and kidnapped in the last twelve hours.

I began rummaging in the bag for some hair product and stopped short when a box fell out. Fingers shaking, I turned it over. Birth control.

What the fuck? Why had he given me birth control?

My throat went dry and I shoved it into the drawer, covering it with a towel. Heat crept over my cheeks. My parents had always told me it was immoral to use any contraception, so I'd never been on it before. Personally, I disagreed with their assessment and I'd intended on using condoms when I finally had sex. But years of conditioning had made me afraid of the pill.

I turned the pouch upside down and some of my anxiety eased. There were other things inside that made me believe the birth control had just been thrown in by someone who didn't know what women needed. Four bottles of Midol, three tampons, and a snickers bar.

I pushed it all into the drawer, hoping my assessment was correct.

CHAPTER EIGHT

IRIS

He sent a housekeeper, a quiet, but pleasant, woman in her sixties who refused to elaborate beyond telling me he was waiting in the dining room. I followed her, the stone cold under my bare feet, down the stairs and to the back of the compound.

He sat on a covered porch outside at the end of a rectangular table. He had mirrored sunglasses on and he wore the same white shirt and dark pants. The shirt was open halfway, revealing a smattering of black hair between his pecs.

He might be an asshole, but he was sexy. Even I could admit that.

I stalled, but the housekeeper pushed me out onto the porch and slid the door shut. Leaving me to the wolves. He glanced up and his lips thinned. His lean hand rose and he beckoned me with two fingers.

"Come here," he said.

I squinted as my eyes adjusted to the light. The sun was setting in a golden haze over the ocean, but it was still much brighter than my room upstairs.

"Why?" I asked.

"Are you hungry?"

I nodded.

"Then come here," he said, pushing out the chair beside him.

Deciding to obey just this once, I crossed the hot deck and sank into the seat to his left. Faster than I could react, he bent and I felt a metal cuff clip around my leg. I jerked, gasping, and yanked my ankle. A little shock of pain moved up my calf.

He'd cuffed me to the table. The fucking bastard.

"How dare you," I hissed.

"I don't feel like chasing you around," he said, sinking back. "This is just insurance that you'll sit there, be good, and we can have a civil dinner together."

I grasped for words, but just then we were interrupted by the housekeeper appearing and setting down a tray of food. She lifted the lids to reveal a plate of fruit and vegetables, hard, flat crackers and bread, spiced oil, olives, cheese, and cold fish and chicken. My stomach rumbled.

"Would you like some wine?" he asked pleasantly.

"Fine," I said, eyes still on the food.

He rose, his lean body bending over the table to lift a bottle of red wine. He poured a little splash in a glass, like we were in a five-star restaurant, and set it down before me. Then, with his bare fingers, he filled my plate with a little of everything and set it before me.

Deciding I was too hungry to be grossed out by him touching my food, I bit into a crusty, warm piece of bread and brie cheese. He sat down with his own plate, shifting his chair so he could face me. We ate in silence and when we were done, he refilled our wine glasses and the housekeeper took our plates away.

"How old are you, Iris?" he said.

I glanced up. "Why?"

"I'm gathering data on my prisoner."

"Oh, okay," I said sarcastically. "I'm twenty-one. I had my birthday a few weeks ago."

His face didn't change, but his brow rose. "Alright, that makes more sense. I thought you were older because you were traveling alone."

I paused, staring at him. "What?"

He reached into his pocket and I tensed, but when he withdrew it all he had was a cigarillo. I watched him closely as he bent, cupping it to his mouth, and lit it. Breathing in the pleasant, earthy smoke and expelling it up into the sky.

"You're still a virgin," he said.

My body went still and a hot, humiliated flush crept up my cheeks.

"No, I'm not," I lied quickly.

"Either you had sex with a man who was blessed with a very small dick or you didn't have sex at all."

"Oh my God, you're disgusting. How would you even know?"

He cocked his head, putting the cigarillo to his lips. "Because I ate you out and you didn't want me to fuck you. So I checked and you appear to be virgin."

The heat radiating off my face intensified, seeping down my neck and making my throat flush. I gathered myself as well as I could, lifting my wine glass and taking a sip. Hoping it would stabilize me.

"You are sick," I said coolly.

"You weren't truthful with me when we had sex," he shot back.

"We didn't have sex," I protested.

"We had oral sex," he said. "We were intimate and I went into it thinking you were acquainted with casual sex and you let me think that. It wasn't until I realized you still have your hymen that I knew I must have been an exception."

"You're acting like you know so much," I said. "You don't know my sexual history."

He breathed out a cloud of smoke. "You can lose your hymen from things that aren't sex, but the likelihood of you engaging in sex and keeping it are low. I've been fucking for quite a while and I know how this works."

"Oh, really?" I sat back, trying to glare at him through his sunglasses. "Is that where the women's clothes and the birth control are from? All your women?"

He took off his glasses and set them aside, fixing his eyes on me. "The clothes belong to Adriana."

"Who's Adriana?"

"Ahmed's woman."

"Who's Ahmed?"

"My friend."

"Oh, okay, this is all making sense now."

"Sarcasm is the lowest form of wit, Miss Scavo," he said coolly.

That was rich coming from him. I pivoted quickly, unsure how to come back from his scathing comment. "If you're Italian, why do you speak French? I heard you speaking it to someone on the boat."

He put his sunglasses on, but not before I saw a flicker of something vulnerable in his eyes. I'd brushed up against a sore spot, I could tell.

"I can speak more than one language," he said. "English, Italian, French, and some Arabic."

"Why did you learn French?" I pressed, sensing a little weakness in his walls.

He was quiet for a moment and then he stood abruptly, stamping out his cigarillo in a bowl. "Someone taught me. Now you need to get to bed because we have a big day tomorrow."

He knelt and his hard hand slid down the back of my calf and he unfastened the cuff. Then he led me inside and up to my room. We didn't speak as he pushed me in, but his eyes brushed over me before he shut the door and locked me in.

I stripped and climbed into the bed, wrapping my arms around myself.

Was he right? Had I technically had sex last night?

I squeezed my eyes shut. Virginity was a confusing concept for me and it always had been. I wasn't even aware of it until my mother pulled me aside when I was fifteen and told me never to let a man who wasn't my husband touch me.

"It's a sin," she said, her voice low like she was speaking of something shameful. "You have to protect yourself from men. They will deflower you and you'll be different. God and your husband will be disappointed in you."

Her analogy was burned into my brain. I went out into the rose garden the next day and sat on the step and stared at the white roses. Picking one and crushing the delicate petals.

I asked my mother a few weeks later to explain that word—deflower—to me. She took me to the roses that had haunted me for days and crushed a white blossom in her hand. Grinding it until it was limp and creased.

"Do you think the rose bushes are prettier in the summer or winter, Iris?" she asked.

"Um...the summer, I guess," I said.

"Why is that?"

"Because they have petals on them in the summer," I said.

"Men will take all the petals off you," she said, sending me a stare that wasn't unkind. It was just blank, disconnected. "Men don't want women who have no petals, who are just thorns."

She put the ruined rose in my hand and left me there. Hollow inside. That night I went upstairs and looked at myself in the mirror and for the first time I felt a growing sense of fear towards my body. How was it possible that I was so delicate that one minute I was pure and one misstep later I was ruined?

"Do men lose their virginity," I asked my mother the next day.

"No," she said shortly. "It's not the same."

That seemed unfair and it made me afraid of men for a while after that. It frightened me that my future was so fragile and so easily lost.

And it took me years to consider that perhaps, it wasn't true.

Perhaps I could have my own opinions about my body.

My eyes were wet. I ran the heels of my palms over them and pushed back my thoughts. I'd spent a long time trying to unlearn the things my parents had taught me about my body. But they were so deeply ingrained in my brain that he'd triggered me just by talking about my virginity.

I slid back and closed my eyes. Forgetting that he'd never answered my question about the birth control.

CHAPTER NINE

DURAN

She took forever to come down the next morning.

I sent housekeeping up to let her know to meet me for breakfast out on the deck, but an hour later, I was still sitting alone watching the waves roll against the shore. It was irritating and I knew she was doing it on purpose. I kept my face grim, unwilling to give her the satisfaction of knowing she'd gotten to me.

The door slid open five minutes after eight. I glanced over and she stepped out, chin up and mouth set in a little pout.

Her feet were bare except for a thin, gold anklet and I wondered if she just liked going without shoes or if Adriana's sandals didn't fit. Whatever the reason, I didn't care. She had great legs and beautiful ankles, so the less coverage the better in my book.

"Hi," she said flatly, yanking out her chair and sitting down.

"Good morning," I said coolly.

She picked up a plum from the bowl and bit into it, chewing as she stared at me with a narrowed gaze. She did have gorgeous eyes, I could admit that despite my annoyance. They reminded me of a geode, glittering when the sun hit them, shifting shades as she turned her head.

"What? No cuff today?" she asked.

I shook my head once. "Not yet. I'm going to put an ankle monitor on you for when we go into town."

I saw her face change, a shiver of excitement at the prospect of freedom and civilization. It bothered me that she was so eager to get away. I didn't enjoy this side of her as much as the other one—although I did find it stimulating. I'd never been one to shy away from a challenge and she was giving me a run for my money.

"I'm not wearing a monitor in front of other people," she said. "That's embarrassing."

"Would you prefer that or being hauled back over my shoulder after you try to run away?"

That glare lasered in on me as she took another bite of plum. My eyes flickered down. God, she was an irritating little thing, but the way her mouth moved as her teeth sank into the purple fruit was doing things to me under the table. She reached up with her middle finger and wiped the juice from her lower lip.

I shifted, the front of my pants tighter than they'd been a minute ago. Annoyance rippled through me and I bit it back. Ever since I'd brought this woman here, I'd been nothing but irritated and hard. It was driving me crazy. Usually, I prided myself on being easygoing.

But since I'd laid eyes on her, I'd found myself feeling...rebellious. Fuck what my brother, my boss, or the rest of the outfit might say when they found out. This was about me and her and everyone else could go to hell.

"You're following your dick again," Lucien would say.

He didn't approve of how much I slept around, of the money I spent with Ahmed and Cosimo, my colleagues. We worked hard, but we also played hard and partook of the finer things in life.

Lucien didn't reward himself with money, women, or other tension relieving activities. He didn't even sleep with his fiancée. He just worked and schemed.

That was probably why he was the boss's right hand. But I didn't give a fuck anymore, I was never going to be the heir. I was always the younger brother, unloved by our late father, with only my mother as my ally during my childhood.

I checked myself.

That wasn't fair to Lucien. Despite his ice cold way of loving me, he'd always protected me. In fact, he'd sacrificed a great deal to ensure I didn't have to taste the worst of our father's abuse.

A ripple of guilt moved through me and I pushed it down. Focusing my gaze back on the woman sitting just a few feet away. She was my most immediate problem and she had to be dealt with before I dealt with the problems that kidnapping her would bring about.

"Adriana's sandals didn't fit?" I said.

She shook her head. There was a spot of plum juice at the corner of her mouth and it dragged my eyes down. Making me focus on her full mouth, filling my mind with the dirtiest image of her on her knees with her lips wrapped around my cock.

"Are you going to make me go shopping barefoot?" she asked.

"I guess so," I said, standing up.

She stayed seated. "I can't do that."

I moved across the deck and pulled open the sliding doors. "What's your suggestion, princess? Shall I carry you so your feet never have to touch the ground?"

She scowled and jumped up, grabbing a bagel and another plum. As she flounced past me, her body bumped into mine and a warm shock moved directly to my groin. She was sexy when she was mad like this, all her feathers ruffled. Stomping in front of me with her thick ass jiggling under her shorts.

"Stop smirking," she called over her shoulder.

I didn't bother replying. Usually I liked compliant women, the ones who did what I wanted without me even having to ask. Who wanted my money enough to say and do everything I commanded. Iris had done nothing but defy me from the moment she'd woken up on the boat to now and I couldn't get enough of it.

I was pathetic.

Neither of us spoke while I led her down the shore to the boat. When I lifted her around the waist to help her off the dock, she sniffed loudly and shook her hair back. Her lower lip pushed out and her arms crossed.

If I hadn't been irritated, I'd have found her defiance amusing. Instead, I pretended I had no idea why she was sulking in her seat and occupied myself with helping the crew of two men get the boat out onto the water.

Her presence was a chilly vortex. Every time I glanced over, she was sitting with her body in a knot and her brow arced.

Clearly she wanted me to make the first move.

I could give her that. It might not be the first move she wanted, but I took the ankle monitor out of my pocket and walked over. Her gaze flicked over me, and to my surprise, she didn't speak when I knelt and snapped it around her ankle.

Heat crackled as our skin touched. Her hips jerked, I knew she felt it.

I should have walked away, but instead I slid my open palm beneath her bare foot. Her toes clenched. Heat spread slowly up my arm, bringing flashbacks of her body writhing under mine.

Fuck, I was getting hard.

My head snapped up. Her eyes widened and her lips parted. Did she see my thoughts in my face?

"What are you doing?" she whispered.

My hand moved up, encircling her ankle. Her toenails were an iridescent white and there was a tan line where her anklet sat. My pulse increased, remembering the other places she had tan lines. I'd seen them when she was naked in my bed. Three little triangles where her bikini covered her pussy and breasts.

"Stop touching me," she said.

I released her, pulling back and rising. If she saw the half-erection in my pants, she didn't say anything. I needed to get control of myself when I was around her because staying constantly hard was getting to be a problem.

"Do you have a foot fetish or something?" she snapped.

"No, not that I know of," I said. "I was thinking about your cunt, not your feet actually."

She gasped. "How dare you!"

"Pretty easily actually. I've got a tendency to dare all over the place."

"What?"

"Never mind, princess," I said.

I sank down on the bench opposite her and crossed my ankle over my knee. She found my stance annoying, I could tell by how sharply her brows arced.

"Are you always this irritable?" I asked.

She tossed her hair. "No, I'm just riddled with PMS."

"No, you're not."

"How would you know?"

"You told me you were ovulating when we hooked up," I said. "That was two days ago, hence why you're not on your period yet."

Her jaw dropped and a faint flush moved over her cheeks. "It's not your business to track my cycle, thank you."

"You brought me into it, princess."

She was livid, blushing to the roots of her hair. It took her a moment to pull it together and throw a poisonous glare at me.

"You're goading me," she whispered.

"So are you," I said. "Maybe that's the one thing we have in common. Mutual hatred."

"I don't hate you," she sniffed, pushing her shoulders back. She tossed her golden and brown hair again. "You're not worth my time."

I planted both feet on the deck and leaned forward, resting my elbows on my knees. "I was worth at least one night of it."

"A mistake I won't repeat."

I reached out and put my hand on her soft, bare knee. Instead of shaking me off, she froze and her throat bobbed. Experimentally, I slid my palm an inch higher and down. Until I was touching the underside of her lower thigh. Her breath hitched and she bit her full lip.

God, she was so fucking annoying and I was dying to drop to my knees and eat her out until she broke and showed me the good girl I knew she was deep inside. The best revenge would be seeing her whimper and beg with her thighs wrapped around my head.

No, that was a terrible idea.

Checking myself, I released her knee and sat back. Putting as much space between us as possible. Her eyes lingered on me, confused. Her mouth parted and she chewed on her lower lip distractedly. Biting it until it turned pink.

Pink...like her pussy.

I cocked my head.

Maybe I should just admit to myself that she wasn't just a hookup. I'd felt something with her, tangled up in that bed, and I couldn't stop subconsciously obsessing over it. The problem was—was it just lust? If she let me fuck her, would I be satisfied and move on?

That didn't make sense because I knew she was virgin and sleeping together wouldn't be simple. It wouldn't be a quick hook up to pump her out of my system once and for all. It would be messy and complicated.

Thankfully, the barriers that stood in my way were stronger than my desire. I knew of the Scavo family and they were traditional people. If I kidnapped their daughter and took her virginity, it would cause internal problems for the outfit. We didn't need infighting and I didn't need to be dragged in front of the boss for disrespect.

"Why are you just staring at me," she said.

I jerked myself back to reality. She was frowning, her arms crossed.

"You've caused me a lot of trouble," I said flatly. "Maybe I should have put you back where you came from."

"Why don't you?" she shot back.

That was a fair question, but I didn't have an answer. Did I really think she was a spy? The chance was there, but the odds were low. Was I just using security risk as an excuse to cover up something else?

"You're not getting off that easy," I said. "You saw things you shouldn't have. If you hadn't snooped, you wouldn't be in this mess. I'm keeping you until I decide you're safe to let go."

She rolled her eyes. "You mafia men think what you do is so important," she said contemptuously. "It's really just not that big of a deal."

I laughed aloud, unable to help myself.

She scowled. "Go ahead, laugh. You're not doing anything that keeps me awake at night. If you were trying to impress me with all your secret spy stuff, you'll have to try harder. So just calm down."

I couldn't hold it together. Shaking with suppressed laughter, I rose and went to the front of the boat with the crew. When I glanced back, I saw her triumphant little smirk. She was so fucking proud of herself. I couldn't tell if I was annoyed or impressed by her attitude.

We docked and alighted in the seaside town. It wasn't large, but it existed mainly as a place for rich tourists to shop so there were plenty of places for her to buy clothes. She walked barefoot beside me as we made our way to the shoe store, but as soon as we got inside she decided to put up a fight.

"I can pay for my own things," she said coldly.

"Really?" I asked, looking around. "With what?"

She put her hands on her hips and turned to face me. "If you give me my phone back, I can pay from there. I have a job and I make my own money."

"I'm not giving you your phone back."

"I'm not using your credit card."

"You've had my cock in the back of your throat," I said. "I'm pretty sure you can use my credit card."

She gasped and ducked into the aisle, away from anyone who might overhear. "It was a mistake I'll never repeat."

I followed her, leaning on the wall and crossing my arms. "Want to bet?"

"I don't make bets with criminals," she said grimly.

"No," I said. "But you do let them eat your pussy."

"How dare you!"

"I'm pointing out your own hypocrisy, princess," I said, my patience finally waning. I reached out and took her elbow and steered her to the women's section and pivoted her to face the sandals. She shivered as my breath fanned over the back of her neck. "You will pick out shoes and I will buy them. Understood?"

She scowled and those eyes rolled again.

"I would like to remind you that you are my captive and you will obey me or else," I said.

She swallowed, eyes straight ahead. "How can you say that when you're hard every time you look at me."

So she had been looking. "Just because I want to lick your pussy doesn't mean I'm a good man," I said, my voice ice cold. "Push me, Iris, but don't push too far."

Cowed, she picked out a pair of leather sandals, black heels, and slip-on sneakers. As she followed me to the cash register, I noticed a faint blush at the base of her throat. Like she'd gotten aroused again when I'd threatened her. If she had, that would be an unexpected reaction and I was interested in learning more.

CHAPTER TEN

IRIS

I was out of my depth. I had plenty of smart comebacks, but not the way he did. He had a talent for flipping the script and making the most scathing remarks that somehow made me shamefully wet. And he had no problem using them like a weapon, just like the gun beneath his belt.

When he'd told me he was part of the outfit, I'd assumed I was safe because of my father. But now I wasn't so sure. Duran Esposito was a powerful man and I was beginning to realize that he did exactly what he pleased.

If he wanted me to be a pawn in his game, I didn't have a choice but to play. Direct defiance wasn't working. I needed to figure out how to outmaneuver him without succumbing to his crooked smirk and obsidian eyes.

He'd handed me a weapon this morning when he'd stood up on the boat. I'd caught the burning lust in his dark gaze, I'd seen the flush creeping up his throat. And there had been no mistaking the hard ridge beneath the front of his pants.

He wanted me badly and I could use that if I was clever enough.

I watched him from the corner of my eye as we walked up the street. He had a bodyguard following us, but at enough of a distance that we still had privacy. I opened my mouth to make another smart remark and closed it. He was more intimidating after that moment in the shoe store.

He was walking a few steps ahead, looking perfect in his dress attire. I wondered if he owned any other clothes that weren't a plain button up made of expensive, light cotton and a pair of flat front, dark dress pants. His shoes were a bit odd, like a mix between dress shoes with the tread of boots.

Like he needed to be well dressed, but prepared for action at any moment. A light shiver skittered down my spine and tingled between my legs.

He was in good shape, lean and muscular, but not bulky. He could move fast if he needed to, despite his strength.

Then there was those mirrored sunglasses that were a permanent fixture of him. It bothered me that he wore them all the time like he was using them as a barrier so he didn't have to let anyone see his eyes. It made me wonder what he was hiding.

Shame welled in my chest and I dropped my head, watching my brand new sandals slap against the pavement. Part of me, the rational part of my brain, knew that it wasn't some kind of sadistic divine punishment to be kidnapped by him. But the other part of me, the child deep inside that still thought I would go to hell for the slightest misstep, was sure I deserved what he was doing.

"What is it?" he asked abruptly.

He hadn't turned around. I stared at his back, wondering how he knew that I was close to tears.

"What?" I said, swiping the heel of my hand under my nose.

He paused, turning. "Why are you crying?"

No, I wasn't going to let this arrogant man see me cry. I took a quick breath and shook my hair back, straightening my shoulders. Leveling my gaze to his impenetrable sunglasses, I sent him a hard stare.

"I'm fine," I said. "Why on earth would I be crying? Getting kidnapped is my favorite thing. It's been a blast."

He shook his head, but I was sure I saw the corner of his mouth twitch. "That mouth is going to get you killed or kissed. Or spanked."

I froze and my lips parted as my jaw dropped. It was one thing for him to want sex, but it was another thing to talk about kissing. And spanking. That was too intimate and it made me shift back and forth, looking over my shoulder for a way out of his conversation.

"Can...can I just go buy some clothes now?" I asked.

He jerked his head to his right. "In here."

I glanced up, scanning the upscale boutique. We pushed through the front door and stepped into the cool front room, I half expected it to be full of work clothes like silk blouses and slacks, but I was pleasantly surprised that it all looked comfortable and relatively casual.

I stalled by the first booth, watching and feeling awkward as Duran crossed the room to speak with the saleswoman. He leaned on the counter and slipped off his glasses, flashing her a smile as he laid his card down. She looked at it and her eyes widened.

They began conversing in French, which bothered me a lot. He was more animated when he spoke it, adding a lazy flick of his wrist and a shake of his head for emphasis here and there. I stared, transfixed, wishing that I could understand them.

After a moment, he shook the woman's hand and crossed back to me, knocking his glasses down. As he approached, a wave of that faint sandalwood scent filled my senses and a trickle of warmth moved to the bottom of my stomach.

"Just get your things and I'll be right back," he said. "Don't leave the shop, I'll have my guard on the door."

Before I could reply, he turned on his heel and strode through the front door. Awkwardly, I turned back to find the saleswoman around my age watching me with an overly polite smile on her face.

"I'm just going to look around," I said. "Am I okay to just go ahead and try things on?"

She nodded. "Whatever you like, miss. Let me know if you need help."

I gave her a small smile and her shoulders eased. I felt bad for her, she looked nervous. Clearly she found Duran's presence intimidating.

Nothing had a price tag on it. Confused, I brought a pair of shorts up to the counter, but the salesgirl just lifted the card Duran had left and assured me it would be paid for. I decided not to argue and gathered an armful of things and went to try them on.

My family wasn't particularly important to the outfit, but my father was paid a decent salary. I'd always had good clothes that fit well, but they were never anything glamorous. I could feel the quality in each garment as I ran it through my fingers and settled it over my body. The fabrics were natural and well made and the fit was so much better than anything I was used to.

I bought a pile of things and laid them on the register, including a handful of nice dresses. As I was standing there, waiting to be rung up, I noticed a necklace in the glass case built into the front desk. I stared down at it and something in my chest shifted, moved by how pretty it was just laying there against the black satin.

"Do you like it?" the saleswoman asked.

I nodded. "It looks really expensive."

She waved a hand. "Mr. Esposito said I should make sure you got what you wanted."

Why was he being so insistent on buying me things? Was he feeling guilty for what he was doing to me? I stared down at the hammered gold and glittering moonstone, strung on a twisted chain, and decided that maybe he deserved to pay up.

"Okay, just add that in," I said quickly.

How much could it be? Maybe two hundred dollars? The Espositos were disgustingly wealthy, both from their businesses and their mafia work. He probably wouldn't notice if I used his credit card to buy a house.

Or a ticket back to the States.

I stared down at the credit card on the desk as the saleswoman wrapped up my purchases and tucked the receipt into the bag. She pushed the bags across to me and I snaked out my hand to grab the card, but she was faster, tucking it out of reach. Her eyes were blank as she offered me a plastic smile.

"Mr. Esposito asked me to hold the card for him," she said.

Fuck him, he'd thought of everything. He probably kidnapped women all the time and brought them here to buy them pretty things. Like lambs, fattened up and slaughtered.

"Didn't he say to give me what I asked for?" I asked, desperately.

She nodded. "Yes, but it's Mr. Esposito's name on the card, ma'am."

Those words hit me like a wall of bricks tumbling down and burying me until my breath felt like it was being squeezed from my lungs. My head spun as I pivoted to look through the glass door to the street outside.

I was helpless. Really, truly helpless. He was the brother of my father's boss, one of the most powerful men in our city. I was nothing, a complete nobody. I didn't have his kind of money or influence and what little I did have wouldn't save me.

He had paid for my clothes just like he'd snapped his fingers and a boat and a private island appeared.

I turned, defeated. He appeared on the other side of the glass door, striding confidently up the sidewalk and entering the shop. He pushed his phone into his pocket and took off his sunglasses just long enough to scan my bags. I balked, suddenly guilty and then confused about feeling guilty.

"Did you get everything?"

I nodded. "I think so."

His gaze slid from my head to my toes and it seemed to warm, like it was slowly heating up until it simmered like coals. It was still hard to glean his emotions from his face and body.

"Do you have panties?" he asked, his voice like silk. "And bras? Or would you like to go without?"

Indignant, I ducked away from the saleswoman and shot out the door only to have the guard step in front of me. Duran followed me at an easy pace and lifted his hand and his guard allowed me move past him to the curb.

"Come on, princess," he said coolly. "Let's get the rest of what you need."

I simmered as I followed him across the street. For the first time, I had no smart remark as a counter punch. He was right, I did need undergarments. I wasn't angry with him about bringing it up. I was just confused by the way my body reacted when he talked about it intimately. And I was even more confused by the way his gaze flickered over me, all dark and warm like his mouth beneath the sheets had been.

We went to a lingerie boutique, which wasn't what I had in mind. I wanted a cotton bra and panties, but clearly he had different ideas.

I stole a glance at him as we stepped inside and it occurred to me that this wasn't the first time he'd bought intimate items for a woman.

"Do you do this a lot?" I asked quietly.

"Hmm?" His eyes skimmed over the room. He was being pointedly dismissive.

"Do you buy kidnapped women lingerie often?"

His jaw worked and then he shrugged. "Not under these circumstances, but this is my first time kidnapping someone so this is all new to me. How am I doing?"

"I wouldn't quit your day job," I said.

He sighed. "That's tough feedback for someone in my line of work."

I shook my head, trying to suppress my smile, but he saw it before I could look away. A flicker of triumph passed over his face and that stopped me short. Was he making smart remarks to hurt me or...was he trying to get a more positive reaction?

And why would he do that?

"Here," he said, pointing to a table at the center laden with piles of folded silk and lace panties. "Pick something out and go have the salesperson help you with your bras. And please get something you can wear with a formal dress as well because that's what you're getting next."

I jerked around. "What? Why?"

"I need a date," he said. "I have a business meeting tomorrow night and I'm taking you. I told you I needed arm candy."

"I'm not going anywhere as your date," I said.

He pushed his hands in his pockets and raked me over with that gaze again. "Yes. You are."

There it was, that edge to his voice. The one that made me remember who he was and all the power he had behind him. My throat tightened. I looked around, trying to decide how I wanted to handle this situation.

I needed to play to his weakest point.

"Fine," I said. "I'll go."

"Good girl."

I felt my jaw drop and our eyes locked. His face didn't change, it just stayed so casually self-assured that it made me itch with irritation.

"What?" I managed.

"I'm calling it as it is," he said, his voice dropping to his chest, as soft and seductive as black silk. "You're being a good girl. I wish you'd do it more often."

I'd reached the limit on my patience and I was going to be the bigger person. Shaking my head and eliciting a quiet laugh from him, I dipped past him and began taking panties off the shelves and dropping them into my basket. He retreated to the waiting area where there was a cream couch and a coffee machine and sank down.

There was something about his lean body, relaxed like a big cat with his ankle crossed over his knee, that was driving me crazy. He was just flipping through his phone, while I spent his money on lingerie.

It was doing something to me that I wasn't sure I liked despite how good it felt between my legs.

I tried the bras on and found one that was simple, but had to be contented with the rest being a little impractical. There was a part of me that enjoyed the silk and lace, that liked the expensive feel between my fingers, even while my brain told me they were ridiculous for everyday wear.

He hadn't given me his card and it wasn't at the register when I went up to pay. I turned around and he was on his phone, speaking French.

"Sorry," I told the salesperson. "Just one moment."

Tentatively, I crossed to him and waited, my hands twisted together. He glanced up.

"I have to pay," I whispered.

He kept talking, but his hand slipped into his pocket and he took out his wallet, flipped through it idly. He had two silver cards and a black one, which he removed and held out between his two fingers. I took it, feeling like a child, and went back up to the desk.

When I glanced back, he was still on the phone, but there was a flush at the base of his neck.

I whipped back around. Did it turn him on to pay for my things? If so, that was not a game I wanted to play with him.

We stepped back out onto the street and I took a beat, fanning my face. The sun beat down and my shirt stuck to my back. He put his phone away and turned to me, opening his wallet again and taking out cash.

"Go get yourself a sandwich or whatever you want for lunch," he said. "I'm leaving my bodyguard with you again. I'll be back in thirty minutes."

He didn't ask, he just handed me money and then he was off, striding down the street on those long legs. Looking every bit like the kind of man I would have salivated over before now.

I scowled all the way to the sandwich shop.

CHAPTER ELEVEN

DURAN

She wasn't a spy. I got off the phone with Cosimo, a made man I worked closely with, and he'd run her background check and followed up with anyone who could vouch for her. As far as anyone could tell, she'd just been in the wrong place at the wrong time.

I mulled over my situation on the way home. We didn't speak. She sat on the deck of the boat with her bags in a heap at her feet. Arms crossed and eyes fixed on the horizon.

Back on the island, I carried her bags to her bedroom door. She stood back and watched me put them down by the bed, her brows arced. I straightened, sharply aware of the last time we'd been in a bedroom alone together. My mind drifted. The image of her naked, blushing, and coming hard on my mouth flashed through my brain.

No, now was not the time. I pivoted and crossed the room to put some space between us.

"Thank you," she said tersely.

I paused in the doorway. "I'll be back in a few hours."

Her eyes narrowed. "Why?"

"I told you I want you to come with me tonight," I said, stepping into the hall. I leaned against the doorframe and her eyes widened, but she didn't shrink back. Instead, her chest rose in a quick breath. Her arms crossed over her chest.

I glanced down, I couldn't help it. Her cleavage was perfect. As annoying as she was, I had to admit she had the prettiest cleavage I'd ever seen.

"What if I don't," she whispered.

"I can put you over my shoulder and take you," I said. "I took you once, I don't mind doing it again."

Her breath hitched. I couldn't tell if it was from indignation or something else.

"You're not a good person," she said wrathfully.

Surprised, I laughed aloud. For some reason, she'd thought that would hurt me and her eyes darkened at my reaction. Her hands balled and she clenched them behind her back. I leaned in, arms still crossed, towering over her until she shrank.

"Tell me something I don't know," I said.

Her temper flared in her eyes like I'd struck a match.

"Really? Okay. I faked the first orgasm I had with you," she snapped.

"When we hooked up?"

"We didn't hook up," she said. "But yeah, I did."

I couldn't bite back my smirk. "No, you didn't. I'm not stupid. Try again and try harder, princess. Next time go after my weaknesses, not my strengths."

She huffed at that, but couldn't answer because my phone rang again. I flipped the screen, shielding it from her eyes, and Cosimo's name appeared. I frowned—I'd just talked to him. What could he possibly want?

"I have to take this," I said. "Make sure you're ready for tonight."

I pivoted and began walking down the hall and she slammed the door hard. Jaw tensed, I swiped the phone and lifted it. "Hey."

"Ahmed wants his boat back," he said. "I just spoke with him."

I cringed. He had to know I was out on the boat at this point. "Why were you talking with Ahmed? I thought he was taking Adriana to see his family in England this week."

"He is, but I called him to ask where you were because you were being so fucking cagey on the phone. And you had all those questions about the Scavo girl," he said. A door slammed in the background.

"Maybe...I'm just trying to help find her," I said, knowing full well how dumb that sounded.

He gave a quiet sigh and I heard a car engine start. "Listen, we've been friends for a long time. You can be straight with me."

"I always am," I said.

"Do you have the missing Scavo girl with you?" he asked, his tone grim like he was gearing up to scold me.

"What?" I said, veering into my office. "No."

"Duran," he said. " The security system is still hooked up to Ahmed's phone. He has a video of her on his boat. Don't believe me? I'll have him send it to you right now."

I closed my eyes, pinching the bridge of my nose. "Fuck. Okay, did you tell anyone?"

The engine of his sports car revved and I knew he was getting on the road. "No, I'm not a dick," he said. "But you better have a good explanation because I'm on this weapons acquisition project with you so if you fuck it up, I have to answer to Lucien too. And the boss."

I hit the button and the doors to my office hissed open. "I won't fuck it up. I'm getting everything tonight and paying the final bill. Then we're good to go."

"I'll hold you to that," he said. "So why run a background check on her? She's eighteen, she barely has a background."

"She's twenty-one," I said. "And yeah, I did. I caught her fucking around with my laptop. I thought she might have been paid to spy."

"So you kidnapped her?" There was a note of exasperation in his tone. "You could have just brought her home and let her father deal with it."

"Do you know her father?"

"No, not well."

"I looked into him as well and he seems like a pussy."

Cosimo sighed, a deep sound that could only be cultivated by years of friendship.

"Are you sleeping with her, Duran?" he said.

I sank down at my desk and propped my feet up on the edge. "We hooked up, but it was just hands and mouths. She didn't want to fuck."

He was quiet for a beat.

"Do you...did you kidnap this girl because you *like* her?" he asked.

"No," I snapped.

"Be fucking honest, man, I know when you're lying."

I ran a frustrated hand over my face. "I don't know, I don't know. All I can say is she's different than what I thought. She feels different and she's driving me insane."

"If you slept with her, would you still feel that way?"

I shrugged. "I don't know, but I think I would."

There was another short silence. The motor of his car quieted and the door slammed again. His feet crunched over gravel.

"As your colleague, I should say don't pursue this," he said. "But as your friend, go for it. You've never told me you felt anything for any woman before now. If this is what you want, go all in. Fuck her—what's her family going to do about it?"

CHAPTER TWELVE

IRIS

He brought me the toiletries I requested and left them hanging on my doorknob. I showered, shaved every inch of my body including between my thighs, and rubbed lotion into my skin until it was supple and shimmery.

I took out the dress I'd purchased for tonight. It wasn't my style, but I did like that it was elegant. It was a simple black dress that went to the ground with a slit up to my lower thigh. The top was a halter with a corset bodice that cupped my breasts and brought them up high. I slid it on and turned back and forth, appreciating the beautiful silhouette.

It needed something else. I went into the bedroom and took out the hard case that held the moonstone necklace. When I snapped it open, a discreet slip of paper fell out. I caught it and turned it over and my jaw went slack.

A wave of shock moved through me.

Fuck, I was in trouble. Twenty-thousand dollars. For this necklace. This one necklace.

I wasn't sure if I was going pale or green. He was going to be pissed. It was one thing to buy clothes, which were about a hundred dollars apiece, but it was another to spend that much money on unnecessary jewelry. I took a shuddering breath, trying to decide what to do next.

Would he be angry? Should I just confess and give it back? Maybe he could return it and we could forget about this whole thing.

My hands shook as I finished my makeup and hair and slipped the heels on. Taking a deep breath, I gathered up the box and forced myself to walk downstairs.

The housekeeper was standing in the hall, getting ready to leave for the night.

"Um, excuse me," I said. "Um…where can I find Duran?"

Her eyes darted over me. "I think he's in his office, ma'am."

"Where is it?"

"Down the hall," she said, pointing. "Please, I would knock first."

Heart thudding, I nodded and headed down the hallway. At the end was a black door with a buzzer and a place to swipe a key card. Confused, I knocked once and then a little harder just in case he hadn't heard me. There was a slight hiss and I jumped back as the doors slid ajar to reveal Duran sitting at a white desk in a minimalist office.

He glanced up, lifting a hand to beckon me inside. I went, my palms sweaty on the jewelry box. The door hissed shut and suddenly I felt stupid that I'd come to him about this. I didn't owe him anything, but I also wanted to be on his good side.

He closed his computer and got to his feet. I couldn't control my eyes and they wandered up and down his body. Taking in his black shirt and pants, his open collar. He still wore that religious medal around his neck. It rested in the dark hair between his pectorals.

"Can I help you, Iris?" he asked.

I crossed to the desk and set the box down with a sharp click. My heartbeat picked up again. No part of me wanted to admit my mistake to him of all people. Not after the way he'd behaved this morning.

"I bought this necklace not realizing how much it was," I said. "I thought it was maybe a few hundred dollars and it's a lot more than that. So...the receipt is in the box. You can take it back."

His lip curled back in a smirk, revealing a flash of his pointed canine. He stood and picked up the box, snapping the lid back, and gazed down at the moonstone.

"How much was it?"

I stared at him. Was that a note of amusement in his voice?

"Twenty-thousand," I said, clearing my throat.

"Oh, I didn't notice," he said.

"Well," I floundered. "Here it is. I don't...want to be in your debt for that much. Even though technically I'm not because you kidnapped me."

His brow lifted. "Do you know any other kidnapping victims who get treated like you have? I don't think you're suffering."

"That doesn't change that I'm here against my will."

He leveled his gaze on me, narrowing his eyes. "Keep it. Wear it tonight. I like the thought of you with twenty thousand dollars of my money around your neck."

I'd never had arousal surge through me so quickly before. It moved in my veins like an electric shock and centered between my thighs. My pussy tingled and I shifted my legs, acutely aware of how slippery my sex was against my panties. His eyes dropped, catching the movement. The corner of his mouth twitched.

"Why?" I whispered.

He took a step closer and I backed up. He was tall and he smelled even better than usual tonight. Up close, I could see the dark hairs on his chest in high definition and my hand itched to reach up and touch them.

Maybe unfasten his top button. I'd seen his stomach before and I knew how firm and warm the ridges beneath his skin were. My brain spiraled back to that night.

His hand came up and the tip of his middle finger touched the side of my throat.

Zing. Heat like lightning moved down. My breasts tingled and my nipples went tight beneath my dress.

His lips parted. The tip of his tongue flicked out to wet them. Oh my God, he was going to kiss me.

Why? All we'd done was fight and threaten each other since he'd kidnapped me.

His lids fell.

I forgot all about my previous plan to use his desire to manipulate him. My heart thumped, out of control. He was looking at my mouth, intently like there was nothing else in the room. Unable to stop myself, I felt my lips part and my tongue dart out. His throat bobbed.

His grip closed around my neck. Tight and warm, but somehow gentle at the same time. His gaze flicked up and met mine and a shiver moved down my spine. Those eyes were darker than usual—pure obsidian. Clouded with lust beneath heavy lids.

He pulled me against his body in a quick gesture. We collided, panting.

"What—"

"Shut up," he hissed.

His mouth came down on mine. Hot and tasting like heaven. My limbs went completely limp and I melted into his chest. His free arm wrapped around my body, bending me back. His other hand had a grip on my throat, holding my head in place.

His mouth—God, his mouth was ruining mine.

My ears roared. His lips moved over mine, forcing them apart. His hot tongue swiped between my teeth. Flicking briefly up and hitting the roof of my mouth. Making my eyes roll back beneath my closed lids.

I'd had the unfortunate experience of dating someone in high school who insisted on pushing his entire tongue into my mouth every time we kissed. It had completely turned me off tongue kissing for years.

In a second, Duran had turned me back onto it.

It helped that he was fucking amazing at it. His mouth moved hungrily over mine, applying the perfect amount of pressure. When my lips parted for him, his tongue flicked between them and brushed mine. Offering me just a taste of him and leaving me wanting for more.

We broke apart. Both panting hard.

His palm came up, eyes still distracted with lust, and gripped my jaw. My mouth parted and he bent. It took me a second to realize what he was doing, but it was too late to pull back.

He spat, just a little bit, onto my tongue.

My body tingled and I swallowed without even thinking about it. He released my jaw and I stared up at him, my mouth hanging open.

"Better shut that," he breathed. "I might get ideas."

"You…you spat in my mouth," I whispered.

The corner of his mouth turned up in a crooked smirk. "Want to spit in mine?"

My mind was completely blank and my body was one fire. I forgot all about how much I was supposed to hate him. I forgot he'd kidnapped me and spent the last few days tormenting me.

"How—what?"

He picked me up, pushing my skirt up around my thighs so I could straddle his lap. He was hard, I saw a flash of his length pushing up beneath his pants. His arm slid around my waist, pulling me close. His lip rose, flashing that sharp canine.

"Go on, you want to, you little slut," he urged.

"I do not," I gasped.

He cocked his head. "Then why are your nipples so hard I can see them through your dress, princess?"

My hand shot up and I gripped his jaw. He opened his mouth and before I could lose my nerve, I spat a tiny bit onto his tongue. He flashed a grin up at me and his throat bobbed.

"You taste good," he said. "Give me more."

My forehead scrunched. This time when I spat past his lips, I gave him a taste of me. He'd asked for it. He groaned slightly, shifting in his seat so he was level with me. His thumb slid over my chin, tugging my lips apart.

And he spat it all back into my mouth.

"Swallow it," he ordered.

Glowing with heat, my throat moved reflexively. That smirk slid into place and his eyes dropped, studying my mouth like he wanted to kiss me again. Like he wanted to consume my breath and meld his tongue with mine.

"If you want to do dirty things to me, princess, all you have to do is ask," he murmured.

"I don't," I managed.

He leaned in before I could say anything else and kissed me again. Heat poured down through my chest and centered between my thighs. My panties were drenched and there was a frustrated burning deep inside.

Without thinking, I brought my hands up. My fingertips brushed his jaw, running through his short beard.

He moaned and his hips shifted, trying to work up against my pelvis. His shirt shifted at that moment and the religious medal slid into view. My entire body froze. My stomach turned and went slightly sick. That familiar feeling of weighing my own damnation settled over me.

"What?" he asked, still breathless.

My brows drew together. "Why do you wear that?"

"Huh?" He glanced down and his hand went up, picking up the medal. "Oh, it's nothing. It was a gift from my mother before she passed."

I chewed my lip, trying to breathe through my anxiety. My fingers tightened on his chest as I pushed back to climb off his lap, but he stopped me. The arousal had left his face, but it hadn't been replaced with his usual mockery. Instead, there was faint concern in his eyes.

"What is the problem with my medal?" he asked.

My wrists rotated involuntarily. My only outlet for my emotions. He glanced down and noticed the repetitive motion and to my surprise, he gripped my hands and held them steady. His palms were warm.

They were comforting.

"I don't have a problem with your medal," I said. "It makes sense, the reason you wear it."

His mouth thinned. "Are you all fucked up with shame, princess?"

I blinked. "What?"

"You're not the first Catholic girl I've met," he said.

I knew that met equaled fucked. A foreign emotion stirred...buried deep down. An ugly, *envious* sensation.

"What does that mean?" I snapped.

He shrugged. "A lot of the Catholic girls I've met from very traditional backgrounds are confused, ashamed, horny, and have eating disorders. It's in the starter pack, I guess."

My jaw dropped. "Generalizing much?"

"It's been my personal experience," he said. "I'm sure there are some that are very well adjusted. I just haven't met them."

I blinked, trying to gather myself. "Well, I don't have an eating disorder," I said.

"I was right on three accounts," he said.

All the fight drained out of me. His words were light, but there wasn't a hint of mockery in them, and his face was...kind. I swallowed, feeling my walls crumble. Suddenly my pride didn't seem so important. I fidgeted, but he didn't release my wrists.

"What are you thinking when you balk at the prospect of sex?" he asked, his voice low.

I swallowed, refusing to meet his eyes. "I dread the shame that comes with it. My mother took me outside when I was young and crushed a flower in her hand and told me that was what I'd become if I let men touch me. She told me that no one wants a rose without petals."

There was a long, embarrassing silence.

"Well, lucky you're not a fucking flower," he said.

I glanced up and shock rippled through my chest. He looked upset...why did he look upset?

"I realize that," I whispered. "But I spent a long time believing it."

He cocked his head, still holding me tight.

"Do you see yourself as a participant in the sexual things we do together?" he asked. "Or are you simply the thing that I do things to?"

My jaw dropped. I'd never been able to pinpoint that feeling exactly, but somehow he'd cut right to the heart of it and laid it bare. In all its ugliness.

"Yes," I managed. "How did you know that?"

He cleared his throat. "I knew another woman a lot like you. Shamed, shaped into what the people around her wanted, used, and ultimately broken. Religion didn't do that to her, but it was used as a tool to make her just a thing to the man who abused her."

I was quiet. There was so much pain behind his eyes.

"She was devoutly religious, but she used her beads to pray for others, not count their sins," he said. "She was a good person."

His mother—he was talking about his mother. Confusion swirled in my chest. Was I supposed to comfort him? Deep inside, I wanted to, but we'd also done nothing but fight with each other up until now. And, although it didn't feel like it, we didn't know each other well.

He broke the tension by pinning both of my hands together and yanking me in. My heart began pattering again. The blood surged to my head and my ears rushed. His mouth brushed over mine and he kissed it. When he pulled back, his eyes were shuttered.

Like frost had settled over him.

"I'll bet I can fix all that," he said forcefully. "Let me take you upstairs and fuck the shame out of you, princess, and you'll be so tired you won't be able to feel guilty about it."

CHAPTER THIRTEEN

DURAN

That was the wrong thing to say, but I needed out. Physical closeness was easy, emotional closeness wasn't my area of expertise. She drew back like she'd been slapped. The familiar scrunch of her brows returned, along with a pout I was familiar with at this point.

We'd gotten too intimate and it was my fault. I'd never intended on telling her anything about me. Much less about my past.

"You're disgusting," she said, disappointment in her voice. "I thought for a second you were human, but joke's on me."

My phone beeped. With her still in my lap, I reached for it and swiped. The boat was here, waiting for us on the shore. She gave a short huff and started to wriggle away. My hand shot out, sliding around her waist to keep her still.

"No," I said. "Keep your ass right where it is."

Another message appeared. This was from Lucien and it was brusque as usual.

Confirm when items are secured.

I typed out an answer and sent it. She sat quietly, her bare thighs still wrapped around my waist. I was surprised she wasn't fighting me to get away. My ego purred at the idea that she liked being in my lap. When I set aside my phone and looked up, she sent me a dark glare.

"May I get off your lap, your majesty?"

I arced my brow. "I like that attitude. Good girl."

Her cheeks went pink. "Shut up."

"The only way I'll be quiet is if you shut me up with your cunt on my face," I said.

Her jaw dropped. This time she jumped from my lap and pushed her tight skirt down her thighs. I dragged my eyes up those curvy, long legs and let them linger on the little dip of her pussy beneath the fabric.

"You're disgusting," she said, lifting her chin.

"So are you."

Her fists clenched as she trembled with annoyance. I rose and brushed off my suit, buttoning it. My hand shot out and closed around her wrist, pulling her against my body.

Her breasts heaved. Fighting the tight neckline holding them back. My mind flitted back to when she'd taken off her bra that night at the resort. There was no doubt in my mind that she had the most perfect breasts I'd ever seen. It was too bad we were at odds.

Otherwise, I'd take her top down and put my mouth on those hard, pink nipples. I'd suck them and curl my tongue around them. I'd cup the soft heaviness of them and leave little marks on her skin with my teeth.

I'd turn her around and fuck her naked in front of a mirror. Just so I could see her pretty ocean eyes grow wide and watch her tits bounce at the same time.

"Hello?"

I blinked, coming down to earth hard. My cock was hard again. I released her and stepped back, leaving her staring at me. Bewildered.

"The boat is waiting. You will stay by my side or within my sight tonight," I said. "This is a business party, which means it's not safe for you to be alone."

"You know what? Fine, I'll go with you," she said, rolling her eyes.

That was good enough for me. I led the way outside and down the beach where the transport boat waited for us. She sat on the deck with her hair whipping in the wind, looking like a fucking goddess in that dress, the moonstone resting just above her cleavage.

My dick twitched.

The sun was setting as we pulled up beside the yacht and I saw her jaw drop slowly. Her eyes were round and she stayed close to me as we alighted the deck and entered the group of partygoers. She kept turning in circles, like she couldn't believe her eyes, and it was making me nervous.

She looked like a target. Like a very young woman completely out of her depth.

I took her elbow, skimming my fingers down and interwove them with her small hand. Her arm tensed and she glanced up at me, eyes glinting in the setting sun.

"What are you doing?" she whispered.

"Keeping you with me," I said, leading her across the deck to the bar. "You need to pretend to be my woman. These men aren't safe and you need protection."

She nodded once. "Okay, I get it."

We both ordered drinks and I stared her down as we waited, amazed by how quickly she oscillated between being a wildcat and a good girl who clung to me for protection. The bartender handed her an Aperol Spritz and me a dash of Japanese whiskey in a short glass and I took her arm and guided her to the railing.

There was a group of men talking among each other a few yards away. Iris leaned down to take a sip of her drink, but her eyes were fixed to them. She swallowed slowly, touching the corner of her mouth with her finger. Smudging her lipstick slightly.

"Those men are speaking Russian," she said quietly.

I dipped my head. "There are people from all over the world here."

"But…our outfit…we're not friendly with the Russians." She cocked her head, waiting.

"Not all Russians are associated with their organization."

She nodded once. I glanced down as she bent forward to rest her bare arm on the railing. God, she was a fucking knockout in that dress with her sun bleached hair falling around her shoulders. She just needed some diamonds on her fingers and her ears and she'd look like a queen. The kind of woman I was expected to marry as an Esposito.

She took a deep drink and released a sigh. "Is this the kind of life you lead all the time?"

"What do you mean?"

She waved a hand. "Kidnapping whatever woman you want, going on yachts, staying on private islands. It's very glamorous."

I shrugged. "I'm working."

Her eyes fixed to mine, narrowing. She'd lined them with dusky black that winged out, accentuating the blue green of her irises. Her full mouth was glossed and it glistened in the sinking sun.

"Do you ever get lonely, Duran Esposito?" she said softly, her voice falling until it was husky.

"No," I said firmly.

"Why? Because you could have a different woman in your bed every night?"

"No, because I'm too fucking busy to get lonely," I said, raising an eyebrow. "Don't tell me you're jealous of who I have in my bed."

She snorted quietly, rolling her eyes in a way that seemed a bit jealous. I took hold of her wrist, circling it lightly and firmly. Reminding her how easily I could simply press her back, pin her down, and rouse the hungry little animal in her that wanted me.

"You like this," I observed. "This game of pushing and pulling."

"So do you," she shot back.

"I like the game where you get on your knees," I said. "I like the game where I come down your throat."

She gasped. "You're disgusting."

I slid my hand up the side of her neck and tucked her hair behind her ear.

"Hate fucking is one of life's greatest pleasures," I said. "Let's try it out sometime. I'm sure you'd love getting your claws in me just as much as I'd like to make you beg for air while I fill your cunt until it aches."

She blushed all the way to her hairline.

"No, we can't," she whispered.

"So you want to?"

"It's a developing situation. I'm not sure it's a good idea."

"Why?"

Her lids fluttered. "You know I'm a virgin."

I slid my hand up her nape and fisted her hair, dragging her head back. My chest tightened with anticipation as she looked up with wide eyes, her pupils blowing as her mouth parted. Before she could squirm, I bent and kissed her mouth.

There was nothing discreet or gentle about the way I kissed her. I meant to hold back, but as soon as our mouths touched, fire shot down my spine and set me alight. Her lips were soft and yielding and she tasted like orange and seltzer with a hint of bitterness from her lipstick.

My cock throbbed and my mind went blank. I kissed her harder, forcing her lips apart and sucking her tongue into my mouth. Biting it gently and returning the favor by making her take my tongue all the way to the back of her throat.

We broke apart. She gasped, her knuckles white on the railing.

"I can fix it for you," I said.

"What?" she whispered, blinking hazily.

"You said we couldn't hate fuck because you're a virgin," I said, unable to tear my eyes from her mouth. "I'll come to your room tonight and solve that problem for you. I can be gentle."

She went rigid, the whites of her eyes flashing. "No, you know why that's a bad idea."

"Why?"

"Maybe it means nothing to you, but it means a lot to me. I get that you're a man so it's not like you would understand."

I released her and stepped back. She brushed her hair over her shoulders and took a sip of her drink.

"I lost my virginity a while ago, but I did lose it," I said, confused by her statement.

"Yeah, but you're a man," she said.

"But I was still a virgin once."

She glared, clearly frustrated. "It's not the same. You probably had people congratulating you the first time you fucked. It's not like that for me."

"The upper classes, people like my brother, they barter with those kinds of things," I said. "But you're not like them."

"Oh, so because I'm not rich, it doesn't matter? This isn't about wealth, it's about…shame."

I cocked my head. "You are an enigma, Iris Scavo. I can't tell which side of you is…you. Are you a good girl or a little slut who lets a stranger eat her pussy?"

She hadn't expected that and she took a beat to sip her Aperol Spritz. My eyes lingered over the frosted glass. The memory of her pussy, all wet and naked, under my mouth surfaced. It clicked into place what she tasted like. My cock thickened.

"You taste like oranges," I said.

She froze, glancing up. "What the fuck?"

I shifted closer until we were inches apart and leaned against the railing. "You taste sweet like fresh oranges, down between those pretty thighs."

Her jaw dropped. "I doubt that."

"Are you even real?"

"What?"

My finger trailed up and under her chin. "Pretty blue eyes and soft lips. A curvy body that fills out that little black dress. A cunt that tastes like sweet oranges. How does it feel to be so fucking perfect?"

There was a moment of shocked silence. Her throat bobbed and a little breath slipped from between her lips.

"I don't know who you're talking about. I'm not perfect," she whispered. "I'm pretty ordinary."

That caught me by surprise. There was nothing ordinary about Iris Scavo. From the moment I'd laid eyes on her, I'd known that she was something special. There was an aura of electricity in her veins and every time I touched her skin, it ran through me like lightning.

I bent and our mouths met.

Fire pooled in my veins. Fuck me, she tasted so good and I needed more of it. She moaned and her mouth was wet when I pulled back.

"What the fuck is wrong with you?" she whispered. "You kidnapped me. You don't even like me. And I definitely hate you."

CHAPTER FOURTEEN

IRIS

I stared at him, my heart thudding and my sex pulsing between my legs. What the fuck was wrong with this man? He'd been distant for the last few days, but after our encounter in his office, he couldn't turn keep his hands to himself.

He leaned in and kissed me again. Filling my mouth with the taste of whiskey. My thighs shifted and my aching pussy rubbed against my soaked panties. Warning bells went off in the back of my mind.

I pulled back, dying of embarrassment. "You need to stop."

The tension broke as we moved apart. I glanced around, grateful nobody was watching.

He shrugged, polishing off his whiskey. "Alright, it's time for me to get some work done anyway. You stay in my sight."

I nodded, relieved he was giving me some space. My pulse was beating out of my chest since his office and I needed a moment to catch my breath away from him.

He joined a group of men several yards away and I heard them speaking French loudly. His entire demeanor changed when he was in a group. His broad shoulders were pulled back, his body relaxed but on guard, and he was a lot more outgoing. I could tell he was cracking jokes even if I couldn't understand him because he had the entire group laughing in minutes.

"Can I buy you a drink?"

I pivoted, startled. There was a bulky blond man in a blue suit standing on my opposite side. He was almost as close as Duran had been a moment ago.

"Do you belong to anyone?" he said, a light Russian accent coming through.

"What?" I stammered.

"Who do you belong to?" he pressed.

"Um...nobody," I said. "Myself."

He laughed. I wasn't sure what was funny. "You're beautiful, let me buy you a drink."

My glass was empty and, honestly, I was feeling a little afraid to refuse him. I nodded and he put his hand on my hip, sliding it around me and pushing me towards the bar.

"Um…I can walk," I said, trying to sidestep him.

He laughed again, but he didn't take his hand off my waist. Holding me against his side as he tapped the bar and ordered me another drink. My heart hammered, not in the breathless way it did when Duran touched me, but in a way that made me feel slightly sick.

"Here," he said. "Drink."

I accepted the glass and took a deep drink, trying to decide if I should just risk it and be rude enough to make him leave. He was staring down at me like a hungry wolf, his gaze eating me alive. I glanced over my shoulder to where Duran had stood a moment before, but he was out of sight.

Fuck, this had escalated fast.

"Hey, thanks for the drink," I said carefully. "But I need to get back to my date."

His brow rose. "You said you belonged to no one."

"I don't," I said quickly.

"So you have no date."

His broad hand slid down my arm and his took my hand, leading me across the deck to the stairs. I balked, but he didn't seem to care. He just kept walking, guiding me down the steps until we entered a low lit lounge on the first floor. Luckily, there were other people surrounding us so it didn't feel as intimidating as I'd expected.

He pulled me onto a couch in the corner, keeping his arm locked on my waist.

"You're beautiful, you look expensive," he remarked. "What's your thing?"

Confused, I took a moment to gather myself. "My thing?"

"Are you expensive?" he pressed. "What do you do?"

"I...I don't know what you mean," I said, taking another drink. It was halfway gone already and I was starting to regret having so much so fast.

A wave of heat passed over me and the room spun. Abruptly, I pulled to my feet and scanned the dim room for the stairs. There they were, at the far end. I felt my glass slip from my fingers and saw it spill out over the couch, but I didn't care. I needed fresh air, I needed to get out of this man's arms.

I stumbled and I thought I heard him laugh. A wave of scorching heat moved through me again, followed by a surge of chills. How much alcohol had the bartender put in my drink? It was hitting me like a ton of bricks.

My whole body swayed. The man stood abruptly, catching me as my knees went out.

"There you go, baby," he said. "Let's get you somewhere you can lay down."

Bile rose in my throat and I flailed one arm out, trying to push him away. He caught it, tucking it between our bodies. My brain was shutting down, so hazy I couldn't think straight to form words.

He'd drugged me. Somehow, he'd slipped something into my drink at the bar. There was no way I was just drunk. I'd been blackout before and it had never felt like I was losing total control over my body. My knees gave way and I sagged, completely limp, over his arm. My head fell back and the ceiling pulsed overhead, darkness creeping into the corners of my vision.

How had this happened too fast? One minute I was just a few feet from Duran and suddenly I was barely conscious and being carried down a dim hallway by a man who was going to violate me.

The drug had kicked in fully, but I was still conscious. I could hear, see, and smell everything, but I couldn't move. My entire body had disengaged from my brain.

He dragged me through another door and into a dark lounge filled with men. Someone laughed and I felt my back hit the couch. A voice barked out something, trying to get an answer from me, but all that came out was an incoherent groan. Laughter filled the room and I wondered disjointedly why that was funny.

What happened next was a nightmare, but not the kind of nightmare I'd expected.

The door was kicked open and Duran entered. He looked strange, all emotion gone from his face. His eyes looked black, even the whites, like he was burning with rage. He had a gun, which he took out and unloaded into the row of men on the couch.

Without a moment of hesitation.

Bang, bang, bang, bang, bang.

They went down neat and orderly, like dominoes falling. Duran's face stayed the same, like it was carved from stone. Gunpowder, heat, and the scent of fresh blood filled the air. He calmly dropped the empty magazine and replaced it.

The only man left standing was the one who had drugged me. He had his hands up and he was backing away, begging in another language. Duran didn't spare him a glance, he just walked past him and lifted the gun and emptied it into his temple. The man dropped like a stone.

Duran's jaw twitched once and he pushed the pistol under his belt and knelt beside me.

"Did they touch you, princess?" he breathed.

His hands slid over me, tugging up my skirt, checking my thighs. I tried to shake my head, but I couldn't move, much less speak. My eyes rolled back and darkness closed in.

He lifted me in his arms and my head lolled back. My necklace slid up, the moonstone falling against my cheek. Overhead, the shadows at the corner of my vision were getting thicker and stronger. Filling everything except the sensation of being lifted. Up and up. Enveloped in warmth and the scent of sandalwood.

I saw the next hour in flashes. We were in a helicopter, there was a pilot. In the back, it was just Duran and I. He'd laid me down with my head on his lap and his fingers stroked through my hair. Then I was in the bathroom at the compound, kneeling on the floor with his arms around me. His hand was on my jaw and his fingers were in the back of my throat.

My body convulsed and I threw up all over his hand and the floor, missing the toilet entirely. A whimper gurgled up and my whole body twitched.

"Shh, it's okay," he said.

His fingers pushed back into my mouth and I attempted to squirm, but I was still no match for him. He took me gently by the hair and guided me back over the toilet. My throat fought him as he forced two fingers past my tongue. My stomach seized and I vomited again. Hitting the toilet this time.

Tears streamed from my eyes and a sob burst out.

"Get it all out, princess," he said, his voice hushed.

I vomited again, dry heaving and sobbing.

"That's my girl," he soothed. "Let's go one more time."

I hated him so fucking much. He gagged me again and I dry heaved painfully over the toilet until there was nothing in me. Even in my drugged state, I knew it was necessary, what he was doing. Neither of us knew what I'd been given and I wanted it out more than he did. But it was still fucking torture.

I sagged, covered in vomit and sweat.

He stripped me naked and put me in the tub. I lay there, my vision spinning and my body limp, staring at him while he made a phone call. Then he cleaned me with gentle hands and wrapped me in a fluffy towel.

I blacked out. Maybe from the blood pressure drop of being in hot water, or maybe I was just reaching a different phase of the drug. But as soon as he finished drying me, my body gave out and my brain closed down.

Shutting everything out.

CHAPTER FIFTEEN

DURAN

My heart pounded. The woman in my arms hung limp, her lashes dark on her pale cheeks. My jaw was set, my eyes darting over the partygoers around me as I carried her up to the deck. Everyone had heard the shots, but they knew better than to intervene. I had all the power of the Italian outfit behind me. The men I'd killed had no organization.

Someone called for a helicopter. We docked briefly on shore and I carried her across a strip of sand and laid her on the back seat. I was dimly aware of writing a check to the boat owner for the mess. Then I fitted my headset and climbed aboard.

She was warm and limp. I pulled her halfway onto my lap and slid my finger to her neck. Feeling for her pulse.

It was steady. As we rose into the air, her eyes fluttered open. The clear ocean depths of them was muddy and confused. I stroked her hair back and she coughed, shifting to lay her cheek on my thigh. Her eyes shut.

I kept my hand on her waist, holding tight. She wasn't leaving my sight after this, not for one goddamn second. The sight of her on her back, surrounded by all those men, was burned in my brain. She'd been helpless, her hands trying to bat at the air, trying to keep them away. One of them had pushed her skirt up to the middle of her thigh.

My stomach turned.

It was good they were dead. I hoped they rotted in hell.

We got back to the island faster than I'd expected. I called our family doctor and sent the helicopter out to retrieve him. Then I carried her up to the bathroom and forced her to vomit everything into the toilet. My hands were steady, but inside, I was more afraid than I'd been in my entire life.

She had to be okay, she had to.

I put my finger in the back of her throat until all she had left was bile and she was begging me drunkenly to stop. Then I stripped her naked and washed her in the tub before pulling my softest t-shirt over her head and putting her to bed.

Dr. Howell, the man who'd delivered both Lucien and I, appeared around midnight. I stayed in the back of the room, arms crossed, and watched while he hooked her up to an IV. He spent a while examining her in silence and then he rose and reached for his bag.

"She's okay, Duran," he said, gray brows creasing. "I'm giving her a lot of fluids and some painkillers, but she'll be fine. Where did this happen?"

"I had a meeting on a boat. She went with me, but she slipped away," I said hoarsely. "I found her drugged with six men standing around her."

He winced. "Do you know if she was sexually assaulted?"

I shook my head. "I don't think so, she still had all her clothes on. There were no marks, no blood or semen on her body."

"If she consents, I can examine her when she wakes," he said.

I nodded. Dr. Howell's sharp blue gaze raked over me and suddenly I felt much younger than thirty. I'd known him for a long time, he'd witnessed me grow up and he'd been my doctor from day one. It was hard to hide anything from him.

"Who is she?" he asked.

I sighed. "I met her at a resort. There was a misunderstanding. I thought she was spying on me so I took her with me and then I found out she wasn't."

"So, why is she still here?" he pressed.

I sighed, studying her sleeping form.

"I didn't want to bring her home," I said quietly.

The corner of his mouth twitched. "Well, there's no prescription I can write to cure what you have."

Frowning, I followed him out into the hall. "What does that mean?"

He shook his head. "I've never known you to stay with any woman longer than a night. There's something special about this one."

"No, I'm just trying to be nice," I said, fully aware how stupid I sounded.

He sent me a disbelieving glance from below raised brows. I followed him into the kitchen and leaned on the counter, watching him make a coffee.

"Who is she?" he asked.

I sighed. "Iris Scavo, the daughter of one of Romano's bookkeepers," I admitted.

Dr. Howell turned and I felt like I was being X-rayed as he raked his gaze over me. "I know the Scavos, not well, but we've spoken. Why is she here?"

Defeated, I let my shoulders sag. I'd been in such deep denial for the last few days that I'd never had admitted it. But after seeing her in danger, watching her fight for consciousness in my lap on the helicopter—I was tired of denying the strange warm feeling that flooded through my chest when I looked at her.

"I don't know," I said hoarsely. "But she's not leaving."

He crossed his arms. "Maybe I'd better prescribe her some birth control."

I laughed shortly. "She's not going to fuck me."

The coffee machine gurgled and began filling his cup. The house was so silent it felt loud.

"Does her father know you have her?" he asked.

I shook my head. "Her family is really religious, she still thinks about herself as a good Catholic girl, so it's going to be a shitshow when they find out."

His brow creased. "Did you hook up with her?"

I nodded and then reconsidered.

"We hooked up, but didn't take it all the way," I said. "But that doesn't matter. I did some digging into her family and they'll be pissed she's been with me alone, much less fucked around."

"Hmm, Lucien isn't going to be thrilled," he said.

"Lucien will be fine," I said. "I'm not concerned with myself. I just…I fucked this girl's life up and now I don't know how to fix it."

He turned to retrieve his coffee and sat down at the breakfast bar. "Have you considered just telling her how you feel?"

"You haven't met her. She's got barbs."

He laughed. "She's got you wrapped around her little finger."

I scowled. Was he right? My mind drifted back to the necklace and how quickly I'd decided seeing it on her body was worth the price tag. But even that paled in comparison to how fucking scared I'd been when she'd been drugged and taken.

"I don't do this," I said. "I don't date."

He sighed, shaking his head. "You can, you're a good man, Duran. Just because your father wasn't, doesn't mean you'll be the same. If you think you feel something real, take a chance on it."

My throat was dry. I hated that he'd hit the nail on the head.

"I don't know how to," I said.

"Start with the basics," he suggested. "Maybe stop acting like she's your enemy and see where that takes you. I have a feeling it'll go pretty far. Oh, and you need to tell her father you have her."

"I can't do that," I said.

"I have daughters and I'd be sick if one of them went missing," he said. "Forbid him from telling anyone where she is, but please tell her father she's safe. She's his only child."

"I'll think about it."

We didn't talk about Iris after that. Instead, I told him about the problem I was having acquiring guns, not in detail, and he listened. After a while, he went back upstairs to check on Iris. I lingered in the kitchen, my mind running a hundred miles an hour.

Had I fucked this up beyond repair?

Or could we take it back to the night we met? What if she hadn't looked at my computer? What if I hadn't acted rashly and kidnapped her?

I knew what I'd have done. I'd have fed her breakfast in bed and gone down on her until she was limp. She'd have moved into my room for the duration of her stay. We'd fuck and eat and swim in the ocean for the next week. I'd have postponed my trip to get the guns in favor of being horizontal with her all day and night.

    I'd have gotten her number and called her the moment I got home.

CHAPTER SIXTEEN

IRIS

The window was open when I cracked my eyes. My hand felt stiff and I flexed it, a prickle going up my arm. My body was propped up on a pile of pillows and there was a knitted blanket over my lap. Fresh, ocean air swept in through the window and there was a tray of fruit and a cup of iced tea on the bedside table.

I looked down, noticing I was wearing one of Duran's t-shirts. There was an IV taped to the back of my hand.

Everything came flooding back and my empty stomach churned. Flashes of the dim lounge, gunshots, and him pushing his fingers into my throat flooded my brain.

I needed to get up, I needed some ice water and fresh air.

Down the hall, I heard a door slide open and footsteps rang out across the stone floor. They moved closer and the door opened, revealing Duran and a graying man with a kind face, his sleeves rolled up to his elbows.

"You're awake," he said. "Good. How're you feeling?"

"Um...fine," I said, realizing slowly that I did actually feel fine. I'd expected a headache after the drugs had worn off, but other than being parched, I was alright.

"Excellent," the man said, drawing up to the edge of the bed. "I'm Dr. Howell. We've had you on fluids to help ease your hangover."

I glanced past him and met Duran's gaze from the door. He wore his usual clothes and his expression was guarded, black eyes narrowed. There was a grimness to his jaw I hadn't seen before except in the room where he'd shot down half a dozen men.

Our eyes locked and the air in the room felt thick. My stomach fluttered as he took me in, lids heavy and mouth parted. The air buzzed with a hint of electricity.

There was a moment of awkward silence and then Dr. Howell unhooked me and brought me a cup of ice water. He sank down on the chair beside the bed. I thanked him, offering him a weak smile and he patted my arm. He reminded me of my father and that sent a heavy wave of homesickness through me. I blinked hard, trying not to burst into tears.

"So, there was no initial visible evidence of sexual assault," he said. "But if it would make you feel more at ease, I can you a full exam."

My stomach churned. "No one touched me, I was conscious, I just couldn't move."

"Good, good," he said. "I want you taking it easy here for a few days. Just relax, don't stress yourself out. Drink plenty of fluids, have some fresh fruit until your stomach settles."

I nodded, glancing over his shoulder. "Duran."

He glanced up, his eyes almost desperate. "Yes?"

"Could we have a minute?"

His eyes narrowed, but he didn't protest. I waited until he'd stepped in the hall and shut the door before turning to Dr. Howell.

"Do you know Duran well?" I asked.

He nodded. "I delivered him, so yes, very well. I practice back in the city, but Duran had me flown out overnight."

Fuck, it was obvious whose side he was on.

"So I guess you won't smuggle me back to my family," I said miserably.

He sighed. "I don't know why Duran has you here, but I signed an NDA so I can't tell anyone anything. All I can say, is that he won't hurt you."

"Why do you think that?" My lips cracked.

Dr. Howell leaned back and released a short sigh. "He was frantic when I showed up. He hadn't even washed the blood off."

My breathing slowed. A soft warmth blossomed in my chest despite my better judgement.

"I think that the best thing to offer you in these circumstances is birth control," Dr. Howell said, standing.

I was about to say I didn't want it, that I wouldn't need it. But the memory of Duran's searing mouth on mine when we'd stood together on the yacht resurfaced. His body was so solid and protective. His hand on my neck had been possessive, demanding, and somehow sweet all at once.

"Duran says you're very religious," Dr. Howell said.

"My parents are," I said. "I'm not sure what I am."

"Well, this is all confidential. No one will ever know. If you would feel more protected on the pill, I would advise to go on it. You don't have to use it, but it's good to have it there just in case."

I'd tried and failed to resist Duran already. The shame if anyone found out would be much less than the shame of him getting me pregnant outside marriage. The thought of having to stand in front of my parents and tell them I was expecting made my stomach churn.

"Duran is a good man," Dr. Howell said quietly.

I glanced up. "He kidnapped me."

"That was a little out of character for him."

I sighed. "I'll take the pill."

He nodded, rising to his feet. He pushed his hands in his pockets, loitering for a moment. "Duran won't hurt you," he said finally.

I swallowed past my dry throat. "We'll see."

Dr. Howell left me three months worth of the pill and went downstairs. I heard him talking to Duran for a while and then the front door shut. The buzz of a motorboat sounded and disappeared. My only link to the world off this island was gone.

Why hadn't I fought harder for him to help me? Guilt rose in my chest, homesickness following quickly behind. Was this some kind of Stockholm syndrome setting in? All it had taken for me to hitch my skirt up and climb into his lap was a bit of light banter, a few kisses, and a necklace.

Was I that weak? Was I playing right into his game?

The compound was silent. I nibbled on the fresh fruit and sipped my ice water and tea. Briefly, I heard his footfalls downstairs and they faded away. Another boat came in, but left an hour later.

I jerked awake when it was almost evening and sat upright. The sun was setting golden over the vast, blue swathe of the ocean. The air had cooled and it was wafting through the window, calling me to get up and go outside.

My legs shook a little as I made my way to the bathroom and turned on the shower. The boxes of pills sat on the counter and the sight of them sent a little twinge of guilt through me.

But it was just a twinge. I could deal with that.

I broke the pack open and put one on my tongue and swallowed it dry.

See, I could make my own choices.

CHAPTER SEVENTEEN

DURAN

She didn't come down that afternoon. I ate in my office and tried to forget the sickening feeling of walking through that door and seeing her limp on the couch. The sensation that filled my chest after had stunned me. Pure hatred, a willingness to kill anyone and anything I needed to get her back to me.

It shook me deeply.

I spent the rest of the evening trying to fix what I'd done. It was past midnight when I finally made my way through the dark compound and up the stairs. Since she'd been locked in the guestroom, I hadn't slept in my bedroom because it was just down the hall. But tonight, I felt like I needed to.

I stripped and sank onto my back in bed. Outside, a nightbird cried out over the water. Inside, my heart thumped so hard in my chest I heard it in my ears. My skin crawled and when I closed my eyes, all I could see was what might have happened if I hadn't walked through that door.

Sitting up abruptly, I reached for my boxer briefs and pulled them on. I needed something, a drink or some sleeping pills.

I moved down the stairs, the cool air in the lower level wicking away the sweat gathered on my back and chest. I rarely stayed on the island for long and I was used to the New York weather, which stayed much cooler during the summer. The humidity had everything in a tight grip, making it hard to catch a breath.

In the hall bathroom, I found an unopened bottle of sleeping pills. In the kitchen, I poured a glass of water and stepped out onto the side deck where the pool was, still and glassy in the starlight.

"Hey."

I jumped, spinning. She was sitting on the deck, wrapped in a blanket.

"What the hell are you doing here?" I asked.

She shook the blanket off her head and pulled it tight around her shoulders. "You didn't lock me in tonight."

I set the pill and the water aside and walked over to where she sat, sitting down and sliding my legs into the water. I felt her eyes on me, watching me warily. Like a little night animal on its guard.

"I suppose I didn't," I said quietly.

There was a short silence and she cleared her throat.

"Who were those men at the party?" she asked.

"Mercenaries," I said, done with pretending I was something I wasn't. "The outfit needs guns and I was sent to procure some from those men. They were the reason I was there…we had a business deal with them."

Her jaw worked and she chewed at her lip from inside. I could tell she was struggling with her moral compass. Wondering what sort of man I was and if I would leave my dirty handprints all over her pretty skin. I sighed internally. This wasn't an unfamiliar scene.

When women found out who I was and what I did, they reacted one of three ways. Fear because they thought sleeping with me would forever attach them to the mafia. Disgust because of what I did. Or excitement because they liked the thought of fucking a criminal.

I wasn't getting any of those emotions from her right now.

"Oh," she said, looking down and working the blanket in her fingers. "Sorry if I messed something up for you."

"No," I said quickly. "They messed it up for themselves."

"Will…will your brother be angry with you?"

I shifted, wondering why she cared. Her lashes lay dark against her tanned cheek and I thought I saw tear stains on her jaw. She had other things to worry about, but here she was worrying about me.

"Lucien won't be happy, but he's not a monster," I said. "He'll understand when I tell him what they were about to do."

"I thought…I heard that Lucien doesn't like women all that much," she said hesitantly.

I felt my eyes narrow. "Where did you hear that?"

"Um… I don't know. Around," she whispered.

Years ago, Romano's daughter had gotten pregnant and falsely accused Lucien of being the father. She was in love with him, he didn't give a fuck about her. Romano had demanded Lucien marry her and he refused without a paternity test.

Romano had tortured my brother. When his daughter finally broke down and confessed he wasn't the father, Lucien had permanent scars on his body. Everyone went on like nothing had happened and Lucien covered his scars with tattoos.

I knew better, I knew that deep inside, he was holding onto his hatred like a lifeline.

But I wasn't going to explain that to her.

"Lucien doesn't hate women, he's just been burned in the past," I said. "I'm…surprised when I see him around his fiancée. He's got some warmth, somewhere below all that ice."

"Are you going to tell him?" she asked. "He'll ask about the guns."

I shook my head. "You are my problem, princess. My self created downfall."

There was a long, long silence. She got to her feet, letting the blanket fall away to reveal my t-shirt. Just skimming the middle of her thighs. I shifted over and she sank down next to me, dangling her tanned legs into the dark pool.

"Duran," she said quietly. "Why am I here?"

"Because—"

"I know you don't think I'm a spy," she interjected. "You have access to all kinds of information. If you haven't used that access yet, it's because you don't want to."

I swallowed. "I know who you are."

"I'm nobody," she said. "You have no reason to keep me here. My parents must be frantic. I was supposed to be home yesterday."

I wasn't sure what to say, so I kept quiet.

She shifted to face me and my eyes fell on the gaping front of her shirt. It was too big, and it had slid from her shoulder. She wasn't wearing anything underneath, just warm, tanned skin that smelled so fucking good. Sun-kissed thighs that parted for me in my fantasies and let me dip my tongue into the paradise between her legs.

"I can't sleep," I said.

"Guilty conscience?" Her brow crooked.

I lifted my head and turned and she was so close. When had she moved even closer? My pulse quickened and my cock went rock hard, making me glad for the shadows. Her lashes flicked down as her eyes moved over my mouth and up to mine, glittering in the starlight. Her breath was hot, I felt it brush my bare skin.

"I want you," she whispered.

My throat went dry. God, how had I not realized how much I was dying to hear those words?

"I thought you were trying to keep your legs closed," I said.

"I didn't say I wanted to fuck," she said.

Her hand came up, her fingertips dipping into my hair. Smoothing it back. Her warm palm slid down my jaw and she ran her touch over my lower lip.

"I need your mouth," she breathed.

"How?"

"You know how I need it."

In one movement, I took her by the waist and lowered her on her back on the hot pavement. Her pupils blew and her lips parted, flashing her pink tongue. I bent, my face hovering just over hers.

"Say it.

There was a forceful, darker note to my voice. Her stomach quivered and my eyes trailed down the front of my t-shirt and down to where it had hiked up to her upper thighs. Her legs were pressed together, covering her pussy.

"No one has to know but me," I said. "Tell me how you want my mouth."

Her breasts heaved.

"On my pussy," she whispered. "I want your tongue the way you gave it to me the first time."

I dipped my head, brushing my mouth over her delicate collarbone. Kissing the few freckles gathered there. My cock throbbed down below and I was acutely aware of the way she smelled and how warm her body was.

"You want me to lick and suck your clit," I murmured.

Her neck arced and she moaned softly. I pressed fluttering kisses up her throat to the little hollow below her earlobe. Her hips squirmed and I couldn't bite back a smirk.

"Please, just take me upstairs. I can't sleep and I need you to make me feel better."

There was a faint warning bell going off in the back of my brain, but the animal parts of me were much louder. My cock was heavy in my boxer briefs and there was a pulsing warmth that reached all the way up my spine to my chest.

Fuck my pride.

Silently, I led her upstairs to my room. Her eyes skimmed over the dark space, almost bare except for the messy bed. I turned her around and moved to lift the hem of her shirt, but she stopped me, her slender fingers gripping my wrists.

Her eyes darted up, her lip swollen from being bitten. Poor girl, she was terrified.

"No sex," she whispered.

I shook my head. "No sex. I swear."

"And this doesn't mean I like you. Or that I forgive you."

I couldn't bite back my soft laughter. "No, you still annoy the hell out of me, princess."

"And I...hate you."

"Agreed."

"I just...I need to get a good night's sleep and so do you. It's more out of necessity."

"Absolutely." My fingers lifted the fabric and pulled it free, dropping it on the floor.

Her nipples were erect, little peaks blushed with pink and edged with pale brown. Heat shot down my spine and my cock twitched. So sensitive I worried I was going to blow my load before I got in her mouth.

"You're just an asshole with a really, really talented tongue," she whispered. "I hate you sometimes. Maybe we shouldn't do this."

"You're overthinking this princess. You can hate me and still come on my face." I lifted her shirt

"Enemies with benefits," I told her. "That's all."

She stood there, naked except for her panties, her fists clenched at her sides.

"That's all," she breathed.

I sank to my knees before her and looked up into her eyes. Her throat bobbed. Without a single thought in my head, I pushed my face into the apex of her thighs and ran my tongue along the edge of her panties. The faint scent of her pussy filled my lungs and arousal burst down my spine, making my head spin. Fuck yes, I needed that.

"Please," she whispered. "Please, just touch me."

My cock ached. "Fuck me," I murmured, nuzzling her thigh. "Beg like that and I'll give you anything you want, princess."

My fingers closed around her panties and she gasped when I tore them down and pushed her onto her back. She lay stunned, her hair splayed out on the bed. Her thighs fell open and...fuck me, I'd forgotten just how perfect her cunt was.

She was already soaked. I leaned forward, still on my knees on the floor, and dipped my fingertip into her pussy. Her warm muscles tensed and she pushed herself upright.

"Not in," she begged.

"I'm not, I swear," I assured her, sliding it back. Watching the strand of her arousal break. Our eyes locked. "You're always so wet? Or is it just me that makes your pussy drip?"

Heat crept over her face. "I don't know. Is it bad?"

I slid my finger up through her soft folds to her clit and tugged the hood back. "More for me. I could drink you with the way you taste."

"I don't taste the way you described," she whispered. "I tasted myself. It's just tangy and sweet, that's all."

Keeping my eyes locked on hers, I bent and ran my tongue over her opening. Heat surged and surged again as I moaned into her pussy, licking the arousal from her skin.

The thought of her dipping those fingers into herself and putting them between her lips had me dripping into my boxer briefs. I wanted to see her touch herself to badly it was more of a need than a want at this point.

"To me, you do. You taste like fucking candy," I told her. "Now lay the fuck back down. I don't want to see you fucking move unless it's to come."

She moaned, sinking back. Giving me access to her spread pussy. I slid my hands beneath her thighs to hold her hips in place and pushed my face into her sex, relishing the hot, sweet wetness.

She whimpered and panted as I ate her out, but she was such a fucking good girl and she didn't move.

It drove me wild how submissive she was in the bedroom. Outside of it, she had claws, she had all the smart comebacks. But in here, she wanted to be a good girl for me, I felt it in her little whimpers and in the way she pushed her sex up to my mouth, giving me everything I wanted.

Her thighs tensed. Excitement flared in my chest and it took everything I had not to change the rhythm of my tongue over her clit.

"Oh God," she breathed. "May I come?"

That brought me right to the edge. I preferred to be dominant behind closed doors and she was giving me my own fucking wet dream on a silver platter.

Not because I wanted it, but because she did. And that made it ten times better.

I pulled back, kissing the entrance of her cunt. Making her inner muscles flutter and tense.

"What do you say, princess?" I asked softly.

Her hips worked. "May I *please* come?" she whispered.

"That's right," I praised. "Are you my good girl?"

Her lower back arced as I licked over her swollen clit. Teasing her with slow circles of my tongue.

"I'm your good girl," she begged. "Please, please, let me come."

Her pussy tensed and a little bit of wetness slid down onto the sheets. She was so close, I could see her pleasure trembling in her thighs.

"If I make you come, whose name will you cry out, princess?" I pressed. "Who are you going to come for?"

"Yours...you," she stammered.

I lightly spanked her clit with the tips of my fingers. Her entire body shuddered and her eyes widened.

"Whose pussy is this?"

"What?" she gasped.

I spanked her clit again and her hips jolted. Another moan slipped from her lips.

"I said, whose fucking pussy is this?" I repeated. "Open that mouth and tell me it's mine or I'll take my cock out and show you who this pussy belongs to."

She gasped, twisting her hips.

"It's yours," she managed. "It's your pussy."

I bent my head and fixed my mouth over her clit, sucking gently and licking at the same time. A sharp gasp burst from her mouth and her thighs clamped around my head. Pinning me into her pussy. From somewhere above, her fingers wove into my hair. Her fingertips dragged over my scalp and closed.

"Duran," she gasped. "Oh, fuck, I'm going to come for you."

It hit her hard, making her lower body lift off the bed. Her thighs were squeezing me so hard I couldn't breath and I didn't care. I wanted to suffocate in her, to drown in the little rush of sweet citrus arousal she released all over my tongue. Until it dripped down my neck.

Her fingers seized, pushing me away, too sensitive to continue. I drew back, dazed and soaked with her scent. She went still, her ankles twitching slightly. When I lay down beside her, her lashes fluttered open and her eyes met mine.

"Fuck you," she breathed.

I cupped her breast and ran my thumb over her nipple. "Did I break you, princess?"

"No…just fuck you for being so good at that."

I laughed, falling back. "Do you think you can get yourself back to your bed?"

She rolled onto her side with effort. "After I return the favor."

"You don't have to," I gritted out.

She struggled to her knees, bending over me. "I'm going to make you come…just do something for me?"

I waited, watching her chew her lip.

"Just tell me it's not really sex," she whispered. "I don't care what you actually think. I just want you to look me in the eyes and tell me it's not sex."

She wanted me to lie to her, to stand between her and her guilt. I reached up and cradled her soft cheek.

"It is sex, princess," I told her. "But right here, in this room, I'm the only you have to obey. If this is a sin, let me take the blame for you."

She swallowed, biting her lip. I could tell her arousal was building again. I got to my feet and pulled her onto hers, bending to kiss her mouth briefly. Letting her taste her pussy off my tongue.

"Be a good girl," I said. "Get on your knees and sin for me."

I was taking a risk saying it like that, but it paid off. Her eyes widened and her nipples went rock hard. A tremor moved down her belly and she locked her gaze with mine and sank to her knees at my feet.

"Take my cock out," I ordered. "Now."

Her hands slid up my thighs, sending waves of heat from her touch, and tugged down the front of my boxer briefs. My cock sprang free, achingly hard and leaking from the tip. I was tempted to ask her what she wanted next, but I knew that wasn't what she needed.

She didn't want to be asked. She wanted to be told. She needed me to stand between her and her guilt, to absolve her of responsibility.

I gathered her hair in my fist, holding her head still.

"Open, princess."

She hesitated. The tip of her tongue darted out.

"It wasn't a question. Open your mouth. Now."

Her eyes locked with mine and her lips parted, her pink tongue visible. Holding her by the hair, I fed my cock into her mouth until I felt her throat convulse a little. Then I stopped, letting her adjust.

"Good?" I asked.

She nodded, unable to speak. Her tongue was so fucking warm and wet and her lips were so soft around the middle of my cock. Pleasure, already built from eating her out, threatened to burst.

"I want you to suck me off until I come in your pretty mouth," I said. "And then you will put your tongue out and show me before you swallow. Understood?"

She nodded again.

"Go on then."

Her cheeks hollowed and my vision flashed as she obeyed. Sucking me eagerly like it was all she'd ever wanted. She pulled back until I slid from her lips with a pop and then she ran her tongue up the underside and dipped it into the slit. My stomach tensed.

My God, she was perfect.

I released her hair. "Use your hands. Get me off."

She spat into her palm and wrapped it around the base, gripping me. Her fingers didn't quite meet, but she was doing so well. Her mouth fitted around the head of my cock and she pushed it in as far as she could take it.

Her head bobbed and pleasure surged in a wave. Her wrist worked and her cheeks hollowed, but she didn't tear her eyes from mine.

My orgasm moved down my spine and burst, my cock going rock hard on her tongue.

"Take my cum," I breathed.

She obeyed, letting me pump it all out onto her tongue. Until there was nothing left in me.

"Go on," I ordered.

She pulled her mouth from my cock carefully and got to her feet. Her lips parted and her curled tongue pushed out. Holding my cum like such a sweet girl, so fucking obedient.

"Good girl," I said, gently closing her mouth. "Swallow it all for me."

She obeyed, her throat bobbing once. My cock went hard watching her, knowing my cum was in her stomach. Where it was meant to be.

I stroked her hair back. "You should sleep."

She hesitated. "Was that wrong?"

"No," I said quickly. "You were only doing as you were told. Now get your ass into my bed and get some fucking sleep."

Peace settled over her eyes as she crawled up into bed, settling herself into the side where I usually slept. I brought her a glass of water and slid beneath the sheets and laid down facing her. Her lids were heavy as she set her water aside and snuggled up.

"Will you spoon me," she asked sleepily. "Not because I like you, just because I'm cold."

She wasn't fucking cold, it was eighty degrees outside. I stretched my legs out, flipping her unceremoniously over and pulling her back against me. Her soft ass nestled against my cock. We lay there in silence for a few minutes before I realized she was already asleep.

I slid one arm around her waist and curled my other hand loosely around her throat.

Holding her close.

CHAPTER EIGHTEEN

IRIS

I woke with a heavy pit of regret in my stomach. Part of me, the rational side of my brain, had enjoyed last night and wanted more. The subconscious half was so conditioned to shame it didn't know anything else. I rolled over, seeking his warmth.

He was already gone, his side of the bed empty. My brain whirled. Both sides argued back and forth while I padded down the hall.

Whore.

Shut up, I can make my own choices.

You really fucked up this time.

Shut. Up.

On the verge of tears, I burst into my bedroom. My hands moved of their own accord, wrathfully scrubbing my face and putting on makeup. I didn't want him thinking I cared what I looked like for him, so I put on plain sweats and a t-shirt. Then I dried my hair and put some light makeup on and padded barefoot downstairs.

He was standing in the living room, talking on his phone in French. When he saw me, he jerked his head towards the kitchen. I frowned, a little hurt by his brusque attitude after what we'd done last night. Maybe he regretted it too?

Slamming the kitchen door, I crossed the room and yanked open the fridge. There was a bowl of cut fruit and bottled iced coffee. I pulled them out and laid them on the counter, climbing onto one of the tall stools.

He walked in and his brows rose. "What's the scowl for? Did I not work that attitude out of you last night, princess?"

Heat shot up my spine and spilled over my face. I ducked my head, unsure how to respond, and popped the cap off my iced coffee.

"No quick comeback this morning?" he pushed.

I glared. "I haven't had my coffee yet."

He crossed the room, tugging his suit jacket off to reveal his usual clothes. His white shirt was open a little lower than usual. I glanced furtively at the dark hair, distracted. Before I realized what was happening, he'd taken me by the waist and put me on the kitchen counter.

I yelped, flustered.

"Sit there," he said smirking. "I'll make us some fresh espressos."

Why was he being so nice? I narrowed my eyes with distrust, but he didn't notice. He turned on the espresso machine in the corner by the fridge and took down two cups. I watched him work in silence, an odd sensation seeping through my chest.

Was this so bad? Yes, I wasn't here of my own free will...but he was the most hospitable captor I could ask for.

"I had Dr. Howell tell your father you were here," he said.

Startled, I blinked. "What? Really?"

He nodded, dark eyes averted. "But if your father tells anyone else, I'll gut him. And he knows it."

I was speechless. He passed me a cup of frothy espresso and leaned on the counter, dark eyes burning into me.

"Lucien doesn't know," he said. "But he does know you're missing."

"Why...why would he care?"

"Because technically you fall within his jurisdiction and now that you're gone, you're on his radar."

"I've never even met him," I said. "And...and how dare you threaten my father!"

"Your father is fine," he said.

I stared at him, trying to figure out what the fuck was going on with him. He'd told my father where I was, so there was at least an ounce of compassion in him, but he was still refusing to tell me why he wouldn't just bring me home. And why was he so adamant that Lucien not know?

It hit me all at once.

"You *like* me," I whispered.

He scowled and his eyes narrowed. "I like your cunt. I like your tits."

Triumphant, I hopped down from the counter, crossing my arms over my chest. "So why can't Lucien know that you *like* me?"

"I don't like you," he said flatly.

"Now you just sound immature."

He emptied his espresso and reached for his jacket. "We're done with his conversation. I haven't brought you back because I fucked up bringing you here in the first place. It's a secure location and now it's been compromised. Not to mention how much it set me back to kill those men. You're here because you're a smoking gun, a liability."

His black eyes were lifeless as he turned on his heel. There was a sudden tenderness in my chest...like his words had hurt me. I followed him out into the hall.

"Wait," I said.

He paused, hand on the doorknob.

"Are you...angry with me for what *you* did?"

He sighed and reached into his pocket and took his sunglasses out. Shrouding his eyes from me.

"Pack your things, princess," he said shortly. "I have a business trip and you're going with me."

"After what happened on the last one?" I said.

"This time, you will not leave my side if I have to handcuff you to my wrist," he said, his smirk appearing. "That's a tempting picture."

"Don't be vulgar," I whispered, blushing.

He left the door, walking slowly back down the hall until he stood so close I could feel his breath. His hand came up and brushed back my hair, tucking it behind my ear. My heart quickened and heat pooled between my legs.

"Would you like that?" he said softly. "Perhaps when we get there, I'll cuff your little wrists to my bed and eat your pussy until you soak the sheets. And when you're so weak with how hard I made you come, I'll fuck you."

My ears roared. I couldn't see his eyes, but I knew they were on fire.

"No," I said, my voice cracking. "No sex."

He cocked his head. "Who are you saving it for? Some well behaved man who thinks it's a sin to eat you out? Is that the kind of man your parents want you to have?"

My jaw was on the floor. He was right...but how dare he speak to me like that. He slid his fingertip up my throat, tilting my chin back.

"You're scared because you know I will fuck you better than your hypothetical husband ever will and when you're laying on your back ten years from now, after he pumps twice and leaves you hanging, you will touch your pussy to the memory of how I fucked you and regret choosing duty over pleasure."

He flicked his finger up, releasing me. My jaw slid open as he strode down the hall and disappeared through the front door.

I wanted to cry, but my eyes were so dry they made sticky noises when I blinked. Instead, I wandered upstairs and sat on the edge of my bed. My chest hurt, but mostly I was angry.

Angry that he was right.

Angry that he'd opened me up and read me like a book.

Angry that every time I closed my eyes, I saw crushed rose petals and naked thorns.

Jaw set, I packed my things into a suitcase I found in the closet. Then I pulled on clothes I thought might be good for traveling—soft linen shorts and a tank top with sunglasses.

Around noon, there was a low hum from over the island and I walked out onto the back porch to see a private plane circle and land a short walk down the beach. The sliding door opened and Duran stepped out onto the deck. He was on his phone again, mirrored sunglasses glinting, the open front of his suit jacket flapping in the wind.

He lifted a hand as an attendant crossed the sand, covering his phone.

"Can you bring the bags in the hall?" he said. "I'll make sure she gets on. Thanks."

The man nodded and Duran turned to me, holding out his hand.

"Come on," he said.

Curious, I slid my fingers through his. They were big, lean, and his warm palms were rough. As we crossed the sand to the landing strip, I listened to him speak French with a little Italian mixed in. I only spoke English, but I found that rise and fall of his voice comforting.

I'd never been on a private flight before, but I was trying not to make that embarrassingly obvious. There were two rows of pale leather seats and an area behind them with a low table and additional seating. Duran led me beyond it and through a curtain at the back to a private area. There was a short, plush bench against the wall.

He pushed his phone in his pocket and took his glasses off. Baring his midnight gaze.

"Are you going to behave?" he asked.

There was something about how stone cold his face was that sent arousal up my spine like a firework. Our eyes locked and the air between us tingled.

"I don't know," I whispered. "Why should I?"

There was a little flush at the base of his throat.

"If I take your bait, will you be a good girl?" he said.

My throat felt dry and my cheeks burned.

"Maybe."

He stepped back, crossing the small space and sinking into the seat in the corner. He spread his knees and leaned back, arms resting on the top of the seats on either side.

"Come here," he said.

I hesitated. Something had changed. Perhaps it had been when he rescued me or perhaps it was the second time we made each other come and slept in the same bed. The walls between us felt so weak now. I could have reached out and pushed and watched the bricks come tumbling down.

I went to him. His big hands closed on my hips and he lifted me into his lap, facing him. My stomach fluttered as he brushed a strand of my hair back.

"Did I hurt your feelings, princess?" he said, his voice low.

My brow shot up. Was he about to apologize?

"I don't have feelings for you to hurt," I said, but my voice didn't sound right. It was flimsy, breathy.

His palms were still on my waist and I was acutely aware of how big his hands were. His middle fingers almost met on my lower back. My stomach constricted as I took a sharp breath. He felt it and the corner of his mouth twitched. Flashing the pointed edge of his canine.

Our eyes locked.

He shifted one hand up and my nipples went hard under my tank top. I'd worn a thin bra because it was hot, but now I wished I'd worn something with an actual cup. There was nothing between him and my breasts but two layers of fabric.

His gaze lowered. His mouth parted.

"You have a beautiful body," he said.

There wasn't a trace of sarcasm or playfulness in his voice. It was honest and quiet. Surprised, I looked down and scanned myself. I'd never hated my body, but I had dealt with a lot of discomfort over it after being told it was a stumbling block. A tool for ruining men.

That had fucked me up for a while.

"Do you actually think that?" I whispered.

He nodded once. His eyes rested on the outline of my nipples. Heat swelling between my thighs and that intense frustration I always felt around him gathered deep inside. It wiped my brain blank.

Fingers shaking, I reached up and peeled my tank top down around my waist. His chest heaved. The triangle of skin showing between his collar flushed around the medal. This time, I ignored it.

"Take my bra off," I begged, my voice hoarse.

Both rough, warm palms slid up and undid my bra in a second. The flimsy silk fell away. My nipples tightened even more as cool air hit them. His lids fell and his expression shifted. I could see desire pool in his eyes like inebriation.

His fingers tightened. My breath hitched.

Then he leaned in and took my left nipple in his hot mouth. Pleasure shot through me and a whimper burst from my lips.

My stomach shuddered. My sex felt wet and incredibly sensitive against my panties.

His eyes closed. His lashes were thick and dark. They lay on his tanned cheek like a feather.

My breath came in a long shudder as he sucked gently, flicking his tongue. God, there was nothing that felt like this. It was so intimate, being half naked in his lap, his mouth on my breasts.

Daringly, I slid my hands up and into his hair. He moaned, a dark, sexy noise in his throat. My fingers clenched, my nails digging lightly into his scalp. My hips began working, desperate for something to rub against.

He pressed his mouth against my neck. His hand pushed between my thighs and tugged my loose shorts and panties aside. The tip of his finger traced down the seam of my pussy and my head fell back.

My hips worked harder. He kept his finger hooked on my panties as he shifted his thigh. Giving me something to grind on. His mouth moved over my neck, the rough fabric of his shirt rubbing against my nipples.

He'd stripped all my inhibitions away in a second. He had a way of doing that.

All it took was his touch, his taste, and I was putty in his hands.

"That's right, princess, grind your pretty pussy on me," he breathed.

I obeyed, clinging to him. He dragged his hot, open mouth back down to my nipples and sucked them. One after the other. Pleasure sparked deep inside and I felt the familiar tightening of my pussy in response.

Moaning aloud, I ground harder on his thigh.

"Good girl," he praised. "Ride my thigh, use it until you come."

My lids fell shut and sparks danced in darkness. The pleasure felt tight and hot and so frustrating I couldn't keep from whimpering. My thighs shuddered. I ground harder, finding the perfect spot and doubling down.

His tongue flicked my right breast.

"So fucking wet," he panted.

He could feel me through his pants. Soaking right down to his bare skin. The thought sent me over the edge. My spine snapped back and I cried out as pleasure erupted between my thighs. My nails pierced him. My hips shuddered and twisted, grinding my orgasm out onto him.

Greedy and reveling in every sensation.

"That's my girl," he said.

I didn't have the presence of mind to tell him I wasn't his girl. I was too busy shaking from how good it had felt to get myself off on his thigh.

"Fuck, I'm hard," he groaned.

I was high on the euphoria of orgasm. My shame still hadn't hit me.

"Let me fix it," I panted, squirming from his lap and falling to my knees.

His eyes widened. "You like that, don't you?"

"It feels good," I admitted. "You taste good."

"Far be it from me to refuse you," he said, fumbling to undo his belt.

His cock sprang out, leaking and rock hard. Not wasting time, I spat into my hand and wrapped it around the base. He gathered my hair and held me bent over his lap. My tongue darted out, wetting my lips.

Then his warm, hard cock was sliding into my mouth. Filling it with his taste and the pulse of blood in the veins running up the delicate underside. My lids fluttered, my eyes rolling back.

Oh God, I had no shame. No dignity.

Fuck it, who needed dignity to have a good time?

Recklessly, I sucked hard and began working my wrist at the same time. He growled, holding my head into his lap. His hands were gentle, keeping me just elevated enough I could breathe. I appreciated that. The only other man I'd given a blowjob had shoved my entire face into his lap and held it there while I gagged until he was done.

That hadn't felt good. And the shame from it had felt worse.

I refused to let my mind wander and ruin this moment. He held my head gently and I pleasured him, soaking in his groans. I barely noticed that my jaw ached or that the plane had lifted into the air.

"I'm going to come, princess," he gritted out.

I didn't pull back. His cock went even harder on the back of my tongue. My palm worked. His thighs went tight and his body shuddered.

Salty-sweet warmth filled my mouth. I swallowed once. Then twice.

My eyes swiped up. Meeting his burning gaze.

"Fuck me," he groaned.

I swallowed again and he was done, sinking back in his seat.

Silence fell. Suddenly shy, I pulled back and rested my cheek on his thigh.

"You're surprisingly nice," I admitted quietly.

"What?" He frowned.

"The only other person I did that for wasn't very nice," I admitted. "You're a lot nicer than he was. I didn't expect that from someone who shot five men in front of me and didn't care."

His brow twitched. "Who?"

"What?"

"Who wasn't nice to you?" he said. "Give me a name and I'll make him suffer for hurting your perfect mouth."

Oh my God. I melted, my cheek pressed against his leg.

"No, that's the past," I said. "He was just inexperienced. I don't think either of us knew any better."

He didn't like letting it go, I could tell. "Did he go down on you?"

"No," I said. "He never mentioned it. I didn't know enough then to ask."

His lean fingers brushed through my hair. "Good. Only I get to eat your cunt."

I swallowed, my chest aching. "What's going on?" I whispered.

"I don't know," he said. "But you're coming with me because that's how I want it. And you're sleeping in my bed at the hotel. I won't touch you unless you want it, but none of this staying in other rooms bullshit anymore."

"But I'm supposed to hate you," I murmured.

"You can hate me in my bed," he said.

There was a knock outside the curtain. I jumped, tugging my tank top up over my naked breasts. He tucked his cock away and got to his feet. My eyes dropped and I flushed hot.

"Your leg," I managed.

He looked down. There was a large wet stain on his thigh, right where I'd ground myself.

"Here, let me clean it up," I said, flustered.

I went to the sink in the corner and moistened a handful of paper towels. He held still while I dabbed at it, only succeeding in getting him wetter. He watched me with a smirk as my frown deepened. Finally he pulled me to my feet and gathered the paper towels.

"I have extra pants," he said. "I'll change before we land. For right now, I'm fine with wearing your pussy on my leg like a trophy."

He grinned and I rolled my eyes, still too flustered to come up with a smart remark. I stood there wordless while he tapped my chin and strode out of the room. Not bothering to hide the mark I'd left.

CHAPTER NINETEEN

IRIS

I fell asleep on the plane and woke up to him nudging my shoulder. I blinked, my eyes gritty. He was kneeling before me, looking fresh in new clothes. His eyes glittered with post-orgasm glow and I could tell he was in an excellent mood.

So a blowjob was all it took. I filed that information away, studying him. He looked good like this, better than when he was annoyed.

"We're here," he said.

I stretched, arching my back and releasing a yawn. "Where?"

"Miami," he said, rising.

"Wait...really?" I scrambled up, pushing past him, and ran to the window. "Can I go home?"

He laughed quietly. "No, not yet, princess," he said. "I've got a dinner and I have business. How about you be my arm candy again?"

This time, when he refused to take me home, it annoyed me a lot less. I turned, leaning back against the wall. "The last time I was your arm candy, it didn't go well."

He moved close and I caught his cologne and the warm, male scent of his skin. Warmth flooded my chest and seeped lower...gathering between my legs. His lean fingers brushed up my neck and his thumb grazed my lower lip.

My stomach pooled like melting lava.

"Nothing will happen to you," he said. "I'll let it be known that you're mine tonight."

"I'm not though."

"That's not what you said earlier when I said you were."

"That's different. I was horny."

"No exchanges or refunds. You're all mine for now."

I gave up, rolling my eyes. He took my hand and led me off the plane to a sleek, black car waiting on the tarmac. I slid into the back seat and watched him through the window. He had his mirrored sunglasses on and he was packing our bags into the trunk, his mouth set in a firm line.

He glanced up and I whipped back around.

But not before I saw his smirk. I rolled my eyes and looked away as he slid into the seat beside me.

"Enjoying the view?" he asked.

"The view out the window maybe."

He was quiet so I shifted to sneak a peek at him over my shoulder. He was leaning back in his seat with his knees apart, totally unbothered.

We drove into the affluent part of the city and pulled up outside a high-rise hotel. The streets were bustling with locals and tourists alike. The air smelled faintly of the ocean and overhead the sky was streaked with clouds. It was close to evening and I was starting to feel tired despite having slept on the plane.

"Can I have a shower and go to bed?" I asked, stepping out onto the hot pavement.

His hand brushed my waist and slid down my arm, his fingers twining with mine.

I looked down, but I didn't pull back.

"I'll make sure you get a good night's sleep," he said.

We stepped into the lobby and I had a hard time pretending like I walked into five-star hotels by the ocean every day. Everything was sleek and glowed with soft light. The glittering floor reflected the dizzying patterns on the fountain in the center of the lobby like stained glass.

In my shorts and creased shirt, sandals slapping on the floor, I felt very young.

Especially with this man walking beside me. I stole a glance up at him, taking in his black jacket and shirt, his open collar. The gold religious medal hung against his bare skin.

He looked a little bit…dangerous.

To my surprise, my nipples tightened inside my bra. I swallowed as we paused by the desk and he took off his sunglasses. The clerk was a peppy brunette who flashed us a smile as she sank into her chair behind the counter.

"What's the name, sir?" she asked.

"Esposito," he said.

Her brows shot up, but her smile stayed plastered on. She typed rapidly and jumped down from her chair to retrieve the key cards.

Duran accepted them. "Thank you. Can I have our bags brought up to the room. And what time does room service end?"

"It's all night, sir," she said. "I'll have those bags brought up right away."

He thanked her and tipped her a hundred dollar bill. My jaw dropped, not at the amount, but at the way my body reacted to it. There was something…sexy about him tipping well. I hadn't expected that from a man in his line of work.

He led me to the gilded elevator on the far side of the room. I hesitated, waiting for him to go first, but his hand absently slid to my lower back and guided me inside. I was pretty sure I could feel my pussy dripping down my leg as the door slid shut.

He glanced down at me and his fingers untangled from mine.

"You had quite a grip on me, princess," he said softly.

"Sorry," I said. "My family isn't…badly off, but this kind of wealth is really new to me. It's kind of overwhelming."

"Do you like it?"

I chewed my lip. "I don't know. I never really wanted more money than I needed to be comfortable. Have a decent house and go on a few vacations a year."

His jaw worked and he fixed his gaze ahead. "Probably better."

I frowned. "Why?"

He sighed, his head falling back. "My brother is marrying for wealth and connections. It's a marriage that's been set up for a long time. He doesn't want to go through with it, she's a lot younger than him. Neither of them seem like they're looking forward to it."

"Oh," I said. "That's antiquated."

He shrugged. "Arranged marriage is more common than you think. It's how people keep money in elite circles."

I swallowed, glad I wasn't upper class. "How old is she?"

"Nineteen," he said. "She'll be twenty when they marry."

"Oh. And he's…thirty?"

"I'm thirty," he said. "Lucien is thirty-five, he'll be thirty-six in a few months."

My stomach felt heavy. "Does she seem okay?"

He shrugged as the elevator slowed to a halt. "She seems terrified. If I'm being honest. But my brother can be a terrifying person from the outside."

I opened my mouth to reply, but he was doing that casually protective thing again and my words dried up. One hand held the door and the other curled around my elbow, helping me into the hallway like I was made of glass.

Why was he doing this? He knew I could walk on my own, that I didn't need help to get on and off an elevator.

I dropped my head, trying to conceal my blush. His hand slid down my forearm and his fingers wove through mine. I followed him down the hallway, aware of every step.

I needed to say something. The silence was deafening.

"Are you going to have an arranged marriage?" I blurted out.

A muscle in his cheek twitched. "I'd prefer not to. I've done my best to cultivate my image so I don't have to."

"What does that mean?"

We paused before room 759. There was a group of men in suits walking past us and as they drew near, Duran shifted subtly between me and them and they curbed their wandering eyes. I stared after them as he took out his key card.

It felt incredibly nice to be protected.

"I'm not serious like Lucien," he said. "I'm nothing more than a playboy, a fuck-up, the kind of man the tabloids like to write about, but no one really thinks about. I'm not a serious person."

I gaped. "But...you are."

"Between you and me, Iris." He swiped his card and the door flashed green. "I manage an enormous amount of money. I negotiate with some of the world's most powerful players. But who the fuck would expect that? And who needs to know?"

"You...make it seem like you're just...fucking around," I whispered. "Why?"

The door swung open. He pocketed his key card.

"So I get left the fuck alone," he said. "So I don't have to damn some poor girl to a life of being married to a man who runs guns and drugs and kills an entire room of men and thinks nothing of it."

He strode into the room and I followed him, pushing the door shut. We were in a luxurious suite overlooking the ocean with the city glittering along the shore. The bed was set against the far wall and made up in thin cotton sheets and a fluffy comforter, pillows stacked high against the wall. The floor was thinly carpeted and there was a mini kitchenette in the corner. The door to the bathroom was ajar and I could see a large tub set into the ground.

"This is nice," I said, feeling awkward after his admission.

He cocked his head. "Did I unsettle you, princess?"

"Maybe," I said. "I didn't expect you to actually have a conscience."

He laughed all the way to the bathroom. I scowled at the shut door and sank onto the edge of the bed. My eyes roved over the room, taking in my surroundings. There was a mirror by the kitchenette and I got up to look myself over.

I paused, noticing I was a little curvier now than before the island.

I looked good. My hair needed washed and my makeup was smudged. But my tits looked great and my ass had gotten bigger since I'd been kidnapped. I wriggled my hips to watch it shake. He had fed me well since kidnapping me.

He stepped out of the bathroom, showered. His dark hair was wet and slicked back.

My eyes moved over him, unashamed. He had the filthy rich, organized criminal look down.

"You know, we never finished having a drink together," he said, rolling his sleeves to the middle of his forearms. "Put something pretty on. I'll take you down to the hotel bar and buy you whatever you want."

My body froze and my mind went blank.

What was he doing? Did he even know what he was doing?

I swallowed. "Why?" I asked hoarsely.

He moved close until I had to tilt my head back to look into his face. One hand came up and brushed my hair back. He smelled so good it was making my stomach glow warm and my toes curl.

"Do you think I'd let you suck me off and not buy you a drink?" he said, his voice soft.

Not a single intelligent brain cell in my head chimed in.

"Uh...I guess not," I mumbled.

His crooked finger curled under my chin. "Good girl."

I stood there dumbfounded, while he went to the door and pulled the suitcases in from the hall. He opened mine and his hands ran through my dresses, my panties, and my bras. Finally he lifted a silk, cowl neck dress and beckoned me over. I went and stood obediently while he held it up to my body.

"Perfect,'" he said. "Go put that on."

I took it and one of my bras and went in the bathroom. When I shut the door, my whole body sagged. My fingers trembled as I slid them down my body and beneath the soaked fabric of my panties.

Fuck him, he knew what he was doing.

Annoyed, I showered, did my makeup, and pulled on the dress. It clung to my body tighter than expected and the little skirt hit the middle of my thigh. I turned in a circle, concerned. It didn't seem like daywear.

I pushed open the door.

"I think I need something more casual," I said.

He looked up from where he stood by the bed and his whole body froze. I shifted, biting my lip. Without a word, he crossed the room and circled me. My eyes darted down.

He was rock hard.

"Fuck," he said, his voice husky. "No, you're wearing that. What are you worried about? I can fight anyone who disrespects you."

Blushing, I watched him go to the suitcase and take my black heels out. He moved close and I reached out to take them, but he sank down to his knees. Startled, I kept still as he put them on my feet and fastened the diamond straps.

"So is this...what you usually do for women?" I whispered.

He kissed the side of my knee and straightened. "Not usually."

It took me until we were halfway down the hall to realize what he'd said. What did that mean? I glanced over at him, but he was moving confidentially down the hall. Walking with his hand threaded through mine, a half step ahead.

I didn't voice my thoughts.

Downstairs, we moved across the glittering lobby to a private area that overlooked the ocean. The bar was halfway full and the group of men from upstairs were leaning on the far end. I felt their eyes on us as Duran guided me to the side closest to the entrance and lifted me onto the stool.

"Aperol Spritz?" he asked.

I nodded. "Japanese whiskey?"

"Old fashioned actually."

"Oh? You're switching it up on me."

"I wouldn't want you to get bored."

He put in our order and sat down, facing me. One foot on the bottom of my stool. His head was cocked and his body draped against the bar.

"Did you feel shame when you woke up on the plane?"

I froze like a deer in headlights. The bartender set our drinks down and I reached for one, taking a gulp to stall for time.

Had I felt shame? I wracked my brain and realized that I hadn't. For the first time I could remember, I'd done something sexual and I hadn't been flooded with shame so overwhelming it made me sick.

There was no dread.

I took another large sip. "No, I think I was distracted."

"That's good," he said.

I arced a brow, the alcohol giving me courage. "Why do you care?"

His gaze narrowed. "I thought we were past that."

"You keep forgetting that you kidnapped me," I said.

His forehead creased. "I didn't kidnap you, I borrowed you. Accidentally."

My drink was halfway gone. He'd barely touched his, he was just holding it on the counter.

"So put me back," I said, but I didn't sound very convincing.

He shook his head. "I set out on this business trip with the intent to secure that shipment. I'll bring you home once I have what I need. I have to do my job before I do you."

"Do me?"

"I meant, bring you home."

I leaned forward, letting him see the line of my cleavage. His eyes flicked down and his lips parted.

"Really? Because you look like you want to do me," I whispered.

He raised his glass, watching me over it. "Are you teasing me with the intent of letting me fuck you?"

I shook my head. "I told you I wouldn't fuck you."

"You must not be very afraid of me, princess," he said. "You've refused me more than once and you're confident I won't overstep."

My stomach flipped. "Overstep?"

He cocked his head. "You know I won't touch you without consent."

My throat was dry. I wasn't sure what I'd expected, but it wasn't the raw emotion in his dark gaze.

"Who kept you from becoming a monster?" I murmured.

He took his wallet out and flipped it open, handing it to me. Gingerly, I turned over the worn leather to reveal a photograph of a tired woman in her thirties. She was pretty, but there was something so haunted in her eyes it sent a shiver down my spine.

His mother.

She looked like she wanted to die. My stomach felt like ice. A slow realization settled over me and my lashes went wet. When I looked up at him, his face was unreadable.

"You feel guilty too," I whispered.

He winced. "Sometimes."

"You were a child when she died," I said. "Right?"

He shrugged. "I was a minor, yes."

"What did she die of?"

He cleared his throat. "She had an official diagnoses, but that was just the final straw. She died of abuse and neglect. She just broke and stopped wanting to be alive. No one ever came to save her."

I folded the wallet and handed it back to him.

"I'm really sorry, Duran," I said. "You should consider seeing a therapist because you aren't in any way responsible for what happened."

His brows shot up. "A therapist?"

I nodded. "To work through it. This is pretty heavy stuff."

He stared at me like I'd grown a second head. "There's no way I can see a therapist. Not that I could find one with the expertise to deal with my circumstances."

I set my empty glass aside. The alcohol was setting in and I was feeling more open and relaxed.

"Thank you," he said quietly.

"For what?"

"For being the only person to tell me you're sorry she died," he said, straightening. He knocked on the table and signaled the bartender to refill our glasses. "Now, I'm fucking done with the emotional shit."

I opened my mouth, but his eyes flashed. Warning me to back off. The bartender set my drink down. My head spun pleasantly. I caught a glimpse of myself in the mirror behind the bar. No wonder he was speechless when I'd stepped out in this dress. I looked fantastic.

I shook my hair back, feeling incredibly confident.

"Want to play a game?" I asked.

His face relaxed and I knew he was glad for the distraction.

"Sure, princess," he said.

"Okay. Truth or dare?"

He laughed, flashing his white teeth. "Interesting choice. I'll play if we don't do heavy shit."

"Agreed," I said, nodding.

"Alright," he said, leaning in until he was less than a foot away. "I'll go first. Truth or dare, princess?"

"Dare," I said, afraid he was going to ask something incredibly embarrassing.

"That's easy," he said. "I dare you to kiss me."

My eyes widened, but he was already leaning in. Capturing my mouth with his and kissing me slowly and thoroughly. Heat flared in my belly and spread down my thighs, making my pussy ache. When he broke away, I was breathless.

"Truth or dare?" I squeaked.

"Truth."

"Alright. Why did you kidnap me?"

"I thought we said no heavy shit."

"It's not heavy, you seem to be enjoying it a lot."

He sighed. "Alright, I actually thought you might be dangerous at first. You did compromise our security."

"Alright...so why not bring me back when you found out?" I pressed.

He shook his head. "Only one truth per turn, princess. Truth or dare?"

"Truth," I said begrudgingly. I'd suggested the game so I had to stick to the rules.

He leaned in, his dark eyes serious. "Have you…ever cheated at Monopoly?"

I couldn't hold back my giggle. "I don't play Monopoly. I'm an only child."

"You've never played?" he said. "I fucking love Monopoly. We'll play."

"I don't like it."

"You just said you never played it."

"I mean, I imagine I wouldn't like it. You actually like it?"

He shrugged. "I love it, it's the only game that I've ever kicked Lucien's ass at. He wins fucking everything else—chess, battleship, you name it."

The lower half of my face was taken over by a stupid smile. "Has it occurred to you maybe he let you win?"

He scowled. "I hope not, that's the source of all my confidence."

I laughed, unable to hold it back and he smirked. Clearly triumphant. It occurred to me that making me laugh had been his goal. That surprised me. His goal before recently had been to bother me as much as possible and get the upper hand in every conversation.

There was a commotion on the other end of the room. Duran glanced over and I leaned around him to look. The bartender was arguing with the group of men, who were clearly drunk. I shook my head, rolling my eyes, and sat back.

"Anyway, where were we?" he said.

"It's my turn. Truth or dare?"

He emptied his glass, eyes narrowed in consideration. I glanced over his shoulder again, the arguing from the group of men growing louder. I was usually at bars on my own so drunk men set off my alarm bells. Slowly, I became aware that he was looking at me, anticipating an answer.

"What?" I asked.

Behind us, two of the men pushed away from the bar and moved our way. I shrank back and Duran turned, his lips thinning. His shoulders went back and something that looked like anger flashed through his gaze. I shrank back, glancing behind me at the doorway.

"Let's just go," I said quickly. "We can sit outside."

He shook his head once. The leader of the group, a man about Duran's age, paused between our chairs. I could smell the vodka on his breath as his eyes raked over my body. Out of nowhere, a wave of shame flooded me. So intense I automatically squeezed my thighs together and put my hand over my breasts.

"Fuck off," said Duran calmly.

The man's head swung around. Until he was inches from Duran's face.

"You taking this girl upstairs? Gonna give her a good time, huh?" he slurred.

Duran's lip curled and his eyes flashed.

"I'll give you to the count of five to fuck off," he said.

The man laughed, along with his four companions. Burning with embarrassment, I slipped off the opposite side of the stool and ducked around him. Hoping to slip out the door in hopes Duran would follow me.

The ringleader's hand shot out and I whirled, ripping my wrist away.

"You gonna let me have a go when he's done?" he laughed.

Before I could respond, Duran stood and seized him by the collar. I squeaked, backing against the wall. The other men surged forward, but not before Duran yanked the man close, kneed him in the lower belly, and punched his face hard enough to send him tumbling into the next table.

I shrieked and clapped my hands over my mouth.

Duran flexed his hand.

"Fuck," he said.

The four other men rushed him. He took a step back and there was a sharp click. Everyone froze.

Duran had his gun out, leveled at the men. Even in their drunken state, they knew better than to keep going.

"I said fuck off," he said evenly.

In that moment, I wasn't sure if they were going to obey or I was about to see a recreation of the last time Duran had defended me. Then, to my relief, they backed up and disappeared back into the lobby. All except for the ringleader, who was rolling over and trying to get to his feet.

"Hey, asshole," said Duran, kicking a chair out of his way. "Apologize."

"I'm sorry, sorry," the man stuttered.

"I didn't mean me," Duran said, jerking his head. "Apologize to my girl."

His girl? I slowly became aware that my heart was beating out of my chest. If I'd worn panties, they would have been drenched. I shifted my hips, feeling the sensitive, soaked place between my legs tingle. Right here, in this moment, I wanted him more than I'd ever wanted anything in my life.

Dimly, I heard the man hiccup.

"Sorry," he mumbled.

"Whatever," said Duran, gesturing with the gun. "Get the fuck out."

He practically ran into the lobby. Silence fell and I glanced over at the bartender, who was watching with round eyes. Duran snapped the safety on his pistol and pushed it beneath his belt. Then he took his wallet out and counted a stack of bills onto the table.

"I'm sorry about this," he said. "If this doesn't cover it, add it to my account. Duran Esposito."

At his name, the bartender paled, but he nodded hard.

"Absolutely, sir," he said. "And I apologize for those customers."

"Not your fault some motherfuckers can't hold their liquor," Duran said. "Have a good night."

He swept me into the lobby. My fingers had a death grip on my clutch purse. Neither of us spoke as we waited for the elevator. Distantly, I was aware of his arm on my lower back. Guiding me aboard and pressed the button for the seventh floor.

The doors slid shut.

My clutch fell to the ground.

I yanked him close and he shoved me, harder. Pinning me up against the wall. His mouth came down on mine and I moaned, parting my lips to take his tongue. The taste of whiskey and Duran filled my senses.

"When you said you could fight, I didn't think you were actually going to do it," I panted.

He laughed, his other hand pushed between my thighs.

"No fucking panties," he groaned. "You little whore."

My head fell back. His mouth moved down my throat, licking and sucking on my bare skin. Maybe he'd leave marks, maybe he wouldn't, but I didn't care. All I cared about was his rough, lean hands stroking over the wet entrance of my pussy.

Begging to be let in.

He pulled back and flipped me around, one hand on the back of my neck. Pinning me to the wall. With his other, he pulled my skirt up, baring my ass. I wondered haphazardly if the elevator had cameras and decided I didn't care.

His palm came down, slapping my ass hard.

"Pretty little slut," he panted, pushing his hard cock against me. He slapped me again and his finger slid down.

I tensed. The tip of it found my asshole and stroked the sensitive skin. Fireworks exploded and my entire body sagged as my knees wobbled.

"Duran," I gasped.

He pulled back and spanked me again. Hard enough to make my back arch. His mouth dragged over the nape of my neck.

"Whose cunt is that between your pretty thighs?" he demanded.

"Yours," I moaned.

My pussy pulsed, painfully empty. My entire body was frantic for him and I couldn't control the way I was pushing my ass into his erection. Practically begging for him to pull his zipper down.

His hand came down again. Heat radiated from the right side of my poor ass and wetness slipped down my thigh. I whimpered. He bit the nape of my neck, holding it for a second before releasing.

"If I were a bad man, I'd lift your skirt and fuck you right here," he said. "If I were a bad man, I'd be fantasizing about having your blood on my cock and my cum in your pussy. If I were irreparable, I'd have been fantasizing about it this entire time."

My stomach flipped.

Why did that make me want him more?

"You want me like that?" I gasped.

He pushed his hand in my hair and gripped hard. Pulling my head back as he ground on my naked ass.

"Princess, you have no fucking idea the depraved ways I want you."

The elevator dinged. Abruptly, he pulled back and adjusted himself and picked up my purse. I brushed my skirt down and the doors slid open to reveal a handful of business people waiting in the hallway.

"Evening," Duran said, taking my hand and guiding me out of the elevator.

I could barely walk straight. He kept his hand on my waist as he swiped his key card and guided me into our room. Before I could speak, he pushed me onto my back on the bed and knelt over me. His eyes narrowed.

"Duran," I whispered, my heart pounding.

"Let's sober you up, princess," he said. "I still have some shreds of decency left."

CHAPTER TWENTY

DURAN

Despite having just fought in the bar, I had nothing on my mind but this girl in that dress. It was one of those tiny silk things that rode up when I caressed my hands over her hips, revealing a flash of her soft, naked pussy.

It took us forever to find a menu. She was all over me and I wasn't going to push her off. For the first time, she wanted me and there wasn't a trace of shame in her big, ocean eyes.

We made out against the wall until my dick was so hard I couldn't take it anymore. I pulled back, head spinning and chest heaving. She nipped at my lower lip and I groaned, cupping her face.

"You need dinner, princess," I breathed.

She giggled. The sound made my ego purr. Knowing that she was happy and having a good time felt so good I was worried I might get addicted. I ran my hand through her hair, brushing it from her smooth cheek.

"Lift your arms," I said.

She obeyed and I slid her dress up and off her body. Without hesitating, she unsnapped her strapless bra and her breasts fell free. Beautiful, full, soft. My hands gravitated towards them and she bit her lip as I cupped each breast and ran my thumbs over her nipples.

"That feels good," she murmured.

I bent and kissed her forehead. "I'll play with you all night if you have some dinner and a glass of water. Alright?'

She nodded. "I am starving."

Spinning her around, I slapped her ass and pushed her towards the bed. She giggled again and clambered onto the bed. Ass up and back arced. I narrowed my eyes, watching as she snuggled beneath the comforter. Pulling it around her waist and leaving her breasts bare.

"I'm not really that tipsy," she whispered. "I'm just really horny and I don't want to stop."

Fuck, I didn't want to stop either.

Instead, I changed into sweatpants and found a menu. She moved closer as I sank into bed beside me, pressing her cheek against my shoulder. I kept my eyes on the menu, trying to play it cool. Inside, my ego purred like a cat.

She was snuggling me, she trusted me.

"Have you ever had caviar?" I asked, dragging myself back and scanning the starters.

She wrinkled her nose. "I did once on vacation with my family. It's okay, but I don't really see what all the fuss is about."

"Not a seafood person?"

"No, I just didn't like the caviar. I love lobster, shrimp, most kinds of fish. We had this great sushi place by my house and I used to go there after school."

"Well, tonight they don't have sushi," I said. "But they have a four-course meal with lobster as the entree."

She cocked her head, thinking hard. "Lobster seems kind of extravagant."

"Good, let's order it," I said, reaching for the phone.

She rolled her eyes while I placed the order and I got her back by flipping her onto her stomach and slapping her ass a few minutes later. She yelped and giggled, burrowing into the fluffy bed.

"Comfortable?" I asked, sliding between the covers.

God, why did her body feel so perfect against mine. I closed my eyes and shifted closer and buried my face in her hair. She moaned and wriggled her ass back against my sweatpants. My cock twitched.

"Don't wake the beast," I murmured.

She wriggled her hips again and my cock went fully hard and I pushed it up against her round ass. Her spine arced and a little moan escaped her full mouth. Almost a whine of longing. All the blood in my head rushed down to my groin and my mind went blank.

"So I shouldn't feel guilty?" she whispered.

I buried my face into the side of her neck, kissing her hard. My hips worked, dragging my cock over her perfect, soft ass. My fingers slid down her waist, up the delicious curve of her hip. She moaned and wriggled, begging for more.

"Duran," she breathed. "I want it so fucking much."

I found the seam of her naked pussy and stroked it gently. Teasing the little nub of her clit before dragging my middle finger down to where her wetness gathered.

"Does this pretty cunt need my cock, baby?" I whispered. "Do you need fucked so badly?"

Her grip clenched above her head, gripping the pillow so hard her knuckles were white.

"Yes," she panted. "God, I just want something."

Her pupils blew as I flipped her onto her back and slid between her legs. My thigh pushed against her slippery clit and I felt her arousal soak through my sweatpants and scorch my skin. Her teeth nibbled her soft lower lip and her gaze dropped as I pushed my waistband down and bared my cock.

"Just the tip, princess," I breathed.

I thought surely she would shake her head or scramble up against the headboard. But she kept perfectly still and her fingers gripped the pillows like she was afraid she would fall off the bed. Then, eyes wide and vulnerable, she nodded.

I laid her on her back and pressed a frantic kiss to her mouth. Her tongue brushed mine and that burning touch went right down to my groin. The intelligent part of my brain was completely dead. There was nothing in me except the animal urge to feel the soft, wet heat of her pussy wrap around my cock as she took me into her body.

Into her perfect, stunning body.

One hand below her knee, I spread her thighs back. She whimpered and her hips worked. Her pussy looked wet and relaxed despite her inexperience. Heart pounding, I slid down over her and gripped myself by the base. Her jaw tensed as the head of my cock slid against her opening and her lashes fluttered as I pushed the very tip inside.

My vision flashed. I gritted my teeth to keep from slamming into her.

She was perfect, even just this half inch of her.

Hot and so sensitive I swore I felt her heartbeat pulsing around me.

She whimpered, pinning her lower lip. Chewing on it hard.

"Are you alright, princess?" I breathed.

She nodded hard. "It hurts. Are you sure that's just the tip and not all of it?"

I shifted to pull out, but her legs wrapped around my waist tightly. Her expression was fierce and drunk with desire. Heavy lids, a swollen mouth, hard nipples flushed pink. I bent and took one in my mouth and licked it once before sucking hard enough to hurt.

Her hips bucked in an involuntary spasm and her pelvis hit mine. The gasp that burst from her lips was more of a strangled cry. It took me a second to find my way through the confusion and burst of intense pleasure around my cock to realize I was inside her pussy.

Almost. There was an inch or two left.

But I'd broken her hymen, I could tell. I'd felt it give way. The faint metallic scent of blood edged the heavy sound of our panting breaths.

"Are you okay?" I whispered.

Her nails pierced my naked upper arms, digging into the skin and muscle. "Yes, but I didn't mean for that to happen," she whispered.

"I didn't either," I said, my voice hushed. "But now that I'm in, let's fuck."

She flushed bright red and her head fell back as I drew out halfway and thrust gently into her slick, little cunt. My jaw went hard and my stomach tensed down to where our bodies joined. I'd fucked a lot before, but never in my life had I felt anything like this.

My cock was made for her pussy, made to fill her until her pretty ocean eyes rolled back in her head and she begged for relief.

I braced my knee and fucked in short, shallow strokes to help her adjust to my size. She squirmed and the pink flush on her cheeks was the prettiest fucking thing I'd ever seen. Second only to her tight pink nipples, straining up from her breasts.

I thrust all the way in and paused.

Her lashes fluttered. "Did you...are you done?"

I laughed quietly. "No, princess."

"What are you doing?" she whispered.

I brushed back her long, blonde hair and gathered it in my fist. "I'm just feeling you from inside. You're so soft...wet...silky. You grip me so well."

Her lips trembled and the corners tugged up in a small smile.

"You like that?" I asked. "When I praise you?"

She nodded and I bent, capturing her mouth with mine. Kissing her slowly as my cock grew impossibly hard deep inside. I'd never kissed and fucked at the same time—it had always felt too intimate. And I'd been right about that because this was the most fucking intimate I'd ever been with another person in my life.

She moaned. Her slender fingers dug into my chest and pain sparked beneath her nails.

We kissed slowly. Mouths moving together, tongues brushing. Our tastes mingling.

I broke away, our lips still almost touching.

"You're such a good girl for me," I told her. "Now let's flip you over so I can see your beautiful, round ass shake while I fuck your cunt."

We broke apart and she scrambled to her hands and knees. Her spine arced as I knelt behind her and she presented her wet, little pussy to me for fucking. I ran my hand up her thigh and gripped her hip to hold her steady before slipping my cock back into her.

She was a little bloody, but that could wait until we were done.

Right now, we both had more pressing things to think about. I reached up and gripped the nape of her neck. Her hips wriggled and she let out the sweetest, breathy moan. Almost a giggle of anticipation.

"Good," I breathed, fucking my hips up against her ass. "Take the whole thing, princess, it's all for you. You've got the sweetest fucking pussy ever made and it's all for me."

"All for you," she panted.

"That's right," I groaned, slapping her thigh. "Tell me whose cunt this is."

"Yours. It's yours, Duran," she moaned.

Goddamn, that made me drunk and high all at once. I pumped my hips and slammed into her until my cock bottomed out. But I didn't relent because I wanted my cock in every inch of her cunt. I wanted my cum to stain every part of her because she was fucking mine.

My girl.

Maybe that was why I'd taken her from the resort in the first place.

Maybe I hadn't really believed she was a spy. Maybe I'd just gotten a taste of her pussy and realized that if I let this woman go I was going to regret it for the rest of my life.

I'd always run from commitment, but right here, with my cock buried in it, the thought of making her mine had the opposite effect. I fell over her and we collapsed into the bed together as I came so hard it knocked the breath from my lungs.

My hips ground her into the bed. Pumping my cum into her pussy.

"Take it all, princess," I ordered.

I didn't want a single drop of my cum leaving her body. She whimpered beneath me, but I didn't relent until I was empty. Then, slowly, I slid out of her and flipped her onto her back.

Her eyes were wide, pupils blown. "You fucked me," she whispered.

"I did," I said with pride.

Her lip trembled. "I didn't come."

Confused, I glanced down at her swollen pussy. Wet with our cum and smeared with traces of her blood. I glanced down at my cock and wicked pride rose in me at the crimson smears down my length.

"We have all night," I said gently. "Let's get in the shower and I'll eat you out until you can't come anymore."

She frowned, confused and a little dazed. "I thought I would come," she whispered. "From being fucked."

"Oh...I'm sorry," I said, sitting up and lifting her gently into my lap. Her lower lip starting shaking and tears seeped to the corners of her eyes. Fuck, this wasn't what was supposed to happen.

I felt like a piece of shit.

Gathering her close, I began rubbing her lower back gently. "I'm sorry, but this is totally normal."

A little sob shook down her center. "What's wrong with me?"

My heart shattered. "Wrong with you? Nothing, you're perfect."

She sobbed out loud this time and her body shook in my arms. "Why do I feel like this?"

This was all new to me. Never in my life had a woman started crying after sex with me and I was scrambling for the right words. It didn't help that my chest ached like I'd been kicked.

"Like what?" I asked gently.

She took a deep shuddering breath. "I thought I wouldn't feel like this after...I feel so fucking guilty. What am I going to do when I get home?"

I lifted her in my arms and carried her to the bathroom. She sat quietly on the counter as I ran a hot bath with bubbles. When I got a warm washcloth to wipe her pussy, she winced and I could tell she was sore from what I'd done.

I brushed back her hair. "Can you use the toilet?"

She frowned. "What?"

It was dawning on me that she'd meant it when she'd said her parents were strict. No one had bothered to teach her about sex or her body and now she was feeling the effects of it. Now, she was all broken and bloody on my sink and I felt like the worst person in the world.

"You need to empty your bladder after sex," I explained gently, making sure she didn't feel patronized. "It'll keep you from getting an infection."

"Oh," she sniffed. "Okay, I can do that."

I turned my back and got into the tub while she used the toilet. Then I beckoned her close and helped her sink into the hot water. She sat opposite me, her shoulders hunched. Her wet blonde hair stuck to her neck.

"Can you talk to me about this?" I pressed.

She shook her head. "I don't want to think about it."

I cleared my throat. "No, I'm not accepting that. You're going to sit here on my lap and be a good girl for me and tell me what went wrong. Understood?"

That snapped her out of it. Eyes flashing, mumbling under her breath, she obeyed. Her soft body slid over mine as she climbed into my lap and laid her head back against my chest.

"That's my girl," I said gently. "Now, who told you that you would come from being fucked?"

She shook her head. "I don't know. I just assumed."

"You masturbate sometimes though," I mused. "You know that most of your pleasure comes from your clit."

She chewed on her lip. "I...I don't touch myself very much."

"Why not?"

Her big eyes met mine in the mirrors surrounding the tub. She swallowed and tore her gaze from mine. There was so much shame and sadness in them.

"Because you were taught it was wrong," I guessed.

She nodded once.

I kissed the top of her head. "That part of your body is for pleasure, whether from yourself or with someone else. It's no one else's business if you touch yourself. Stand up."

Surprised, she rose. Her naked body stood over me, dripping soap and bubbles.

"Sit on the edge of the tub and spread your pussy so you can see it in the mirror," I told her.

She shook her head. "Absolutely not."

"Why? You've never seen your own pussy before?"

I'd meant it as a joke, but she blushed and I regretted my words instantly. I pulled her back down into the water with me.

"It's okay," I assured her. "And it's normal for you not to come just from being fucked. I'd have been surprised if you did. Some women can come from having their G-spots stimulated, but the majority of women need their clitoris touched."

"So...I could come from being fucked if I touched myself while you did it?" she whispered.

"Yes, I'm sure you can," I said. "But expecting your body to go from zero to a hundred right away is just not realistic."

She released a shaky sigh. "I think...after growing up being taught that sex was for men's pleasure, I think I thought the opposite end of that was fireworks and rainbows for women."

"Did you watch porn?" I asked, keeping my tone neutral.

She looked instantly guilty, but she managed a flushed nod. Poor girl, she'd had it ground into her so deeply that anything to do with her sexuality or desires was something to be ashamed of.

This was going to take time and patience.

But for her...I was willing to do that.

I turned her around and wrapped her silky thighs around my waist. She looked up at me earnestly. Like she was waiting for me to offer her absolution.

"Porn isn't very realistic, Iris," I said, struggling to find the right words. "Those women aren't having multiple orgasms just from being fucked. It's for show, no one really acts or looks like that in the bedroom."

Her jaw worked. "Okay, that makes sense."

She was too young to be this broken.

I kept my face empty of emotion. She didn't need to deal with the confusion I was experiencing right now.

"It also just takes time to learn someone's body," I said. "Everyone is different and what one person likes might feel like shit to another. Everyone has certain things they like and ways they can orgasm. Trying to apply a broad brush over giving and getting pleasure just doesn't work."

"What...what are you into?" She looked up at me shyly.

"During sex? Or foreplay?"

"Either."

I leaned back, running my hands up her thighs and circling her waist. "I like women with eyes the color of the ocean and blonde hair long enough I can wrap it around my fist."

A little smile ghosted over her mouth.

"You're just describing me," she whispered.

My throat and mouth went as dry as sand. Deep inside, my heart thumped like a drum. I'd realized it when I was balls deep in her pussy and if I wanted to tell her, now was the perfect time.

"I like you, Iris," I said. "A lot."

She swallowed hard and her fingers came up to slide over mine so we were both holding her together. I could feel our hearts thumping in the silence between us. In this moment, there was nothing but our just-fucked bodies all slippery with soap and the realization that her next words could break my heart or bring me to life.

"You like me?" she said. "Is that why you kidnapped me?"

I shrugged. "Maybe."

"You kidnapped me and now you've dragged me halfway around the world, Duran," she said. "I certainly hope you like me."

That word, despite it being mine, didn't sit well with me. *Like* wasn't a good enough word to describe the rage I'd felt every time she'd been in danger. It was a poor way of describing the overwhelming warmth in my chest as I held her naked body against mine.

The truth was, I never wanted another man to be in my position. Ugliness rose in me at the image. My fingers tightened, gripping her hard.

Mine.

There was a heavy knock on the door. I'd completely forgotten that we'd ordered dinner over an hour ago. She scrambled up to let me step out of the tub and wrap a towel around my waist. I shut the bathroom door and went to let the concierge in, staying back while they rolled the cart into the room and parked it.

I glanced over at the bed.

It was a mess. Rumpled sheets stained with cum and blood. Our clothes littered the floor.

Grimacing, I took three hundred dollars from my wallet and handed it to the man.

"Sorry about this," I said. "I forgot we ordered dinner."

He accepted the money, backing into the hall. "It's no problem, sir. Enjoy your meal."

"Thanks," I said.

"Would you like me to have fresh sheets sent up, sir?" he asked.

"Yes, please," I said. "Thank you."

He nodded curtly and disappeared and I locked the door. I stood there for a moment, realizing what this must have looked like to him. Undoubtedly he knew who I was so he probably assumed I did this all the time. He probably thought I was some rich asshole who deflowered women almost ten years younger on hotel sheets regularly.

Was he right?

She wasn't the first virgin I'd fucked in a hotel bed.

But she was the first that I'd fucked and decided that no one else would ever do the same.

The bathroom door creaked open and she appeared. She was in my t-shirt and it swamped her, coming halfway down her thigh. I paused and took a moment just to take in the sight of her in my clothes.

It looked right, it felt right.

"Hungry?" I asked, my voice oddly hoarse.

CHAPTER TWENTY-ONE

IRIS

We hadn't resolved anything in the tub, but I felt much better when I joined him in the bed. Maybe it was because he'd listened to me and he hadn't laughed or dismissed me when I'd dumped all my messy emotions out onto him.

Or perhaps it was because he'd told me he had feelings for me and then he'd gotten oddly quiet.

A concierge knocked on the door and handed Duran a stack of sheets and a comforter. I stood back awkwardly, my head spinning, while he made up the bed. He tucked the comforter down and pointed to the bed.

"Get in," he said.

"You're being a little demanding," I teased, offering a shy smile.

His brow crooked. "Get your ass into bed, princess."

This time, I listened. He set the platter of food down between us and lifted the lid. A cloud of steam rose and revealed a whole lobster decorated in lemons and smelling of butter. There was a bowl of rice, a dish of steamed vegetables, and a plate of crisp rolls with butter.

My stomach growled and twisted. I'd forgotten I was starving.

I reached for a roll and his hand closed around my wrist. Shocked, I looked up into his midnight eyes and a shudder moved through me. Sometimes he could look so stern it was scary.

"What?" I frowned.

"You let me," he said. "Open your mouth."

Surprised, I felt my jaw drop open. He tore off a piece of bread and dipped it in cinnamon butter and put it on my tongue. I chewed carefully and swallowed, not taking my eyes off his fingers. There was a bit of butter on his thumb.

I leaned in and captured it between my teeth.

His pupils dilated. "Fuck," he murmured.

Keeping my eyes locked with his, I sucked the butter from his finger and pulled back.

"Do you know what I think, Duran?" I whispered.

He cocked his head, lip lifting just enough to flash those white teeth. That fucking pointed canine. My hips shuddered, wishing I could feel it sink into the soft flesh of my ass.

"I think you like dominating me a lot more than you're letting on," I said. "You pretend you're so easygoing, but I can see who you really are."

"Oh?" His mouth barely moved.

"I want you to help me," I said quietly. "I don't want to feel this shame anymore. If I have to do whatever you want, that's fine with me. Just fix me."

I knew it was too much to ask, but if he couldn't fix me, no one could.

"Alright," he said. "Let's start by getting you fed."

My stomach fluttered and I swallowed past the lump in my throat. This time it wasn't from tears. It was from breathless anticipation.

"And then?"

He kissed me. "And then we're going to sleep."

I almost protested, but his eyes flashed. Demanding obedience. Cowed, I began filling my stomach with tender, buttery lobster and more rolls than I could comfortably fit. Afterwards, he rolled me onto my stomach and I kept perfectly still while he jerked himself off onto my lower back.

It felt good. Sweet and a little humiliating, but not in a way that triggered my shame. More in a way that made me feel owned and protected.

He rubbed the cum into my back and lifted me up just enough to tease my nipples with it. I gasped as my pussy ached with the need to come.

"Mine," he said, lightly slapping my ass.

"I want to come," I panted.

His fingers kneaded the sore muscles in the center of my back. "When you wake up. That's your punishment for talking back so many times."

I pouted silently as he slid into bed beside me. He pulled me against his chest and nestled my ass back against his groin. His fingers began working down my lower back, massaging me gently. I melted, knowing I was done for.

"Goodnight, princess," he said.

It was early when I woke and flipped over in his arms to watch him sleep. His face was relaxed and his lids were slightly cracked, his eyes rolled back. I ran my fingertip over the short hair of his beard and down his stubbled neck.

He moaned in his sleep. I glanced down and froze as my eyes fell on the rise beneath the sheets.

Was that normal?

I stared at it, remembering how thick and full it had felt inside me yesterday. The memory triggered a ripple of shame. But, for the first time, I took a deep breath and forced my mind not to spiral.

I was going to focus on the warm, naked man in my bed because it was positive. Because he'd never once shamed me for wanting him.

His lids fluttered. He cleared his throat.

"Take a picture, princess. It'll last longer," he said hoarsely.

I giggled and stretched, sitting up in the cloud of white bedding. My whole body felt so relaxed, better than I'd felt in a long time. I cracked my neck and back and yawned.

"Feeling good?" He cocked his head.

"I feel amazing," I admitted. "Honestly, I thought I was going to feel like shit, but I don't."

His hands closed on my thighs and before I could protest, he lifted me over his face and set me down. I wobbled, my mind flashing back to that moment in the elevator when he'd stroked my asshole with his fingertip. This was only slightly less embarrassing.

"What are you doing?" I gasped.

"Grab the headboard and sit on my face, princess," he demanded.

Heart pounding, I sank down and gripped the headboard for support. He looked up from between my thighs and a slow smile curled over his mouth. Flashing me with that canine and a thoroughly dirty expression.

"Stay still," he said. "If you can."

He pressed me down onto his mouth and the wet heat of his tongue slid over my clit. Licking it slowly until my tensed muscles relaxed and I sank down onto his face. He moaned and the vibrations felt like heaven.

"I don't think it's going to take much," I whispered.

He kept licking, his eyes fixed on me from down below. Dark, dangerous, and glittering. His tongue lapped at my clit, pausing only so he could suck on the sensitive bud. His right hand slid over my ass and dipped between my thighs.

It circled the tender opening of my pussy. Something about the pain felt good this time. Perhaps because he'd done that to me, he had left his cum and his bruises behind.

Pleasure moved along my spine in a rush and tingled down to the soles of my feet. I curled my toes, my hips going tight. My head fell back and the ceiling swirled overhead.

He pulled back, taking my orgasm with him.

"Eyes on me, princess," he ordered.

He gripped my ass and slapped it. I yelped and obeyed, letting my hips relax. Giving him all my weight. He groaned and worked my clit in quick circles with the blunt tip of his tongue. Dragging the pleasure back up to the surface.

"Oh my God," I moaned.

I knew he must be rock hard and I wanted to look, but I didn't dare break eye contact. He would slap my ass hard if I disobeyed him. Delicious anticipation shuddered down my spine and pleasure burst slowly through my hips and thighs.

My stomach went tight and I felt my eyes widen as it hit me. Slow, long pulses of pleasure that I felt in every part of my body. My hips writhed and my knees gave out. He caught me before I fell backwards and flipped me roughly onto my back.

"Spread your thighs," he ordered.

His lids were heavy and there was nothing but the driving need to fuck in his eyes. I shuddered, with pleasure and anticipation, and obeyed him. Spreading my legs wide and baring my pussy.

He slid between my legs and into me. My lower back arced off the bed—God, he was so big and I was tender from being fucked last night. I gasped and my arms wound around his neck. Clinging to him as he pushed himself ruthlessly into me until he was sheathed in my pussy.

"Mine, my perfect slut," he murmured. "I want to fuck you like this forever."

My head spun. He drew back and slammed into me, clearly not caring if he made me sore. My nails dug into his skin, tearing my pleasure into his hard shoulders.

"Fuck me," I begged.

This was crazy, this wasn't normal. I barely knew this man and after all he'd done to me, he had no business talking about me like I belonged to him.

But I knew right then if he ever talked about anyone else like that, it would break my heart.

We fucked frantically, our breaths loud. I wanted him so deeply inside me I could feel him for days. He clearly wanted the same thing because he stopped and flipped me onto my stomach, lifting my hips. His cock filled me before dragging out and slamming back in.

"That's right," he said through gritted teeth. "Take my cock, take all of it. The way you were made to, princess."

I whimpered and his hand came up and tangled in my hair. He drew my head back in an arc and his mouth brushed down the side of my neck.

Kisses pressed into my shoulder and sent flutters through my stomach and thighs. Just as his lips reached my upper arm, I felt his stomach ripple and his cock went so hard in me I whimpered into the bed.

"Take my cum," he breathed, riding me with short strokes as he emptied himself into my pussy.

We both went still and his warm body sagged over mine. His breath was heavy and his mouth felt extraordinary as he pressed kisses between my shoulder blades.

Who was Duran Esposito?

At first, he'd been nothing more than a villain. My kidnapper, a playboy mafia man without empathy.

But I was completely wrong about that.

There was a gentleness to him that I'd never expected. And beneath that gentleness ran a secret current of sadness. I wondered if I was the only person he'd ever revealed it to.

"Are you alright?" he murmured.

"Yeah," I said, turning my head to the side. "I'm okay. Want to let me up?"

I could feel him smile as he pressed one last kiss into the crook of my neck and eased his cock from between my thighs. A dull ache moved through my hips. Behind me, I heard him walk into the bathroom and turn on the shower.

Feeling shy, I went after him. He stood beneath the two nozzles built into the ceiling, letting the hot water pound down on his upper back. His eyes flickered open and fixed on me.

"Come here," he said.

I obeyed, stepping beneath the water with him. He gathered up my hair and brushed it behind my shoulders. His finger trailed down my throat and traced my collarbones.

"Did I ruin you, princess?" he asked quietly.

"Yes, a little bit," I admitted.

His lids flickered. "In a bad way?"

I shook my head. "No, I think I wanted to be ruined. I think I needed to cut the cord in a real way. Now I just have to…rebuild."

He swallowed and ran his hand up over his face and slicked his dark hair back. He had a fascinating kind of handsomeness about him. He had traditionally masculine traits—a square jaw, a short beard, a thin mouth, a heavy nose.

But there was something so pretty about his face that I couldn't look away. Maybe it was the rare moments of softness.

His mouth turned up in the corners. His smile was a little bitter this time.

"I hope you know you're not different after last night," he said, a catch in his voice. "What men do to you, Iris, doesn't define you. It doesn't change your worth if you've been fucked or not."

It sounded so simple and easy when he said it, but no one had ever said that to me. My entire world shifted a little on its axis.

"My father was an asshole," he said suddenly. "He was the worst person I've ever met and I never wanted to be like him."

His honesty surprised me. I took a beat, formulating a careful response. I didn't want him to pull back.

"What was he like?"

His eyes narrowed, fixed to the ground. "He was a serial cheater, a rapist, an abuser, one of the most narcissistic, manipulative people I've ever met."

"Is...that normal? Like for men in those kinds of positions?"

Duran let out a slow sigh. "It can be. Upper classes from all walks of life tend to marry for alliances, for money, for fame. What we do among the highest social rungs isn't unusual, but it can result in women being paired with men who hurt them. My father wanted my mother so he took her and he resented that she didn't love him their entire lives."

"So he did all those things to her?"

Duran dipped his head, probably to hide his eyes.

"Yes," he said.

"Why?"

He lifted his chin and there was a lingering coldness in his face.

"Answer this riddle for me, Iris, because I've never been able to figure it out for myself. Perhaps I know the answer, but I'm too much of a pussy to say it aloud."

"Okay," I faltered.

"A man has two sons. One is his heir and the other is the spare. Around the time the spare is born, the father becomes increasingly cruel and abusive towards his wife and essentially ignores his youngest son. The oldest son grows up with everyone telling him how he's the spitting image of his father, how they have the same shade of brown hair and hazel eyes. The second son has black hair and black eyes and no one has ever said he looks like his father. What do you think the answer to that riddle is?"

I stared up at him, my mouth dry. I cracked my lips.

"Infidelity," I whispered.

The look in his eyes was glacial.

"Perhaps that's the most likely answer," he said. "But we'll never know. She went to France for a summer when she was eighteen. Sometimes I wonder if the reason she was so insistent that Lucien and I learn the language had to do with someone she met there."

"You can get tested."

He shook his head. "Lucien and I have always bonded over how unfortunate it is that we were related to our father. I think it would hurt him if he found out we only shared a mother."

He surprised me yet again.

"You really love your brother," I pointed out.

He shrugged. "Eh...he's kind of an asshole, but he's all I've got."

"Is he an asshole the way your father was?"

"He's not...or he's what my father might have been if he'd been born with a conscience," Duran mused. "He doesn't want to get married, I don't think he likes being pushed into an arranged marriage, but he won't treat his wife badly."

"So..why can't he just not get married?"

"It's not that simple. Our family has had an agreement with the Barones, his future wife's family, for quite a while. We're both wealthy and we both have substantial assets. Marrying outside of that would spring a leak in generations of wealth. Plus, there's some bad blood between the families and it would smooth that over…or maybe make it worse. I don't know."

"It's kind of weird and archaic," I mused.

"Look around at upper classes everywhere," he said, shrugging. "It's not uncommon. Politicians, heirs and heiresses, even actors, do it all the time."

A slow realization was sinking over me and it wasn't a pleasant one.

"So…you're an Esposito," I said.

"Yeah, I am," he said.

"So…are you supposed to marry a rich girl?"

His jaw twitched. "Technically, yes."

We looked at each other and the things we'd said in the heat of losing my virginity to him hung heavy between us. A surge of heat passed over his face and he gripped my upper arms and turned me around. His lean body pressed against my back and his cock hardened. Pushing hungrily into my ass.

"I will do whatever the fuck I please," he said grimly.

In that moment, I believed him.

He washed my hair and I sagged against him, too blissed out to continue our conversation. I'd never had anyone do this for me except my hairdresser and it felt amazing. Then he washed my body, taking a suspiciously long time to clean my breasts and between my thighs. His cock stayed hard, but I didn't offer to do anything about it.

My pussy needed some recovery time before he fucked it again.

No one had ever spent so much time focused on just me. He'd fed me well, he'd fucked me thoroughly, eaten me out until I wasn't sure if I could come anymore, and then he'd washed me clean. I was feeling like a princess as I dried off with a fluffy towel.

Naked, I crawled back into bed.

I heard him laugh quietly as he walked out to get dressed. Sleepily, I cracked an eye.

"What's so funny?"

He cocked his head. "So you can be a good girl if you've had all the fight fucked out of you."

"Don't be an asshole," I mumbled.

"I'll order you breakfast," he said. "Then I have to go out. Be ready in something nice for dinner at five."

I was already fast asleep, curled up with the sheets wrapped around my body. A knock on the door woke me thirty minutes later and a concierge brought me a platter of breakfast. I burrowed against the pillows and lifted the lid, revealing waffles, strawberries, sausages, and a cup of coffee.

In the center lay a single red rose.

I couldn't keep from giggling and curling my toes. He was making me stupid and I didn't mind.

When my belly was full, I slept some more. There wasn't anything else to do because he'd apparently instructed the hotel staff not to let me leave the premises. There was a bulky man with a stern face outside the door and when I peered out, he shook his head ominously.

I lay in bed and thought about him for a while which led to my fingers sliding between my thighs. This time when I masturbated, I didn't feel such an overwhelming sense of guilt afterwards.

Instead I just stretched and rolled over and fell asleep in a haze of satisfaction.

By the time he'd returned at a quarter to four, I was up. My hair was pulled into a sleek, tall ponytail and my makeup was done with a razor sharp cat-eye. He strolled in and saw me and gave me a slow once over.

"Fuck," he said.

I glanced over my dark blue, skimpy panties and bra like it was nothing. "What?"

He shook his head, taking off his jacket and going to the closet to select a new suit.

"Should I go slutty or good girl?" I mused, looking over the dresses I'd laid out. "Will you get jealous if I show some skin?"

"Maybe," he said thoughtfully. "But you'd like that, wouldn't you?"

I turned to conceal the smirk on my face. "Slutty it is then."

I had a dress at the bottom of my bag that I'd picked up the day he'd taken me shopping. Never in my wildest dreams did I think I'd wear it. I'd just grabbed it to fill my basket.

I pulled it on and settled the straps on my shoulders. Over the tiny silk lining was transparent, beige chiffon with a faint blue print. Before I stood, I slipped on my black heels and straightened.

The dress was even skimpier and shorter than the one I'd worn last night. And that one had driven him wild. I did an experimental pirouette before the mirror. It floated up around me and flashed my dark blue panties before settling around my hips.

He walked out of the bathroom in a casual black suit with a dark shirt, open at the collar. His gaze flicked over me and his mouth thinned. Jealousy brought a flush to the base of his neck.

"Turn around," he ordered.

Heart thumping, I obeyed.

"Bend over. Grip your ankles."

I glanced back. "What?"

"Now, Iris." There was a sternness to his voice I hadn't expected.

Obediently, but blushing hard, I bent over and wrapped my hands around my ankles. There was a long silence and then his footsteps drew close and his finger ran up my exposed ass. It hooked my panties and pulled them aside.

"You'll keep these on," he said. "And don't bend over in public."

I went to straighten up, but before I could, he tugged my panties aside further and gave my pussy a little spank.

I gasped and jumped up, spinning. He smirked and turned away to button his cuffs before the mirror.

"I fucked it, princess," he said casually. "So it's mine."

"What about your cock? I guess the same doesn't apply to it."

"You fucked it so it's yours. Want me to write your name on it?"

My jaw dropped. I was self-aware enough to know he'd out maneuvered me this time. My cheeks burned and I was acutely aware of where his fingers had slapped my pussy. Leaving a sensitive, tingling spot. All I could think about was what it would feel like if he spanked me in earnest.

I shivered.

His brow crooked. "Do you need to come before we go?" he teased.

I shook back my hair. "No. I'm ready to go."

"Actually, I have one more thing," he said, taking a long, thin case from his pocket.

My heart flipped. He had bought me a gift?

He snapped the lid open and lifted a thin, diamond encrusted tennis bracelet with a bow made of more diamonds over the clasp. It wasn't my style…at least it hadn't been my style before I met him. I'd never been confident in girly things, but he was making me like them a lot more.

"Hand out," he said.

Without a single thought in my head, I put my wrist out and he fastened the bracelet around it. His gaze flicked up as he clasped it and stayed, not breaking contact.

"It's beautiful, but not as beautiful as you," he said.

"Oh," I said, blushing and shaking my head. "You are a smooth operator, Duran Esposito."

"Remember how you panicked when you accidentally spent twenty thousand on a necklace?" he said.

I nodded.

"Well, this is twice that, princess."

My jaw dropped. Smirking, he led me downstairs and out to the waiting car. It took a lot of work to sit down and slide into the car without flashing my panties to everyone. In the end, he stood over me, his broad body a human shield between me and passersby. When he slid in next to me, I saw the rise beneath his pants.

Smiling, I crossed one leg over the other and tucked my hands together over my clutch. He had his sunglasses on, as usual, and he was swiping on his phone. I could tell he was reading by how his lips were moving.

He put the phone away abruptly and his palm rested on my thigh. The gesture was shockingly possessive. Like he already owned me.

Like he'd just taken my virginity and regretted nothing.

I stared out the window. Had that actually happened or had I dreamed it up? Last night was a blur. I knew for certain he'd fucked me because I was sore and when I clenched my inner muscles, I swore I still felt his cock in me.

But…had he really said he felt something for me?

My fingers drifted down to the absurdly expensive bracelet and twisted it absently. The city lights flashed by as we drove out on a peninsula and the driver pulled up outside a brassy, modern hotel on the water. I stayed still while Duran circled the car to help me out.

"Your panties flash every time you sit up," he said, lifting me to my feet.

"Are you jealous?" I murmured.

He kissed the side of my neck. Butterflies burst in my stomach.

"Fuck, yes, but I don't mind," he said, taking my hand. "Let them look. Everyone knows whose cock you ride."

My brows shot up to my hairline and I admitted defeat once again. He led me up the paved walkway and through the sandy garden out front.

We entered a dimly lit room set with classy tables and a large, black orchid display over the fountain in the middle. Duran ushered me beyond it and out to the balcony over the water.

I shrank back. There was a long, oval table with men dressed like Duran seated at almost every place. At their sides were elegant women, many of them glittering with thousands of dollars worth of diamonds. They were all stunning with their perfect makeup and elegant clothes.

Suddenly, I wished I'd picked a little black dress or something more sophisticated.

"What's wrong?" Duran murmured.

"I don't know if this is my crowd," I squeaked.

"Don't worry, you'll be by me," he said, guiding me across the patio to two empty chairs beside the head seat. I sank down to his left and he leaned over to shake the hand of the man at the head of the table.

The man greeting him was incredibly tall and broad. His hair was cut short and his bright blue eyes flicked over me for a second before focusing on Duran. He was handsome with a hint of boyishness to his face.

A flurry of words spilled from his lips. A language it took me a moment to recognize and even then it confused me. He was speaking French with a Russian accent.

I swallowed, glancing to my other side. There was a willowy, young woman with an ash blonde French twist sitting next to me. She was beautiful, like one of the women I saw on my reality shows, and her hands and neck were laden with jewels.

"Hi," she said shyly.

"Hi, I'm Iris," I said, offering my hand.

She shook it. "I'm Raina."

The waiter slid between us and filled our glasses with white wine. Grateful for a distraction, I sipped a little.

"Are you Duran's girlfriend?' she asked.

I shook my head and then nodded. "I don't know. It's complicated. Are you here with anyone?"

Her eyes darted up to the man at the head of the table. "I'm with him."

"Oh...his wife?"

I was just trying to make small talk, but I realized too late this was sensitive topic. She swallowed and offered a thin smile.

"He traded me," she said.

"Oh," I said, my mind whirling. What did that mean?

"My father owed him," she said quietly. "He couldn't pay up...so here I am. Tale as old as time."

She smiled ruefully and I was speechless. I glanced sideways at Duran as he conversed easily with the man at the head of the table.

They knew each other, that was clear, and the realization sent a shiver down my spine.

How was it possible that the man who had held me in the bathtub while I cried consorted with people like that?

"Hey, it's okay," she said, smiling. "It could have been a lot worse. He's completely smitten with me so I get whatever I want. And his dick is huge."

My jaw fell open and she laughed, shaking her hair back. Her eyes flicked past me and ran over Duran. Her brow crooked.

"So Duran Esposito finally picked someone," she said.

"He kidnapped me," I admitted.

She shrugged and tapped her glass so the waiter would refill it. "And he probably tried to make it better by letting you run up his credit card bill, didn't he? That's what Leonid does. Every time he fucks up, he spends a ridiculous amount and considers it forgiven."

"Not exactly," I said. "He gave me a sandwich and shut me in a spare bedroom."

"Oh, maybe he's losing his touch," she said, frowning.

"We got off on the wrong foot."

"How are you getting off now?" Her lips curved in a smile.

I blushed. "Frequently."

She glanced back up at the man at the head of the table—Leonid, I assumed—and a look of thinly veiled desire passed over her eyes.

Her lids lowered as he glanced up and their gazes locked. The air between them was electric and it gave me the sudden feeling I was intruding on something private.

I turned away, rotating my wrists nervously. Duran glanced at me, leaning in.

"You okay, princess?" he asked.

I nodded. "This is a bit overwhelming."

His hand slid over my thigh again and an inch under my skirt. It went still, his fingers gripping me firmly. The heat beneath his palm spread up until I felt it in my clit...like a sweet, torturous heartbeat.

My pussy ached. I took a large sip of wine and leaned back in my chair.

"So, where are you from?"

I turned back to Raina and pulled myself together. "New York. What about you?"

"LA," she said. "But Leonid has a lot of business overseas so we travel now."

"Oh, that must be fun at least," I said. "I've never left the country."

Her eyes narrowed. "Can I ask...how old are you?"

"Um...I just turned twenty-one."

Her brows raised and she glanced at Duran, eyes narrowing. Then she pushed back from the table. "I have to go to the bathroom. Want to come with?"

"Sure," I said, leaning towards Duran. "I'm going to the bathroom."

He nodded once and I felt his eyes follow Raina and I as we disappeared down the hall and into the bathroom. It was a big room with a line of mirrors and marble sinks. Raina sat on the counter and took a little bag of makeup from her purse.

"You okay, Iris?" she asked lightly.

I leaned on the counter, watching as she applied lipstain. "Duran doesn't hurt me."

She turned her head to the side, admiring her work. "I'm just checking on you, babe. I remember what it was like to be as young as you and suddenly be surrounded by men like that."

My throat felt tight out of nowhere. I didn't have any sisters and I didn't have a lot of close female friends. It was something I'd always wanted, but struggled to get.

My chest felt too full, like there were so many pent up words inside me I just had to let them out. My eyes smarted and my lashes were wet.

"He took my virginity," I said.

She froze, looking at me in the mirror. Her shoulders sagged. "Oh, honey. I'm sorry."

I swiped a tear off my cheek without smearing my makeup. "It's fine. It's not like I didn't enjoy it…it's just been a lot."

"When?" she asked gently.

"Last night."

She slipped off the sink and wrapped me in a brief hug. Then she took a tissue out and dabbed my cheeks carefully. I kept still while she touched up my lipstick for me, comforted by being fussed over.

"Did he give you birth control? Or use protection?"

I nodded. "I'm on the pill."

She smiled encouragingly. "Just make sure you don't forget to take it."

I nodded. "Sorry, I didn't mean to just dump my feelings on you. Are you okay? I know you're not in an ideal situation."

She shrugged her bare shoulders. "I'm not afraid of these men anymore. I know how to work Leonid like a puppet. He'd get down on his knees and beg like a dog if I told him to."

"Oh my," I said, surprised, but incredibly impressed.

She tucked her bag over her shoulder. "It's all in what you're willing to do and what you're willing to withhold from them, honey. Just make sure you don't catch any feelings."

She ducked into the bathroom stall and I stood there, staring at my reflection as a sudden realization hit me. In my head flashed dozens of images of Duran—him on his knees, face buried between my legs; his crooked smirk as he looked me from head to toe; the way he'd held me while I slept last night. Too late.

CHAPTER TWENTY-TWO

DURAN

My body was on high alert the moment she stepped out of my sight. I took my phone out and swiped the screen. The bracelet I'd given her had a tracking chip in it so I could watch her little red dot move on my phone. After the night on the ship and our evening at the bar, I was never letting her out from under my protection.

I kept my eyes on the screen for my entire conversation with Leonid.

It felt like forever before her red dot moved. I glanced up and saw her walk out alongside Leonid's mistress, Raina. They took their seats and I slid my phone in my pocket and put my hand on her thigh. Back where it belonged.

She glanced up at me. "Hi," she said.

I leaned in, my mouth brushing her ear. "Open your legs, princess."

Her eyes widened. I pushed my fingers between her thighs and she shifted her chair forward to conceal her lap. Her legs inched apart and I ran my fingertip over her warm panties.

"Alright, if we've got a deal, I'll send over the documents tonight," Leonid said in French. He didn't speak a lot of English and it was the one language we had in common. "It's good to do business with you, Esposito. I look forward to it in the future."

I leaned over and shook his hand. "A pleasure."

"Now, who is this girl you've brought with you?" His bright blue gaze fell on Iris. Beneath the table, I peeled her panties to the side and slipped my finger into the silky wetness of her sex.

Her hips stiffened.

"She's nobody," I said quickly.

His brow crooked and I could tell he didn't believe me. He lifted his whiskey glass and took a slow sip. "Do you share her?"

"No," I said.

"So she is somebody."

"She's just arm candy, I don't fuck her," I said, glad that Iris couldn't understand our conversation.

He leaned back, clearly enjoying my discomfort. "So you just like looking at her, but you don't enjoy her at all? Not even a little bit?"

I shook my head once. "Not even a little bit. Why are *you* so invested in who's fucking her?"

He lifted his hand, waving it once. "Relax, I have my hands full with the one I have. I don't want your woman."

"She's not mine," I said. "But she's also not available."

No one could know what she meant to me—it was too dangerous for us both. I didn't admit to it around Iris, but what had happened at the party on the boat had shaken me and left me feeling deeply guilty. If it hadn't been for me, she wouldn't have been there and she wouldn't have been drugged.

I'd been wary of bringing her here, but I also didn't want to keep her locked up in the hotel room. Especially after I'd fucked her and taken her virginity.

It killed me to think she might feel used.

She shifted in her seat and her clit slid beneath the pad of my finger. God, she was so soft. I circled my fingers slowly beneath her panties, feeling her grow steadily more wet. Her hand came up and gripped the edge of the table.

"Is she sick?" Leonid asked.

"She's fine," I said.

"She looks very warm, she's blushing."

"Perhaps I should take her home," I said, sliding my finger down and pushing it into her cunt with one thrust. Her slick muscles contracted around me and she bit her lip. "She does look a little unwell."

"You may go," Leonid said. "I think we're all squared away. I'll speak with you later after all the papers have been signed about when to expect the shipment. It'll be soon."

I nodded, sliding my fingers from her pussy. She glanced over as I stood and pushed back my chair. Leonid shook my hand—not the one I'd just fingered Iris with—and I helped her to her feet. Her food was half eaten, but she'd finished her wine. She swayed slightly as I led her from the table.

"You're filthy," she said as we stepped back into the restaurant.

"You're soaked."

Her cheeks went pink and her lashes dropped. As I ushered her out to the waiting car, I noticed she had a faint tear stain in her makeup. I slid into the seat beside her and turned her to face me.

"Did you cry?" I took her chin and forced her face up.

"No."

I sighed. "Don't lie to me."

"I'm not. I'm fine."

"Iris, I am going to put you over my knee and spank the truth out of you."

Her eyes widened and I saw the gears in her head turning. Beneath her thin dress and lace bra, her nipples went so hard I could make out the outline through the fabric. Her hips shuddered, working against nothing.

I leaned over and pulled the privacy screen between us and our driver. The windows were tinted black so we were completely alone. Hidden in this little space for the next few minutes. Her lips slowly parted and her breath caught.

I slid back in the seat and spread my knees.

"Would you like it with your panties up or down?" I asked, letting her feel like she had some control.

Her cheeks were so pink and her breasts heaved. She shifted like she needed release...and I knew she had to be soaked. I lifted two fingers and beckoned her and this time she obeyed.

"Over my knee, princess," I said.

Face burning, she bent, sinking down until she was over my lap. Her fingers braced on the leather seat and her hair fell around her face. I trailed my gaze down her back to the hem of her skirt. It was hitched up, showing her round ass and a bit of panties.

"Panties up or down?" I asked.

She moaned quietly and her hips wriggled. When she didn't answer, I slapped her across the ass just hard enough to sting. The recoil shivered down her thighs and she gasped.

"Answer me," I ordered.

"Down," she burst out.

"Good girl." I slid my hand up over her ass and flipped her skirt up to her waist.

Slowly, I peeled her panties down and pushed them to the middle of her thighs. Between her legs, her bare pussy glittered with arousal. With my middle finger and thumb, I spread her open. She was still a little swollen and pink from last night.

"Are you still sore, princess?" I asked.

She nodded. "It's not too bad."

"All you have to say is stop," I said, dipping my finger into her wet entrance and sliding it in to the middle knuckle. Her hips raised and her perfect asshole clenched in response.

"I understand," she whispered.

I pulled my fingers free and spanked her soft, round ass until she writhed. She gripped my thigh and whimpered, but she didn't beg for relief. She just took it, whimpering and wriggling on my lap with every slap. Her pussy got wetter and wetter until it stained her inner thighs.

My cock was rock hard in my pants.

"I'm done," she managed.

Instantly, I withdrew and flipped her up into my arms. Her thighs slid around my waist and she wrapped her arms around my neck. Her breasts heaved against my chest as she clung to me.

"Good girl, princess. You took that so well," I said, stroking her hair.

She took a deep breath and pulled back. Tear tracks ran through the smudged makeup on her cheeks.

"Are you ready to talk?" I asked.

"I was just feeling upset because in the bathroom I talked to Raina about sex," she said. "And I guess I just got triggered by it. This is all really new and I still feel so fucking guilty out of nowhere. Like...sometimes it's fine and I feel good, but then sometimes I feel so shitty about myself. The guilt is so intense it feels like dread."

"Can you tell me why you feel guilty right now?"

"Because you fucked me and I liked it. And now I'm...I'm used and I didn't do anything about it. I should have said no."

My chest ached. She didn't necessarily need me to fix this for her, she needed therapy. But right now the one thing I knew I could offer her was a positive experience right here and now.

"Let me take you somewhere tonight," I said.

She leaned back and wiped her eyes. Delicately, with the pad of her finger so she didn't smear her already running mascara.

"Where?"

I ran my fingertips down her forearms and cradled her palms. "I think maybe the root of your shame isn't what you think it is. I...I think part of you would feel less guilty if you'd hated it."

She chewed her lip. "Maybe you're right. But why?"

Fuck, my chest hurt.

"Well, you told me that you feel like sex is something that's done to you for my...benefit. Like you don't have an right to enjoy it," I said. "Maybe it would help you if you could see yourself. See how pretty you are when you're enjoying yourself, that it's a good thing."

"I don't think seeing how I look when I'm getting fucked is going to help," she said tiredly.

I cleared my throat. Why was I getting emotional right now? I cleared it again and brushed her hair back. Cupping her chin.

"You're not a side character," I said softly. "You're the real thing."

Her brow quirked. "What does that mean?"

I shrugged once. "It means, you get to write the narrative. You get to pick whatever it is that you want the sex you have to be. It's that simple."

She stared at me and I wasn't sure she understood. "How do you know all this stuff?" she whispered.

"Those beliefs are not particular to your upbringing," I said. "They're often passed down from father to son, from mother to daughter. It takes an incredibly strong person to break that cycle and pick what they want. Like, actually pick who they want to be."

"You did," she said. "You must have."

"No," I admitted. "I wasn't the one...my brother shielded me from a lot of my father's cruelty. He taught me about some basic concepts that I never heard my father even mention."

"Like what?"

"Like consent," I said. "Like respect."

"Oh," she said quietly. "I'm sorry."

I shrugged, shoving down all those complex emotions. "This isn't about me, this is about you and what I can do to make you into the dirtiest little slut I can and make you proud of it."

Her jaw dropped and she gave a little gasp. I couldn't conceal my smirk and she flushed, climbing out of my lap and tugging her panties back up. I shifted lower in my seat so I could adjust my cock beneath my zipper.

She crossed her arms. "Alright, just how are you going to do that?"

"I'm taking you out for a real dinner," I said. "I know you're still hungry. Now, how comfortable are you taking your clothes off in public?"

CHAPTER TWENTY-THREE

IRIS

An hour later, I found myself in a dimly lit room in nothing but my bra and panties. I'd never felt more vulnerable before in my life.

The table was rounded and fit into the corner of the tiny room. The walls were a thick velvet curtain that shielded us from the rest of the club. My heart was pounding, I had a glass of red wine in my hand, and I was almost naked in Duran Esposito's lap.

Who was I?

Apparently I was his because when we'd entered the club, the hostess had offered Duran a plate of ribbons. He selected a gold one and tied it around my wrist before leading me through a sea of people to the dining section of the club. I was floored, staring around at the men in handsome suits and the women in an array of beautiful lingerie.

"Don't worry," said Duran, smirking. "They like it."

Our attendant brought us to a private room and Duran turned me around and unzipped my dress. My mouth felt dry and my stomach fluttered, but I kept still and let him strip me down to my lingerie. He gathered the dress in one hand, tossed it aside, and gave me a sharp little spank with the other.

"Sit down," he said. "Time to eat."

He had red wine, a platter of olives, cheese, prosciutto, and buttered bread brought in. I was starving, having barely eaten since lunch, and I devoured a plate of it. He put me in his lap for the next course and made me sit there while he fed me the most tender cuts of roast chicken.

His cock was hard the entire time. I felt it pushing against my ass and it wiped all the memory of my guilt to the side.

It was strange how as soon as I got out of my own head and just let him take charge, let him focus on me, I felt so much better.

Did that mean I *trusted* him?

For the last course, they brought out a dessert wine and two plates of tiny desserts with artfully placed chocolate sauce. Duran turned me around to face him and pulled the right cup of my bra down. My breast fell out and he bent, catching it in his mouth.

"I want to show you something," he murmured.

He nuzzled between my breasts and I let my head fall back. My body was loose with wine and between my legs, my pussy was soaked and desperate for release. I nodded and I heard him laugh softly.

"You perfect, little slut," he breathed. His hand came up and gripped my throat. "Walk out into the club with me like this."

I faltered. "I'm not dressed."

"You're in your bra and panties," he breathed, lifting his head. His dark eyes were starving. A strand of dark hair had fallen over his forehead and I brushed it back instinctively.

I wanted to be desired this way.

Like he would die if he didn't have me.

Swallowing back my nerves, I nodded and he rose, lifting me to my feet and helping me stand. He tugged my cup back over my bra and I turned to where the curtain opened. Before I could slip out, he snagged my waist.

"Mine," he said, his mouth almost brushing mine. "Every inch of you is mine. They can look at your pretty tits and your ass, but I'm the one who fucks you. Do you understand?"

I nodded, panting as he scored my throat with his teeth.

"They can look, they can want you," he growled. "But if anyone touches you, I'll fucking gut them. I've killed plenty of men before I don't mind adding another body to that count."

My clit pulsed between my legs. He slid his palm down my stomach and into my panties and cupped my sex. Heat gathered where our skin collided. My eyes widened as my head fell back against his shoulder and his lip curled back, flashing that sharp canine.

"This wet, little cunt only comes for me," he murmured.

His finger dipped into me, pushing deeper until I gasped and cried out. Then he withdrew it and licked it clean, bending down to kiss me so I could taste myself from his lips.

He took my hand and pulled me out into the main room. Suddenly we went from being Iris and Duran to being just another of the handsome men in black suits with a barely covered woman on his arm. There was something so dirty and thrilling about walking through the crowd in nothing but my tiny panties, bra, and heels.

I understood immediately why people did this sort of thing.

It felt like being set free.

It felt like the opposite of shame.

At that thought, guilt tapped me on the shoulder like an unwelcome specter. I took a quick breath and brushed it back. I wasn't going to let it ruin tonight. He guided me past the bar and I felt men watching me. I turned my head as we floated through the crowd and I saw their eyes linger on my body.

I saw flickers of envy.

My head buzzed and I wondered if it was the high of being desired or just the wine. All around me, the music pounded, making it hard to think.

"Come," said Duran, pausing outside a door with a gold light overhead.

"Where are we going?" I asked.

He pushed the door open and guided me through. It closed and the music cut off abruptly, leaving us standing in silence. I turned in a slow circle, taking in the large glass window that looked through to a couch in the center of the adjoining room.

"What is this?" I whispered.

He tugged me to the couch and pulled me into his lap. There was a little screen with a countdown on it above the window and it was making me nervous. There was ten seconds left.

"What is this?" I asked.

He leaned forward, his mouth brushing my ear. "This is a place where people who like watching others can go. On the other side of the window is a place where people who like being watched while they enjoy themselves can fulfill their fantasies."

My eyes widened. "People like that?"

"Some people love it," he murmured.

He rose and pulled me with him as we drew closer to the window. I watched the clock countdown to zero as he pulled me against him. His cock pushed achingly hard against my ass, rubbing desperately.

"Watch," he murmured in my ear.

The light on the other side glimmered and came on. It was a bare room with a black silk bed in the center. I could tell it was arranged so that anyone using it could be easily seen from our side. My stomach fluttered and I turned, looking up at him.

"What's going to happen?"

His hand slid over my waist and lingered on the waistband of my panties. His eyes narrowed, fixed through the glass. "You're going to watch two people enjoy each other. Without any guilt or shame."

The door opened and a gorgeous woman with a curtain of dark hair entered. She was followed by a large, muscular man in a tailored black shirt and pants. They were both stunning, especially the woman who wore a set of wine red lingerie that left her sex bare. I had trouble not staring as he led her across the room and laid her down on the bed.

"Can they see or hear us?" I whispered.

Duran shook his head. "That's the thrill for them. They know we're watching, but they can't see us."

"Is that a kink?"

"It can be."

The man knelt between the woman's thighs and leaned in. His mouth skimmed up the curve of her stomach and my breath caught. She moaned as he tugged her bra down and took her nipple into his mouth.

Duran's fingers tightened on my hip. His hot mouth brushed the side of my neck.

"This scene is all about her, princess," he said. "I want you to watch her and try to put yourself in her place. Try to see yourself the way you see her."

My cheeks burned, but I couldn't tear my eyes from the woman on the other side of the glass. She was gorgeous, her breasts spilling from her bra and her thick hips covered in a tiny, transparent pair of open panties.

Did I look like that when Duran went down on me?

Beautiful, powerful, sexual.

Shameless?

Duran's hand moved to my stomach and into my panties. I stiffened and he kissed my shoulder.

"You don't have to come," he said. "But I'm going to touch your clit while you watch. If you need to come, you may."

My entire body was on fire, but in the most delicious way. His fingers slid between my thighs and dipped into my pussy. Gathering my wetness and using it to circle my clit. I bit back a moan and let my head fall against his chest.

We both watched through the glass.

Entranced.

The man sank to his knees and pushed her legs further apart. From where we stood, we could see everything. Her pussy was spread and wet enough that the light glinted from her sex. I trailed my eyes down to the rise in his pants. He wanted her the way Duran wanted me when he ate me out.

"Watch as he eats her cunt," Duran murmured. "Watch the way she enjoys it without feeling any shame."

The man buried his face between the woman's thighs and I stared in awe as he ran his tongue over her pussy. From her entrance to her clit. The way Duran liked to do to me.

I swallowed, my lips parting.

This didn't look dirty or shameful. In fact, it was lovely. Like a painting or a statue of lovers entwined. A lump rose in my throat. Would it ever be possible for me to be so unapologetic about my pleasure? Would I ever see it as beautiful instead of something to be feared?

Duran's warm palm cupped my pussy beneath my panties. His mouth brushed my throat. Kissing up to the little hollow beneath my ear. He wasn't watching through the glass, he was too distracted by what he was doing to me. I shifted, glancing down.

"No, you watch," he said. "I'll work."

"Duran," I whispered.

He circled me and knelt at my feet, his hands on my hips. "Yes, princess?"

My teeth gnawed absently at the inside of my cheek. Inside, arousal and something less enjoyable battled in my chest.

"What is sex to you?" I whispered. "Just fun?"

His jaw worked. "That depends on who I'm with. I've had sex before where it was just for fun. But...the sex I had with you was not that."

"It wasn't fun?" I faltered.

He shook his head. "It wasn't just fun, it felt heavier than that, but in a good way. It was pleasure, but it felt...it felt important."

That wasn't the answer I wanted. My stomach twisted. Important was complicated and it meant that there was a right way and a wrong way.

"I grew up thinking that sex had to check all these boxes to be considered sin-free," I admitted. "I just want it to be simple. I want to enjoy it, to feel good, and I don't want to hate myself afterwards."

"It can be that," he said quickly. "If what you need is for sex to be just for pleasure, for intimacy, that's perfectly good sex."

That word—intimacy—felt right. I recalled when he'd taken my virginity, remembering how incredibly intimate that experience had been. Powerful, pleasurable, and...well, all in all, it was actually fun. Despite my panic afterwards. I hadn't expected how much fun it was to sleep with him. There was something so exciting and vulnerable about experiencing him like that.

I wove my fingers through his hair, barely aware of the woman writhing on the other side of the glass. He held my gaze, those big, dreamy eyes filling my vision.

"Intimate feels nice," I whispered.

"Intimate is enough," he said. "Pleasure is enough. A chance to be vulnerable. That's enough."

My throat was so dry and the lump just kept getting bigger. I blinked hard, my hand sliding to the back of his neck.

"I don't think I'll ever be...as adventurous are you were," I said huskily. "I think I need to...feel something to feel safe and enjoy it. Does that bother you?"

"Whatever you choose. You just have to pick," he said. "That's the point, princess. No one tells you how to feel about your body, your orgasms, ever again."

"Thank you," I whispered.

He bent and kissed the front of my thigh. "If anyone makes you feel shame for wanting to be loved on your terms, I'll fuck them up."

I was speechless. Did he mean loved as in *loved*? Or in the physical sense of the words? I opened my mouth to reply, but my eye caught the couple in the other room. She was flat on her back and he was on his knees. Eating her like there was nothing that tasted better.

Arousal surged. My nipples tightened.

He glanced over his shoulder. "You watch, princess, and let me do what I do best."

I nodded, heart thumping. His gaze dropped and his hand slid up to draw back my panties. His head bent and his hot tongue slid between my thighs. My vision flickered.

"Watch," he ordered.

Obediently, I focused on the man and woman. She was whimpering, her arms stretched out above her head. Gripping the edge of the bed. He shifted and spat into his hand and ran it over her pussy. His two fingers slipped into her entrance and the muscles in his forearm worked. It must have felt amazing because her lower body arced off the bed.

Between my thighs, Duran found my clit and began sucking with gentle pulses.

"Oh my God," I breathed.

A tremor moved down my stomach. On the other side of the glass, the woman arced and her eyes flew open. A shudder shot down her stomach. Her mouth parted in a silent cry. Then she shook hard and arousal glittered down the man's wrist.

She was beautiful.

And so was I.

Maybe this moment of pleasure wasn't complicated after all. Maybe it was simple. Maybe the things that happened in bedrooms weren't dirty and shameful.

Maybe they were as beautiful as the dark eyes of the man on his knees at my feet.

My hands tangled in his hair. Pleasure tightened and my eyes barely focused on the couple as she flipped to her hands and knees. He stood and spanked her ass once and her pussy twice. Leaving little blush marks behind. His hand gripped her hip, rubbing her soft skin gently. The way Duran did.

She smiled, bending back. He leaned in and kissed her mouth, slowly and thoroughly. Only pausing to spit between her lips and urge her to swallow. Her throat bobbed and I knew she could taste herself.

Oh God, that was going to send me over the edge.

My hips shuddered. Duran moaned, his tongue working quickly as he felt my orgasm approach. It came in a wave instead of a storm. The pleasure rushed clear and slow, pumping through my hips. Letting me feel every second of it.

My fingers dug into him.

"Oh, don't stop," I breathed.

He pumped his tongue between the folds of my sex, letting me grind on it until my pleasure faded. Then he pulled back, eyes drunk and mouth wet with arousal. He ran a hand over his face and got to his feet.

"Did that feel good, princess?" he asked quietly.

He was so close and I was already weak. I fell into his chest and he wrapped his arms around my body.

"Yes," I murmured. "It felt so good."

"Then that's good enough," he said.

CHAPTER TWENTY-FOUR

DURAN

My heart was still pounding as I ushered her out to the car. Her cheeks were pink and she was flustered. I was rock hard and on cloud nine, my foot pressing too hard on the gas. We sped through the empty streets toward the hotel, not a thought in our minds except getting back to the bed.

I pulled the rental car into the parking garage. She turned as the engine died, but before she could open her mouth, my phone rang. Frowning, I pulled it out of my pocket.

Lucien.

Fuck.

"I have to take this," I said.

She nodded, chewing her lip. Her eyes went from hazy to worried in a second. I swiped the screen and put it to my ear. Bracing myself.

"You have the girl," Lucien said.

"On a scale of one to ten, how fucked am I?" I asked. "Can I just get yelled at and call it day?"

A door shut with a click. "I've never yelled in my life," Lucien snapped. "And Olivia's asleep."

"So I guess your era of celibacy is over then," I said.

"It is not," he said curtly. "Sound echoes through the house at night. I don't want her to hear us down the hall."

Part of me had hoped he'd broken his resolve and fucked her before the wedding. It would have probably lessened my repercussions if he'd loosened up and gotten laid.

"Do you have the guns?" he said.

"I just signed the deal," I said. "We're good, you can tell Romano to calm the fuck down. The supply is back up and running."

"Do I want to know where you got them?"

"V's right hand."

"Fuck," said Lucien softly. "Alright, I'll create a paper trail to keep Romano from asking questions."

"A thank you would be nice."

"Not likely. You did your job."

I sighed. "The guns are secured. Can I just go mind my business right now?"

Lucien's desk chair creaked and I knew he was in his office upstairs. "No, you have to bring that girl back and give her back to her father. You don't have any claim to her, Duran."

I glanced over at Iris. I had every claim to this woman—I'd fucked her, I'd knelt at her feet, I'd called her mine. My throat went tight. If I was a lot braver, I'd have admitted the reason I had claim to Iris Scavo a long time ago.

I loved her and that made her my girl.

The realization pulled me out of the present moment like I'd been thrown from the car. In this moment, all I saw was the years of wondering if I was broken, if I was too fucked up to love anyone. If I was just the son of an evil man and I deserved to always be alone.

I hadn't expected love to feel this good. Like pure euphoria, like a drug coursing through my veins.

I also hadn't expected love to bring all my pain to the surface. I hadn't expected it to feel like the most uncomfortable kind of healing.

"Duran?"

I blinked, jerking back to reality. "What?" I asked hoarsely.

"I want you back home right now," he said. "Bring the Scavo girl."

He hung up and I lowered my phone. Her hand slid over my arm and I looked down as her fingers gripped me. Her eyes were wide and tender, full of concern.

"What's wrong?" she whispered.

"Lucien wants us back in the city," I said. "We need to go get our things from the hotel."

"Both...both of us?"

"If you want, I'll bring you home," I managed. "You don't need to face the consequences of what I did."

Her palm slid down and met mine. Our fingers twined together. It turned out, I did have a heart after all because the thought of being parted from her was breaking it.

"I'm going back with you," she said.

CHAPTER TWENTY-FIVE

IRIS

My heart pounded on the drive from the airport to Lucien's house. Duran was quiet and his jaw stayed locked. Fire simmered in the depths of his lowered gaze. Like he was already rehearsing what he was going to tell his brother in his head and it was making him angry.

His silence scared me.

We pulled up at the end of a circular drive and my jaw dropped. The house was enormous and shockingly lavish. There was a brand new Tesla parked by the fountain outside. Duran didn't seem to notice—but then this was his childhood home. He just got out and circled the car with a grim expression.

He wore his sunglasses, his black button up, and his black pants and shoes. There was a closed off aura about him.

Like he was preparing for something unpleasant.

"Are you okay?" I whispered, letting him help me out onto the gravel.

He nodded once. The warm, hardness of his palm hovered on my lower back and ushered me up the front steps to the porch. I paused to smooth my hair and push it back, wondering if my simple, short sundress was fancy enough.

I hadn't realized we were going to a palace.

Duran hit the bell and I heard it echo in the hall.

"I thought you lived here," I said.

He shook his head. "Sometimes I do, but since Olivia moved in, I give them some space. I have an apartment in the city."

"Olivia?" I murmured.

"My brother's fiancé," he said.

"Oh, right, I remember."

There was a short silence and a woman in jeans and a sweatshirt pushed the door open. She was carrying a bag of cleaning supplies.

"Mr. Esposito," she said, stepping back. "I'm just here for the day. Usual staff will be back tomorrow."

"Did Lucien give them the day off?"

She nodded. "It's a federal holiday, sir."

"Oh, right," he said, taking my hand and leading me into the foyer.

My eyes weren't big enough to take in my lavish surroundings properly. This house looked like a mini Versailles. Heavy draperies, polished floors, a spiral staircase. Everything had a fresh, clean scent and there was a faint breeze moving in from the hall.

"Where's my brother?" Duran asked.

"Upstairs," she said, shutting the door behind us. "He asked that you wait in the living room. I set out food and coffee there, sir."

"Thank you," Duran said.

She disappeared down the hall to my right and complete silence fell. Duran flicked his wrist to check his watch.

"Your family's house is nice," I commented.

"Well, all the money in the world still can't buy you a stable childhood," said Duran, an edge to his voice. "It's not my favorite place in the world."

He strode across the floor, his dress shoes clicking, and opened a large door to the left. He gravitated towards a bar on the far side where he poured himself a drink. I ducked through and found myself turning in slow circles to take in the opulent living space as I moved to join him.

"It's nine," I said, frowning at his drink.

"I know," he said, taking a sip of whiskey. "Have some coffee."

He poured me a cup of coffee and I stirred cream and sugar in. We stood in silence by the bar for what felt like forever. Then I heard footsteps on the floor above us. Crisp, firm, like someone was striding with purpose.

They faded for a moment and then I heard them on the steps. The door pushed ajar and a tall man who looked a little like Duran strode inside and stopped short.

My stomach tightened.

Right away, he frightened me to my bones. I could tell they were brothers, they both had the same structure to their handsome faces. The same jawline, the same lowered brows, the same heavy, arched noses, the same thin, soft mouths. But the resemblance stopped there. He wore a charcoal gray suit and his dark hair was slicked back over his head. It was a few shades lighter than Duran's.

Lucien's eyes dragged over his brother and rested on me.

My heart pumped. It felt like all the heat had drained from the room. His eyes were a pale, hazel color and there was nothing in them. No matter how hard I stared into his gaze…it was just emptiness and ice.

Pure coldness.

A gust of barren wind over a winter shore.

"Lucien," Duran said.

His brow twitched and he reached into his inner pocket and took out a cigarette. Was he going to smoke inside? No, he put it to his lips and let it hang there for a moment. Then he took it out and pointed at me, cigarette between two fingers.

"That's the Scavo girl," he said.

His voice was smooth and flat with a little bite. Like iced vodka.

"It is," Duran agreed.

"Why the fuck do you have her?"

The words seemed like there should be an accompanying emotion or gesture to them, but Lucien's face remained firmly in place. Like he'd been carved from stone.

Fuck that. He gave me the chills.

"Her father knows she's with me," Duran said, emptying his whiskey and setting it aside.

"So that's why he called off the search," Lucien said.

"I asked him not to tell anyone if he valued her," Duran said.

Lucien's jaw twitched and there was a long, long silence. Finally he released a heavy sigh and shifted his weight.

"She pregnant?"

Duran's brows shot up. "No."

"Alright," said Lucien. "If she's not pregnant, you can put her back where you found her."

My jaw dropped, but Duran didn't seem phased.

"No," he said. "Please let me talk through this with you in private."

Lucien released another short sigh. "Alright, we'll talk after lunch. Olivia will be back soon and we're eating in the dining room. The guest bedroom is made up for the girl."

"Her name is Iris," Duran said.

"Alright. The guest bedroom is made up for Iris," he said, dipping his head. There was the tiniest bite of sarcasm through all the coldness.

"She's staying with me," Duran said.

Lucien shook his head and said something in French. Duran answered in the same, his words short and almost irritated. I thought I saw a flicker of exasperation and then he shrugged once.

"What's done is done," he said in English.

He left and the warmth seeped slowly back into my bones. I turned to Duran and he slid his arm around my waist and bent to kiss my mouth. The kiss was brief, but it made me feel a lot better.

"Come on, I'm sure they've already brought our things up," he said.

He led me up the opulent stairway to a large, comfortable bedroom at one end of the second floor hallway. We passed by a series of doors, all shut. I couldn't keep from gawking at everything.

"Where is your room?" I asked.

His gaze flickered behind us. "It was a few doors down from Lucien's."

"But you moved out when Olivia moved into his room?" I asked.

"Olivia sleeps on the far side, not with him," Duran said.

A little bit of guilt wormed its way through me.

"So…they're waiting?" I whispered, setting my purse down on the bed. I sank onto the edge and looked up at him.

He sighed. "It's more complicated than that."

"So tell me."

When he dragged his dark gaze up to mine, there was pain in it. For a moment, I wished I wasn't so curious because I had a feeling he was about to tell me something awful.

"It's because of what the boss, Carlo Romano, did to him. A long time ago, his daughter accused Lucien of getting her pregnant," Duran said, his voice low. Like he was afraid we'd be overhead.

"Oh," I said. "Did he?"

"No, he's never fucked her," Duran said. "I was there the night in question, it was during a party at the Romano house. We went outside and had a smoke and left early. But Romano was furious and he tried to force Lucien to marry his daughter to make things right."

Duran took a beat, his eyes averted.

"You don't have to talk about it," I whispered.

"No, you should probably know," he said, sinking down beside me. "Lucien refused unless he had a paternity test. Romano put him in a cell and tortured him…tore the skin off his back in chunks. It was horrifying. I tried defending him, but I didn't have any sway."

I clapped a hand over my mouth.

"Romano's daughter couldn't take the guilt and she confessed. She'd been knocked up by one of Romano's soldiers. Lucien was set free, but he hasn't slept with anyone in years."

"That's awful," I whispered.

"He and Olivia are celibate, as far as I can tell," Duran said, his voice strained. "But it's not because they're religious people. I think he's terrified he'll get her pregnant."

I thought back to the coldness of Lucien and for the first time I felt a spark of empathy for him. No one deserved that. I ran a hand over my face and took a deep breath.

"What did Lucien say in French downstairs?" I asked.

Duran sighed, rising and crossing the room to the bathroom doorway. "He said that he knew how religious your parents were and he asked if I had...deflowered you, is the term he used. Not my words."

My jaw dropped.

"I said he was a few days too late if he wanted to return you untouched."

"Was he mad? I can't read his face."

"Oh, furious probably," Duran said, yawning. "But like he said, what's done is done."

He ducked into the bathroom and I heard him showering. It took me a moment to pull myself together. Everything about the house and the people in it was overwhelming and a little uncomfortable. I looked down at my suntanned feet and legs, the straps of my sandals dirty.

I needed to change.

Duran came out, wrapped in a towel, and I got into the shower. When I returned, he was fully dressed in a dark blue suit with a tie.

"So…are we getting dressed up for lunch?" I asked.

"Lucien likes things to be formal," he said. "He wears a suit most of the time so when I'm here, I do the same. It's his house."

He went to brush his hair back and I opened my suitcase. Most of my clothes needed washed, but I did have a dress with quarter length sleeves that came to the middle of my thigh. It was dark blue and had a little choker I hadn't noticed before pinned to the tag. I slipped it on with a pair of black pumps.

Duran reappeared and his eyes dropped to the velvet choker and lingered on the little gold bow.

"That's not the sort of thing you usually wear," he said.

"I know, but I need to do my laundry," I said. "Plus, it matches my bracelet."

I flipped my wrist, jingling the diamond bow. He beckoned me and I obeyed. His lids fell halfway as he raked his gaze down to my heels and back up again. Warmth gathered deep inside.

"I'll fuck you tonight," he murmured.

I shook my head, eyes widening. "Not here, that seems disrespectful."

He kissed my mouth, tongue brushing mine. My nipples went tight and the memory of his fingers on my clit in the club resurfaced. My hips felt warm and desperate, like I had an emptiness between them that ached to be filled. He broke away.

"Be a good girl and I'll fuck you quietly," he murmured. "Disobey me and I'll make you scream."

There was a faint chiming sound from downstairs. I picked my jaw up and pressed the back of my hand to my burning cheek.

"That's lunch," Duran said, spinning me around and spanking my ass.

He didn't give me a chance to retort. I darted into the bathroom and quickly swiped on some makeup and pulled my hair into a high ponytail. Hoping it would help me blend into this gilded house.

Downstairs, the dining room was dizzying. The table was spread with a half dozen platters of food, including fresh fruit, vegetables, and cheese. There were two bottles of wine and a decanter of water at the center beside a short bouquet of white roses. It was all very foreign to me in its elegance. I hadn't been raised in this level of wealth.

Duran pulled out my chair and I sank down just as footsteps sounded to our left. We both glanced over and I felt Duran tense.

Lucien walked in, still in the same suit, and a tiny figure appeared at his heels.

I tried not to stare. She was beautiful, but timid like a mouse. He pulled her chair out and I saw his hand guide her to sit down. It seemed excessive, but when I glanced at Lucien, it made sense. His face was blank, but around the edges of it I saw intense protectiveness. Like the most precious thing in the world sat next to him.

Shaken, I glanced at Duran. He didn't seem to notice anything.

"This is Iris," Duran said, sinking down. "And this is Olivia."

I smiled at her and she smiled back, her dark eyes uncertain.

"It's a pleasure to meet you," she said softly.

She wanted to be warm, I could tell, but she was locked in a cage of anxiety. I smiled at her, trying to let her know I wasn't a threat. She glanced up at Lucien and I saw his forearm flex like he was patting her thigh.

Lucien and Duran started talking about something I didn't understand. Warehouses, people I didn't know, deadlines for shipments. I saw Olivia's eyes glaze over as she watched the housekeeper fill our plates, and I took the opportunity to look her over.

She was obviously underweight. Her hair was thick and wavy and she had curtain bangs that framed her oval face and sharp chin. Her pointed nose had a little curl to her nostrils that I liked. It was charming. Overall, she seemed sweet, but nervous.

Lucien took the spoon from the housekeeper and portioned out Olivia's food. I noticed he gave her less and spread it into small piles on her plate. I tried not to stare, wondering what he was doing and why she couldn't get her own food.

Was he controlling her portions?

She was rail thin already.

A surge of anger moved through my chest. I chewed my food in silence and watched her from the corner of my eye. She used her fork to break the food up and shove it around her plate. But she didn't eat anything.

I cleaned my plate, confused.

Duran poured a glass of wine for me and sat back in his chair. "Can we meet and talk after lunch then?"

Lucien nodded, his eyes falling on his fiancée's plate. He bent and whispered something in her ear and she swallowed, nodding. I pretended I was occupied with refilling my plate, but I saw her scoop up a forkful of food and put it in her mouth.

She chewed miserably, like she was eating sand.

I was dumbfounded. What was going on in this house? Lucien was ice cold, barely human, and his fiancée was starving despite the opulence around them. I kept quiet and watched as she laboriously cleaned her plate and set her fork aside. Lucien bent and whispered something into the crook of her neck.

Her eyes lit up, flickering with light for a brief second.

I'd heard him. He'd called her a good girl.

It hit me all at once and a wave of guilt moved over me. Lucien wasn't controlling her portions, he was ordering her to eat. Olivia had an eating disorder. Sick, I set my fork aside feeling like I'd done something wrong. Did it trigger her to watch the rest of us eat?

Lucien's mask was back. He lounged in his chair, one hand on Olivia's thigh.

"Have you spoken to your parents, Iris?" he asked.

I shook my head. "No, sir."

I wasn't sure why I said it like that. Lucien just felt like someone who demanded a certain level of respect and it made me nervous to speak directly to him.

"Would you like to see them tomorrow?"

I nodded, glancing at Duran. He dipped his head and I took it as a permissive gesture. Lucien caught the exchange and his brow twitched.

"She listens, I guess that's something," he said.

Anger flashed. "I do not," I retorted.

"Oh really?" Ice curled through his words. "Is that supposed to be an asset?"

"I don't have to listen to Duran," I snapped. "Or you. I have my own money and I can do what I like."

Lucien's eyes flicked to his brother, who was watching like he was a spectator at a cage match. Clearly he didn't think I needed help and I was grateful that he had at least that much respect for me.

"Where do you work?" Lucien asked.

"I do social media," I said. "Brands pay me to represent them."

His eyes narrowed. "Have you had access to your phone since meeting Duran?"

Duran shifted in his seat, crossing his legs. "I took her phone the night we met. She hasn't had it since."

"Good," said Lucien. "Don't give it back to her until we have a chance to discuss. I assume you mean...you model or something along those lines?"

His cold gaze swung back to me. Nailing me to my seat.

"Yes," I said, shaking back my hair. "I make fine money. And I would like my phone back soon."

"No," said Lucien. "It's a security hazard."

"Oh...so no women in your millionaires club have phones?"

"None of the women who are married to or fucking men in my inner circle have access to social media," Lucien said. "And while you are sleeping with my brother, neither will you."

Olivia was staring at me, her eyes big. Like she couldn't believe I had the guts to talk back to Lucien.

"It's my private property," I snapped.

"And now it's Duran's," said Lucien. "See how easy that is?"

"Lucien," said Duran in a reasonable tone. "Don't fuck with her."

My jaw was on the floor. I got to my feet, nearly shaking with rage, and tossed my napkin on the table. Lucien's glacial gaze snapped to mine and his eyes narrowed.

"Sit down," he said coolly.

I sat, but before I could open my mouth, Duran was on his feet. There was fire in his eyes that I hadn't expected.

"Don't speak to Iris like that," he said.

Olivia gasped and Lucien lifted a hand and inclined his head. Everyone took a beat in the tense space and Duran sank back down, but his crackling eyes were still fixed on his brother. One brow crooked in warning.

"Let's finish this conversation in private," Lucien said.

Duran jerked his head, but he didn't speak. I sat completely still with my hands gripping the edge of the table. Beneath my clothes, my body was burning and I was positive my panties were soaked. Seeing Duran get angry and stand up for me had to be one of the sexiest things he'd ever done.

Other than the time he'd pulled a gun in the bar. Or the time he'd shot six men to save me.

I frowned, glancing at him.

Maybe he felt more than he was willing to admit.

CHAPTER TWENTY-SIX

DURAN

Lucien paused beside me, his mouth a thin line. His cold gaze was narrowed and fixed on the quiet lake. He had a shotgun over the crook of his arm and we were both wearing boots and outdoor clothes. The sun burned and sent sweat trickling down to soak my t-shirt.

"Do you like this girl?" he said flatly.

"Yeah," I said.

"How much?" he asked, turning to face me.

We stood at the edge of the pond. We'd left Iris and Olivia in the library, taking a tour of the house, and gone out to the pond. Like the unusual person he was, Lucien decided he wanted to shoot a pheasant for dinner so he'd taken the shotgun and told me to walk with him so we could talk.

"Olivia likes pheasant," he said, snapping the shotgun together.

I studied him, noticing a shadow of softness in his tone when he said her name. Was it possible my ice cold brother had feelings after all?

"How is she settling in?" I asked casually, grateful to postpone the conversation about my situation.

"Good," he said. "Doesn't eat very much, but I found she'll eat pheasant better than chicken so here I am. Shooting some goddamn pheasant."

"You can just order it from the grocers," I said, frowning.

He shook his head. "She seems to like it fresh better."

I stared at him for a second and then a sudden smirk split my face. My hands shoved deep in my pockets and I rocked on my heels. I couldn't help myself.

"You like her," I said.

A muscle in Lucien's cheek twitched uncontrollably for a second.

"Let's talk about your woman instead," he said firmly. "Are you planning on marrying her?"

Into my mind spun every moment I'd spent with Iris. From the first time I'd laid eyes on her from my room at the resort to her flushed face and little gasp as she came in my arms at the club and all the arguments and orgasms in between.

But what stood out most starkly was the fear I'd felt when I saw her drugged and surrounded by mercenaries.

I'd fucked a weapons deal right then and there and killed the men we were doing business with. I'd do it again, a hundred times over because her safety meant everything to me.

I cleared my throat. "Are you planning on trying to stop me?"

"No," he said.

I wasn't prepared for him to say that. His eyes narrowed in the afternoon sun and quick as a flash, he lifted the shotgun and fired it. There was a sharp squawk from the tall grass at the edge of the woods and silence. He cleared his throat.

"Well, that's dinner," he said.

We trudged through the grass to where the limp bird lay in the grass. Lucien gathered it up and put the shotgun over his shoulder. He took a short breath and sent me an impatient stare.

"How do you feel about another man fucking her?" he asked.

Lucien had never been tactful, so I wasn't surprised. Anger rose in my chest so fast and hard my head spun.

"Not good, it's mine," I snapped.

"What's yours?"

Confused, I shrugged. "Her cunt, all of her. When I ask her who she belongs to, she says me. I don't want her to fucking say that to some other son of a bitch, ever."

Lucien's jaw twitched. "Word of advice. Don't ask her if her pussy is yours unless it's fucking yours. That goes for everything else."

I scowled. "Easy for you to say. Your situation is cut and dry."

"Do you want to marry her?" he asked.

In another life I would have balked. But after the last few weeks, monogamy sounded perfect if it was with Iris. Getting to sleep in bed with her every night, fuck her endlessly, maybe get her pregnant someday and raise our kids together—it sounded like paradise.

"Yes," I said.

Lucien's jaw twitched. "Go back to Miami," he said. "Get drunk as fuck, make sure people see you, and make it look like you married her by accident. Don't let her see her parents first. Everyone needs to think it was an impulse decision."

I blinked, confused. "What?"

Lucien's eyes darted to the house and back. "I'm not the one who wanted you to marry someone important. I'm just an underboss. Romano likes keeping money and power up at the top and he asked me to make sure you picked someone who fulfilled those designs. I don't give a fuck, personally, who you marry."

"Okay," I said quietly, his words sinking in. A wave of guilt moved through my chest. "What will Romano do if I marry her?"

"He won't be happy," Lucien said grimly. "But I'm marrying Olivia at his request. My obedience should be payment enough."

I hated it. For as long as I could remember, Lucien had always been there as a shield between me and the world. He stepped between me and my father. He took the punches for me from bullies at school. He'd taken on responsibility for the Esposito name and rose to shoulder the burdens that went with it.

Even if it meant he couldn't choose his wife.

"You do have a heart in there, I guess," I said.

Lucien's ice cold eyes narrowed and he put a cigarette to his lips.

"Fuck you," he said.

We went back to the house and Lucien sank onto the porch steps in his shirtsleeves, rolled to the elbow, and began dressing the pheasant. I loitered, my hands in my pockets. After a moment, he looked up and jerked his head.

"Best go pack," he said. "And let her know you're marrying her."

I went inside and stood in the hall. For the first twenty years of my life, this house had been a cage. A dismal reminder that I'd known nothing but fear and abuse, that I wouldn't get the love I craved. Here, in this house, I'd learned to pack all my pain and feelings up and squash them down into nothingness.

Into a blur of work, alcohol, and strange people and places.

It didn't have to be that way anymore. Even when we were enemies, Iris had always softened as soon as I opened up to her. She was beautiful and empathetic and funny and perfect.

And I loved her.

If I let her walk away, it would be the biggest mistake of my life. The problem was, I wasn't sure if she was ready to get married tonight. In fact, I was pretty confident she wasn't. So that left me with two options.

I could give everything up and send her home.

Or I could *tell* her she was marrying me.

I stared up at the ceiling, mulling it over. The second one sounded a lot better than the first.

Marrying her sounded like everything I'd ever wanted.

CHAPTER TWENTY-SEVEN

IRIS

"What?" I asked.

It was seven at night. We'd had a pheasant dinner and ice cream for dessert. Lucien and Olivia were downstairs in the living room. Probably sitting a proper few feet apart on the couch in silence. Duran and I were upstairs, getting ready for bed.

I was standing in the shower, sopping wet and patting my hair with a towel, and he was by the sink, fully dressed.

"I said, put on something slutty because we're going out to get wasted and married," he said.

My heart thumped in my ears. I reached up to wipe my wet hair from my face. His brows shot up.

"That was supposed to come out more...romantic," he said.

"You want to marry me?" I whispered.

"Fuck, yes," he said, a flush appearing at his collarbone. "I want to fuck that pussy forever. I feel like I've made that pretty clear over the last few weeks."

"So...can we just do a normal wedding?"

We both froze. Had I just said that? Then the slowest smile curled over his mouth and a wave of pure euphoria rushed through me. I wanted this—I had no idea how long I'd wanted this, but I wanted it so much that I couldn't fathom having any other response.

"You...you want to marry me?"

"I mean...yeah, I guess I do," I said, flustered. "I'm just wondering why we can't just go get married at a church?"

He explained his plan and I dried off and put on a skimpy pair of lingerie. It made sense when he laid it all out like that. Did it sound like it would work? I wasn't really sure and that made me anxious.

"You said Romano tortured Lucien," I said. "What will he do to you?"

Duran's mouth thinned. "I'm the spare, so he might be angry, but he won't be livid. Romano has always had a strange obsession with controlling Lucien. I think he's kind of...everything Romano has always wanted to be and that pisses him off. People couldn't give two shits about Romano personally, but despite being a bit of a dick, everyone likes Lucien."

"I don't get that," I admitted.

"On the outside he's a cold motherfucker," Duran said. "But if you're on his good side, he'll always come through for you."

I wasn't sure what to think. The last few days were a whirlwind and suddenly I was facing a drunk wedding with a man I'd met days ago. Stunned, I moved into the bedroom and began numbly searching through my clothes for something suitable.

"Hey," he said softly, leaning in the bathroom door. "You okay, princess?"

"Yeah, I just don't have anything to wear," I stuttered.

My hands flew and the clothes and shoes tumbled onto the bed. My eyes burned. I squeezed them shut and released a short breath. His arms were around me in a moment, turning me to pull me into his chest.

"Do you love me?" I whispered.

"I love you, Iris," he said gently, stroking my hair.

I didn't speak, unsure how to respond. I knew what my answer was, what it had been for a while now. But part of me was too scared to believe that he really did love me. Maybe everything was just a dream and I would wake up in my bed at any moment.

"Are you sure you love me?" I asked again.

His arms slid down and he knelt in front of me. His dark eyes fixed on mine, big and dreamy as the night sky. They glittered like starlight, with an endless depth I wanted to get lost in forever. He reached up and pulled my panties down around my thighs and pushed me back onto the bed.

"Open up, show me that beautiful pussy, princess," he murmured, kissing up my thighs.

My eyes closed. His tongue slid across my clit and then down and across the opening of my pussy. Then the tip dragged from my clit and across again. The next swipe was a perfect oval and my eyes widened. Heat surged down my spine and burned deep inside.

"Are you...are you writing that you love me with your tongue on my pussy?" I whispered.

He didn't answer until every word was spelled out on my drenched sex. Then he kissed my clit and lifted his head, his eyes hazy.

"I'll do that every day until you believe me," he said thickly. "I'll tattoo your name on my cock if you want, princess. Just let me have you forever."

He sounded so desperate. I looked down between my thighs. His chin rested on the rise above my sex and his fingers dug into my inner thighs. My God, he had the biggest pair of puppy eyes when he wanted something. They were pleading silently with me, almost groveling.

"Be my wife," he said, turning his head to kiss my inner thigh.

I had to admit, I liked seeing him on his knees like this. I slid my thighs open a little more and wove my fingers through my hair. His mouth curved slightly as I pushed his face back down into my pussy and held it there.

"Lick and I'll think about it," I murmured, sinking back.

I already had my answer, but he deserved to work for it. After everything he'd put me through, I was going to get the satisfaction of being in control.

He ate me out with slow strokes, a low growl of pleasure rumbling in his chest. Teasing my clit with his flattened tongue until I felt myself drip onto the bedspread. Then he spat on his fingers and slid two inside me and I felt them work gently as he located my G-spot.

I couldn't hold back a whimper when he found it.

My spine arced and I forgot all about making him grovel. His free hand slid up and gripped my throat and my hips worked against his tongue as he licked my clit. The fullness of his fingers felt so good, especially at my entrance where I was most sensitive.

An orgasm started in a different spot this time, lower than I was used to, and grew quickly. I barely had time to react before my muscles clenched and bore down around his fingers. My hips trembled as I went over the edge and the best orgasm of my life ripped through my body.

He growled, pushing his mouth against my clit so I could ride his face until the last bit of pleasure had ebbed away.

Then he rose, pushed down his pants, and thrust his cock into me. I gasped and my spine lifted off the bed. My hands went around his body and my nails latched into his back. His pupils blew until his eyes were pure black and his hips pumped hard. Taking me like he was starving.

"Mine," he panted. "Say you're mine."

I moaned, incoherent. He pulled out and flipped me over onto my knees. His knee sank into the bed and his cock thrust into me from behind. I gasped, almost yelping as a ripple of pain moved through my hips. His hand wrapped around my throat and pulled me back against his chest.

"Mine," he growled, his hips slamming against my ass.

His cock bottomed out against my deepest point. I choked, gasping. I wasn't wet, I was dripping. I swore there was arousal streaming down my thigh.

His breath burned in my ear. "Say it."

Thrust.

"Say it."

Thrust.

My vision popped. My body lay limp against his, but I'd never felt so safe in my life.

"Yours," I burst out.

"Oh—fuck," he groaned, his hips stuttering. I felt him pump his cum into me as his teeth sank into where my shoulder met my neck. His hips worked in short thrusts as he shuddered and there was a distant, ongoing growl in the back of his throat.

Silence fell. His hand eased up on my neck and my breathing slowed.

He unclenched his teeth and kissed the side of my neck.

"That's my girl," he murmured. "When I say that to you again, you really will be my girl. My wife, my woman."

The thought was dizzying. He pulled his cock from me and stood back and made a noise of surprise. I whipped around and stared at the bedspread in horror. I was kneeling on a soaked patch and all down my thigh was creamy arousal. Smirking, he cracked me across the ass with the palm of his hand.

"Enjoy yourself?"

I blushed to the roots of my hair. His eyes narrowed.

"That's a good thing," he said. "Sex is for pleasure, not duty, not for anyone else in the world and their opinions. I fuck you because I love you and it feels good. Is that enough?"

A wave of intense relief flooded me. Deep in my chest was the peace I'd craved for so long. It flickered and wavered, but it was the beginning of something good.

I nodded, chewing my lip. "I love you too," I whispered. "And it's enough."

He bent and cupped my chin. When he kissed me, I tasted myself on his mouth.

"Good girl," he murmured. "Now, put on something pretty and let's go get married."

We had to stop at the store on the way out of town. None of my clothes were clean and Olivia was too small for me to borrow her things. There was still a classy, little boutique open. It was disgustingly expensive and I balked at the price tags, but my brand new fiancé just put his card down. Then he spun me around and pushed me towards the intimate section. Blushing, I picked out a satin lingerie set made of creamy silk.

It was my wedding night after all.

Heart pounding, I fumbled through the racks trying to find something I wouldn't regret getting married in. It couldn't be white—that would look deliberate, but I didn't want to get married in black. My fingers slowed and I squeezed my eyes shut until my vision swirled.

"Wear red," he said quietly.

He reached out and pulled a little red dress off the rack. It was tight with built in cups and off the shoulder straps. The short, floaty skirt would hit the middle of my thigh and leave my legs bare.

"You look beautiful in red," he said.

My stomach fluttered as I held it up to my body and gazed at my reflection. Behind me, he was watching me with his lips parted. A smile curved over my mouth.

"What are you looking at?" I asked lightly.

"My wife," he said distractedly. "Go put those clothes on while I pay. I'm not waiting any longer to marry you."

All my fear melted away in that moment. Somehow, despite seeing my worst side right from the get-go, despite all the guilt and shame I'd carried inside, despite the tears and arguments, this man loved me.

My hands shook as I pulled on my lingerie.

He wanted to spend the rest of his life as my husband. Heat crept up my cheeks and a thrill like I'd never felt before rose in my chest. I wasn't sure when I'd first loved him, but if I had to guess, it was that moment he'd walked into the door and gunned down several men for me. Right then and there I should have guessed that I wasn't just a casual acquaintance to him.

I stepped out of the dressing room in my dainty, red heels. He was sitting on the bench and when he saw me, his brows shot up. His chest heaved. He swirled his finger, urging me to spin, and I obeyed. Giggling and burning up with excitement.

He rose, catching my hand, and pulling me into his chest. His hand cradled my chin, turning my face up.

"You are mine," he murmured. "From the first time I laid eyes on you."

He kissed me deep and long. When he broke away my head was spinning.

"Is that why you kidnapped me?" I teased.

"Absolutely," he said, lifting my hand and spinning me again. "I didn't see it then, but clearly I wanted you all to myself."

"I won't condone your methods," I said. "But they were effective."

"Should I tell our future sons that's the way to go?" he mused, tugging me towards the door where the car waited on the curb.

"Absolutely not!" I gasped.

He laughed, his head falling back and yanked open the door. I tumbled into the backseat with my heart thudding and my stomach fluttering. He slipped in beside me and pulled the privacy panel down. Before I could speak, he pushed me onto my back on the leather seat and moved his body over mine.

His mouth brushed my lips. That pointed canine flashed. "God, I want you so fucking badly," he groaned.

"I'm fully aware of that," I breathed. "Unless that's just a large phallic vegetable in your pocket."

He laughed again, this time against my mouth. His hips moved, rubbing himself against my thigh. Begging me silently to pull my skirt and panties to the side and let him in.

I broke away. "Not until you make an honest woman out of me."

"I've never wanted anything more," he said.

CHAPTER TWENTY-EIGHT

DURAN

I married her in a dark room at the courthouse an hour after midnight.

We were both tipsy and sweating from dancing at the club. We ran into a group of my friends from the city and we stayed with them until evening. They would be my witnesses. I knew as soon as our marriage became public, they'd spread the story of how drunk and reckless we were all evening.

We spent most of the time on the dance floor. Her gorgeous, tight body moved against mine, her fountain of blonde hair falling down her back. I couldn't keep my hands off her waist. I wanted that perfect ass up against me the entire night.

The club cleared out at half past midnight. My phone buzzed with a text from Lucien's friend at the court house. I took her hand and we ran recklessly out onto the pavement and across the street to the back entrance of the building.

Head spinning, I signed my name. She couldn't stop giggling and I had to hold her steady by the waist so she could print her name. The sleepy clerk officiated the rest and signed at the bottom.

I was a married man.

I paid the clerk several thousand and he shooed us back out onto the street. Her cheeks were flushed and her eyes glistened. I reached for her, but she darted back, spinning once. Her skirt flared and showed me a flash of her round ass and thong.

Fuck me.

She lifted her hand, flashing her bare ring finger. "Do I look married to you, Mr. Esposito?"

"You're about to look very married," I said. "On your back with your husband balls deep in your pussy."

She gasped, like that was the dirtiest thing I'd ever said. "Oh, you're so bad."

She was adorable when she was tipsy. I snatched her around the waist and buried my face in her neck. She smelled so good it made my head spin. Perhaps that was just the drinks, but I doubted it.

"I'm about to get a whole lot worse," I groaned.

Right in the middle of the dark street, she slid her palm down and cupped my cock through my pants. Heat roared through my body and thumped in my groin. It was all I could do to not thrust into her hand.

"I'm going to fuck you right here," I murmured. "So if you don't want that, then come with me because there's a honeymoon suite, a bottle of champagne, and a bed waiting for us at the hotel."

Her eyes were big and hazy when she turned them up to me. She cupped the side of my neck and her face went sober.

"I love you so much, Duran," she whispered. "You make me so...free."

My throat felt tight as I kissed her forehead. All I ever wanted for her was for all the broken, painful bits inside to heal. I wanted her to leave behind all her shame and fear and always be this beautiful, carefree woman. If I could do that, that would be enough.

"You make me feel like I've finally come home," I said.

We kissed until it turned into laughter and then we ran through the streets to find the car. I managed to keep myself off her in the back seat, but it took all my willpower. She was the most beautiful I'd ever seen her tonight.

Eyes glistening and hair mussed from dancing.

Long legs bare.

A mark on her neck from my mouth.

The hotel was simple and classy, but the honeymoon suite didn't let her down. I'd sent her bags on ahead of us and had the manager set up our things for a few hundred dollars tip. It was worth every penny to see the look on her face when I pushed the door ajar.

Everything was pure white—the bed, the floor, the walls—but the six dozen roses were a deep crimson that matched her dress. That was a happy accident. Through the bathroom door I could see the tub full of bubbles and champagne chilling in a bucket of ice.

She turned in a slow circle, taking in the room with her lips parted. Then she did a little jump in her heels and clasped her hands together.

"It's so pretty," she whispered. "But you didn't have to do all this."

I shut the door and locked it. Tonight, I'd given instructions that we weren't to be disturbed under any circumstances.

"You deserve everything," I said. "Come here."

She obeyed and I led her over to the bedside table. Sure enough, they'd placed the little velvet box right where I'd asked in the top drawer. Her eyes widened and her pupils blew as I turned it around and snapped the lid open.

I sank to my knees and she clapped her hands over her mouth.

"Will you marry me?" I said. "Although, technically, you're my wife already. So…will you always be mine, Iris Esposito?"

She nodded, her lashes wet. Wordless, she held out her hand and I slipped the large, square diamond with a thin, gold band around her finger. I rose before she could move and took two more rings from the drawer and slid her wedding band up against the engagement ring.

"Let me guess," she managed. "Three times as much as the necklace?"

"Please," I said. "Try twenty times."

Her jaw dropped, her eyes wide as she soaked in the glittering diamond.

"Will you do the honors?" I asked, holding out mine.

Her hands shook, but she managed to get the plain gold band up over my knuckle. I'd gone out to the family jewelers, because I knew they would be discreet, and bought a full wedding set in the afternoon. By some twist of fate, the perfect ring had just been put out for display that morning.

She was simple with her clothes and jewelry, but I could tell that when it came to her engagement ring, she wanted something substantial. And I was right.

She was entranced by the three carat diamond. It gleamed as she rotated her hand slowly, biting her lip. There was a pleased glint in her eye.

I snagged her waist and pulled her in. "My rings look good on you, princess," I said. "But they'd look even better if you were naked."

She slid her hands up my chest and her red nails dug into me until I winced. Her teeth pinned her lower lip and her eyes bored into me through heavy lashes.

"May I please have a glass of champagne?" she said.

I poured two and joined her at the foot of the bed. She took one and swept her hair to the side to present the zipper of her dress to me. I tossed back my glass and set it aside, more interested in seeing her in her lingerie than anything else.

She kept still for me as I slid her zipper down and pulled the straps of her dress over her shoulders. She wriggled her hips and it dropped to the floor.

My cock went rock hard. I'd underestimated what seeing her in bridal lingerie would do to me and all my hope of lasting more than a minute vanished.

I took her half-empty glass and set it aside. My hands were on my shirt, tearing down the buttons, and on my belt. My clothes hit the ground and I picked her up in my arms.

A soft gasp escaped her mouth. Her pupils were wide and her lower lip was swollen from being bitten. I laid her on her back and knelt between her spread thighs to tug her panties to the side.

My wife's pussy—my God, it felt so good to say that—was the prettiest thing I'd ever laid eyes on. Naked and glistening with sweet arousal. Head empty and cock throbbing, I bent and buried my face in it.

She tasted like my woman. Sweet like ripe oranges, salty like her sweat, and musky like pure arousal. Her hips worked and her fingers tangled in my hair. Time felt like it was slipping through my fingers like water and I didn't care. I was in heaven.

She came hard and there was no shame afterwards. Just wide, sparkling eyes and panting breaths. I made her come again, this time around my fingers, and one more time with her soft, little pussy on my face and her thighs tight on either side of my head.

I would have kept going if she'd let me. Finally, panting and soaked, she pushed my head up and pulled me up to kiss my mouth. Our tongues collided and I drew back just enough to spit past her lips. Letting her taste how sweet she was.

"Little drunk, princess?" I asked.

She giggled. "Let's announce our marriage."

My brow shot up. "How do you propose we do that?"

Her lips curved and she wriggled beneath me until I slid aside. "Give me my phone. Do you still have it?"

"I was just about to give it back to you," I said, leaning over and pulling it from the suitcase. I dropped it in her lap. "We'll talk about privacy and boundaries to keep us both safe later. Don't post anything until then."

She bit her lip. What was that mischievous little glint in her eyes? She snatched the phone and swiped the screen.

"Oh my God, I have literally millions of notifications," she groaned. "And my email is flooded."

"Who cares?" I said, falling back on the pillows. "Tonight is about us."

She took her champagne off the bedside table and drained it. "Take a picture with me," she demanded.

I snatched her around the waist, pulling her back against my chest. She tilted her camera up and smiled the most beautiful, drunk, euphoric smile. I slid my arms and the comforter up to cover her breasts fully. My hand rested at the base of her throat. I buried my face in her neck and I heard her take the photo. Our first photograph together, as a married couple.

"God, you smell so fucking good," I murmured.

She wriggled. "I'm going to post it," she teased.

She turned the camera around, flashing what was clearly a post-sex photo of us. In the background was the rumpled bed, the hotel window, and the city skyline.

Wait a minute.

That was clearly a drunk picture, we both looked like we'd been dancing and drinking for hours. We looked reckless and we glowed like we'd just fucked each other's brains out.

"Post it," I said.

Her brow crooked. "Huh?"

"Post it, it's perfect," I said. "Caption it with something like...something about how you made a mistake, but it's a good mistake."

She bit her lip, sobering a little. "Really? It's kind of racy."

"I know," I said. "It's a mistake to post it, but you need to."

"Oh, it's evidence," she said. "Okay, okay, let me see."

Her fingers flew over the keyboard. There was a faint bloop and she flipped the phone around with a triumphant grin on her face. Almost at once, her notifications turned red. My eyes darted down to the caption and I couldn't keep back a snort of laughter.

Just met and just married!!!

Comments started streaming in and she flipped it around. I peered over her shoulder.

Oh my God. Is that Duran Esposito??

Isn't he kind of a slut?

Damn, those forearms though.

She burst out laughing and clapped her hand over her mouth. I snatched her phone and tossed it aside. She wriggled after it and I snatched her around the waist and tossed her playfully against the pillows. Her mouth met mine in a slow kiss that left us both breathless.

"I'd like to finish what I started," I murmured, dipping my hips to drag my erection over her pussy. "Time to make you mine."

CHAPTER TWENTY-NINE

IRIS

I felt like shit when I finally cracked an eye open. The room was far too bright, but I could smell waffles. I was just hungover enough that I wanted to stay huddled under the covers, but not enough that I wasn't starving. I poked my head out.

He walked out of the bathroom, already dressed. I could tell he'd showered because his slicked hair was wet.

My heart pattered, despite my headache.

I lifted my hand, the giant diamond glittering on my finger. For the first time in my life, I felt free and secure.

"Having regrets?" he asked, brow raised.

"Nope," I said, flipping my hand and wriggling my fingers so my ring caught the light. "Are you?"

"Never."

He knelt on the bed and kissed my forehead. My brain went still and I slid my arms around his neck and buried my face against his chest. He held me for a long time before pulling back.

"How're you feeling?"

"Honestly, not as bad as I anticipated. Breakfast and Tylenol will fix me up."

"I ordered you both," he said, gesturing to the other side of the room. By the door was a dining cart with a silver cover. My stomach rumbled as the smell of coffee hit my nose.

"You're the best," I said, kissing him and snuggling back against the pillows.

"Huh, not so long ago I was the worst."

"Well, you were back then. I changed my mind."

"A few dozen orgasms will do that to you."

I rolled my eyes. "You're so full of yourself."

"No, I'm just a fool for you, princess," he said, his eyes going soft.

I rolled my eyes. He was so smooth and he knew it. I couldn't stop blushing as he brought me a plate and a cup of hot coffee with cream and sugar. I took the Tylenol and washed it down with some ice water before digging into waffles and eggs. He lingered by the window, distracted by something on his phone.

"Is everything okay?" I asked.

He looked up. "Better," he said. "We're in the clear."

"Wait…really? Just like that?"

He shrugged, a look of disbelief on his face. "Just like that. You saved our asses with the picture you posted online last night. The boss thought it was funny."

My jaw went slack. "He thought it was…funny?"

"Apparently he was pissed at first, but after Lucien showed him the photo, he laughed," Duran said. "He said as long as Lucien goes through with his marriage, he's willing to let what we did slide."

I chewed my lip. "I feel bad for Lucien."

Duran's brows creased. "Don't."

"Why?"

My husband set aside his phone and sank down on the edge of the bed. "Lucien is an ice cold motherfucker, he's hard to read, but I know him. He's been down bad for Olivia from the first day he went to her father's house to meet her. I'm not sure he realizes how far gone he is yet."

I swallowed. "I hope he's nice to her. She seems really hurt."

"She is," Duran said quietly. "She's fucked up, just like the rest of us."

Warmth crept through me as I realized that despite how filthy we'd gotten last night, I'd opened my eyes without a trace of shame. I knew I wasn't completely cured, but he'd gotten through to me when nothing else could.

"Thank you," I whispered.

He leaned in. "For what?"

"For loving me."

His hand slid up my bare leg and squeezed it. "I should be thanking you. I never expected it to happen...especially after how royally I fucked up with you."

"Why not?" I frowned. "You're gorgeous."

He laughed and then sobered. "I think I've always been scared of commitment because...I never wanted to be my father, but with you, it's always been about forever. I never want to hurt you, Iris. I swear I'll love you the way you deserve."

My eyes filled with tears and I blinked hard to keep them from falling.

"You're nothing like him," I whispered.

He swallowed. "You make me happy and that's worth everything to me. Anything you want is yours, just be my wife forever because I can't fathom what life looks like without you." There was a catch in his throat.

"Are you okay?" I asked.

He sighed. "We should go face the music."

"I thought Romano was going to let it slide."

"He is, but your parents are going to want to murder me," he said. "I kidnapped their only daughter, popped her cherry, and married her while drunk. I don't think your father is going to like me much."

I chewed my lip, my stomach turning. I'd been so preoccupied with trying to get Romano's approval that I'd forgotten about my parents. Guilt rippled through me and I felt like the worst daughter in the world.

"Yeah," I said hoarsely. "We should probably go home and figure that out."

We finished our breakfast in silence. The atmosphere had gone from celebratory to tenuous. We packed our things and Duran drove us to the airstrip outside town where the private plane waited.

"You okay, princess?" he asked, that protective hand on my spine.

"Yeah, just a little nervous," I admitted. "You have my back?"

He kissed the nape of my neck and warmth prickled all the way down to the bottoms of my feet.

"I've always got your back," he said. "Always, without question."

That stopped me in my tracks. I'd never had anyone in my life who was always and unequivocally on my side. My parents, despite their good traits, were often my advisories. They both preferred rules and proper behavior over who I was and what I wanted.

Maybe that was why I'd fallen for Duran. He'd only ever wanted me to be myself. Even when I was grumpy and snarky with him, even when we were fighting. He'd never once asked me to change the things that made me Iris.

He walked past me, oblivious to the realization crashing down around me. I stood with my mouth hanging open. Watching him pack our bags in the luggage rack.

The tumultuous beginning of our relationship had made me brutally honest. And yet, he stayed.

He didn't just stay, he made a point of keeping me.

I swallowed, my throat dry. My feet felt heavy, but the rest of my body was light as a feather. He noticed I was frozen in place and he looked up, frowning.

"Are you okay?"

I nodded, offering a watery smile. "You really love me," I whispered.

"Of course," he said. "I said I did, so I do."

"Am I the first person you've been in love with?"

He nodded, not hesitating for a second. "The first and last. It's just you and me, princess, until the end of the road."

I laughed, tearing up. He was impulsive, and a little wild, but he was apologetically honest and I loved that. He saw my tears and he pulled me into his chest and kissed the top of my head.

"Why do you think you're so unlovable?" he murmured.

"I don't, it's not that," I sniffled. "Love has always come with conditions and I can't wrap my head around getting it for free."

"Fuck, do I understand that." He stroked my back. "I think I always knew it was you. Some part of me lit up when I saw you for the first time and it never stopped burning. I don't give a fuck what your parents say or what anyone else says. You've always been mine."

I wiped my eyes and he kissed my mouth.

"Let's go home," he said.

CHAPTER THIRTY

DURAN

I was in a suit and tie and she wore a demure, black dress that covered her upper arms and reached her knees. She looked stunning, her hair tucked into a neat bun, but she didn't look like herself.

We pulled up to the curb outside a row house in one of the city suburbs. Her father was a bookkeeper, so he was no millionaire, but he had a comfortable house in a nice neighborhood. I took off my sunglasses and glanced it over, stalling for time.

"We should probably go in," she whispered.

I cupped her chin and bent to kiss her mouth. When I pulled back, she offered me a weak smile.

"Your parents better behave themselves," I said. "If anyone speaks disrespectfully to you, I'll put a stop to that and escort you out. Nobody fucks with my girl, not even your parents."

"They aren't really like that," she said. "My mom is going to cry and talk about how she failed as a mother and how could I do this to her and so on. My dad...I'm not sure. He won't yell at me, but he might yell at you."

"I can take it, it's you I'm worried about," I said.

"I'll be okay," she said, smiling shakily.

She was terrified. Anger bubbled in my chest, but I concealed it and circled the car to help her out. She clung to my hand, her palm sweaty, while we walked up the narrow path to the house. I slid my arm around her waist and hit the doorbell.

Her mother must have been on the other side of the door because she pulled it open instantly. She looked like an older version of Iris, but her face was pinched and her eyes sharp like an animal on high alert. When she saw us standing together, she huffed and stepped aside.

"Come in," she said.

"Hi, mom," Iris said weakly. "This is Duran."

"I know who it is, dear," she said, beckoning us into the hallway. "I'll go get your father. You can go into the kitchen. I made tea and scones."

The house was dark and smelled faintly musty, but otherwise pleasant. As we moved down the hall, I noticed there was a lot of religious artwork on the walls. Icons of saints and angels stared at me with flat eyes, dust gathered on their edges. There was a shelf right before the kitchen door and on it was a statue and a heap of little drawstring bags.

I was about to ask about it, but we walked into the kitchen and her father stood by the sink. Waiting for us. His eyes fell on me and narrowed. He was a tall man with a thin face, easily twenty years older than her mother. He was wiry with age, but still in good shape.

"Duran Esposito," he said.

I held out my hand. "A pleasure to meet you, sir."

He looked down at my hand and his brow twitched. I dropped my arm.

"Where is your mother?" he asked, turning to Iris.

"She said she was getting you," Iris faltered.

"She's been very stressed about this whole thing," he said pointedly. "She's probably in the bathroom crying."

Iris's lip quivered. Instinctively, I put my hand on her lower back. "Sorry, dad, I just didn't have my phone. There was a lot going on," she said. "I would have called if I could."

Her father's eyes swiveled to me and his mouth thinned.

"I know you didn't have your phone," he said. "Duran contacted me with it after he compromised you."

"Compromised?" I echoed.

"Yes," he said. "And now you've embarrassed my daughter."

"Embarrassed?" I struggled to follow his train of thought.

"My daughter is a good girl, she doesn't do things like that. I know you must have had a hold on her—I know what kind of man you are."

"With all due respect, sir, she's my wife before she's your daughter."

I could tell that pissed him off. He took a second, his fists balled at his sides. The door swung open and her mother walked in, going to the stove to bang the kettle down. She turned around and crossed her arms over her chest.

"This is really embarrassing for us, Iris," she said.

Her eyes filled with tears. "Sorry, mom," she whispered.

"Don't shame my wife," I said firmly. "She's twenty-one years old and she made her own choice. No one cares what she does with her body or who she marries."

"We do," her mother snapped.

"She's not you," I said. "We didn't do anything wrong. We fell in love and got married. You should be happy for her."

Her mother opened her mouth to speak, but her father cut her off. His eyes were glued on Iris, who was miserably twisting her wedding band in circles.

"Are you happy, Iris?" he said.

She nodded, lifting her tear-filled eyes. "Duran is very kind to me. I know things didn't go down the way you wanted, but we're both really happy."

I wasn't sure what I'd expected to happen, but it wasn't for her mother to burst into sobs and throw herself on her daughter. Iris was so shocked she just stood there with her arms out. Her mother was mumbling unintelligibly into her shoulder, patting her back. Slowly, Iris's arms closed around her mother. An awkward silence fell.

"Mom...are you okay?"

Her mother pulled back, wiping her face. "Yes, I'm sorry. I don't like it, Iris, I'm not going to lie to you. I wish you'd done it differently. But I'm so glad you're safe."

I glanced at her father, but his eyes were lowered.

"Sorry, mom, I didn't mean to embarrass you," she said.

"I'm supposed to be mad at you," her mother said, stepping back. "Everyone at church keeps telling me how embarrassing this is for our family. But...I'm so glad you're back. I don't support you staying with him before marriage though."

"I know," Iris sighed.

Her father cleared his throat. The sound echoed and we all went quiet. He turned to face me, his hands in his pockets.

"Are you going to take care of my daughter?"

"Yes, sir," I said.

"And any children you have with her?"

"Yes."

He took a step closer, brows raised. "I know your reputation, Duran. If I hear that you stepped out on her, I'll make you pay. I don't care who your family is. She's my baby."

The emotion in his voice surprised me. I could tell by Iris' face that it shocked her too.

"I won't," I said. "I'll treat your daughter like a princess."

"Good," he said. "Because if you don't...." He drew a line over his throat.

"Dad!" Iris gasped.

"He's right," her mother chimed in. "I can take the embarrassment of everyone knowing my daughter was living in sin, but I can't take hearing that you hurt her. So you'd better walk it straight and narrow."

I understood what kind of people they were now. They loved her, but they clearly had no idea what damage they'd caused and I wasn't about to tell them. Shaming her felt like love to them because they saw it as protection. As doing what was best for her.

I knew better. I'd witnessed her tears and her shame. But those things were private. I doubted she would ever want to bring them up to her parents.

"Your daughter will always be safe and treated well," I said firmly. "But I don't want to hear anyone making her feel ashamed for her choices. She didn't get married the way you wanted her to and that's fine. She's not you."

"It's okay," said Iris quickly.

"No, it's not."

"I understand," her father cut in. "That's fine. You're protecting her and that's fine. Let's...let's have tea."

I was pissed, but Iris sent me a pleading stare, so I backed off. The rest of the visit was incredibly awkward. Her parents asked where we would live and we didn't know yet. I could see the disapproval in her father's eyes that I didn't have a house set up for her. I couldn't explain myself to him, he didn't know why we'd had to get married so fast.

It was an hour and a half later when Iris hugged her parents goodbye and promised to come by to get her things once we were settled. Her father shook my hand and I felt the threat behind his grip.

That was fine. As long as he kept his distance, he was allowed to not like me.

We drove away and Iris let out an enormous sigh.

"That wasn't awful," she whispered. "My parents do love me, but they just can't help themselves."

"They did better than I anticipated."

"I don't think they're ever going to change. Not really."

I shook my head. "I think we should visit them if you want to, but I don't want them offering their opinions on how you live."

"Boundaries," she said quietly. "I'm not good at those, but I need to start getting better."

She leaned back against the seat. I could tell an enormous weight had lifted off her shoulders. I slid my hand up her thigh and gripped her smooth skin.

"I love you," I said.

She smiled, that gorgeous smile that had taken me out the first time I saw it.

"I love you too."

CHAPTER THIRTY-ONE

IRIS

A Month Later

I padded down the hallway of the Aqua Resort & Spa, feeling incredibly refreshed after my facial and message. It was early fall and the resort was less crowded than before. Everything felt more peaceful than the first time I'd visited.

Perhaps because Duran was here with me.

We'd taken a couple weeks to get a townhouse at the edge of the city, a few minutes from Lucien's home. We spent a lot of time there because Duran was working on something with his brother that he never talked about. I'd learned from Olivia that there were some things we shouldn't ask about. Not because we were women, but because it was better not to know.

Ignorance was bliss.

After we'd moved our things in, Duran had surprised me with a two week honeymoon in Miami at the place where we'd met.

"So is getting kidnapped part of the trip?" I asked. "Or do I need to pay extra for that?"

"You'd like that," he said.

"I must have bought the VIP package last time," I said.

"I've got a VIP package for you," he said, spinning me around and pinning me to the counter so he could grind on my ass.

We fucked on the floor of our brand new kitchen, deliriously happy. I was always delirious now, there was no high better than the feeling of being a newlywed.

Every morning the sun shone, the birds sang, everyone was happy and polite. I had so much sex it hurt to sit down and he spent hours at night with his face between my thighs soothing me with his tongue.

He bought me a new wardrobe and took me to Miami the next day. For the first time in my life, I turned my brain off.

Being taken care of didn't come naturally to me, but it was my honeymoon. If I was going to let him spoil me, now was the time.

Every morning we had breakfast in bed and he ate me out and fucked me afterwards. We swam in the ocean until lunch where we ordered champagne and ate our fill of seafood. He bought me anything I wanted. If I wanted a massage, he handed over his credit card and let me do as I liked.

The entire time I was completely distracted. He was gorgeous and I was still in shock that he was my husband. He looked at me with those dark eyes and I was a mess, my panties wet and my heart thumping.

I felt my pulse quicken as I stopped outside our door. I'd forgotten my key card so I knocked lightly. He pulled it open, dressed in just his boxer briefs. I dragged my eyes down his torso, enjoying the sight of my husband. Hard muscles and burning dark eyes.

"Feeling good?" he asked, pulling me inside.

He pushed me against the back of the door and shoved his hips against my lower belly. I slid my hand down and under his waist band. My fingers wrapped around his warm, hard length. Enjoying the way he pulsed in my grip.

"Fuck me," he groaned.

I tossed my wallet aside and dropped my dressing gown. "Lie back."

He fell onto the bed lengthwise, pushing his boxer briefs down. His cock sprang out and I wasted no time straddling him. Our eyes locked and his lips parted, flashing his teeth.

"Come on, wife, sit on my cock," he said. "I want you to ride it till you come for me."

I was wet for him already. The thick head of his cock slid down my pussy and I sank onto it. Letting it fill me slowly until he bottomed out. God, he felt so good when he stretched me as much as I could take. I whimpered, rocking my hips to adjust to his size.

His eyes glittered. His hands slid up my thighs and gripped me hard.

"You've got a tight, little cunt. Show me what you can do with it," he breathed. "Show me how you fuck your husband like a good girl."

I shuddered, rocking. His cock moved inside me, hitting my G-spot as I shifted back and ground forward on him. His ridged stomach went hard and he groaned, his jaw clenched.

"Fuck—right there," he panted. "Just like that, princess."

He shifted up, taking me with him, and propped himself against the headboard. Our faces were inches apart. The air between us crackled and I bit my lip, stunned by how sexy he looked. Buried in me with sweat trickling down his chest.

His hand gripped the back of my neck and pulled me in. He kissed me hard, his tongue swiping mine. His other hand slid up and cupped my breast, circling my bare nipple with his thumb. Pleasure shot down and my inner muscles clenched.

"Oh fuck," he said, his lids flickering. "God, your pretty, little pussy grips me so well, baby. You keep riding it, just like that. You're doing so well, you're being such a good girl."

My head fell back. My brain went empty of anything but the glowing realization that I *was* a good girl. *His* good girl. My hips worked and his hand left my neck and slid down to find my clit. Pleasure burst under his touch and my eyes flew open.

"Oh my God," I gasped.

Our eyes locked.

"Come for me," he urged from between his teeth. "Give me all your pretty orgasms, you little slut."

My nails dug into his biceps. My hips locked. My nipples were so hard they ached. There was something about coming on his cock that felt better than almost anything. My orgasms were always so intense they left me breathless and weak.

This was no different. Pleasure tore through my body and I couldn't do anything but shake wordlessly on his cock. Wetness slipped out of me and I heard it between us as he fucked up into me. His eyes burned, soaking in my whimpers.

"You want my cum?" he panted.

I whined, gripping him.

"I'll take that as a yes," he groaned, gripping my hips and slamming me down on his length one last time.

His eyes shut, his jaw went tight. I felt him twitch as he emptied himself inside me. His teeth flashed and the most satisfying groan worked its way up his throat. My orgasm ebbed until it was gone and I sagged against his chest.

Completely spent.

He stroked my hair. "You alright?"

"More than alright," I said. "And I don't feel ashamed at all. You were right."

"About what?"

I sighed. "Sex doesn't have to be so complicated. I love you and it feels good to fuck and that's enough for me."

He kissed the top of my head. "It's more than enough for me."

We fell asleep, tangled up together. A few hours later, we both woke with a start and realized it was almost dinner time. He carried me to the shower and we cleaned up and got ready.

I stepped out of the bathroom, my makeup and hair done. In one of those skimpy dresses he liked putting his hands under. He looked amazing, his dark hair and short beard almost the same shade as his tailored suit. He wore the silver watch on his wrist that I'd bought him as a wedding gift.

"Fuck me, you're sexy," he said. "Give me a twirl, princess."

Blushing, I obeyed. My dress was short with a thin skirt that floated up in an elegant swirl. It had a classy top with a deep V that ended past my breasts. Hanging between them was a diamond necklace he'd bought to match my ring and bracelet.

"No panties?" he asked.

"How'd you know?"

"When you twirled, I saw your bare ass and pussy," he said, grabbing me by the waist. His mouth brushed mine. "Not that I'm complaining. Just make sure no one else sees that cunt. Otherwise, I'll have to kill them and that'll be messy."

"Oh?"

He cocked his head, eyes flickering. "You have a jealous husband. Get over it."

"You like calling yourself that," I observed.

His hand slid over my ass, slipping under my skirt. His two fingers slid between my thighs and pushed up into me.

"I like saying it because it's true," he murmured against my neck. "I'm your husband and proud of it."

I wanted to have a snappy comeback, but it was so hard to even think with his fingers fucking up into my pussy. Working hard, the wet sound of them filling the room. Instead, I bit my lip to hold back the moan in my throat. He laughed and pulled them free, putting them to my lips.

"Lick them clean," he ordered.

Eyes locked, I opened my mouth. He pushed his wet fingers past my lips and my arousal spread over my tongue. Sweet and tasting of him from where he'd fucked me earlier.

"I'm rock hard, but we need to go have dinner," he groaned.

"You can wait," I said heartlessly.

Downstairs, he'd requested we have a dinner that looked out over the beach. The sun was set and glowing lights hung in lines over the patio. There was a bottle of champagne on ice by the table when we sat down. Duran ordered something in French to the waiter, who knew us by now and spoke both French and Italian. I made a mental note to ask about Italian classes when we got back to the city.

When we were settled and our food was on its way, I took a package from my purse and laid it on the table. Duran glanced down, brow crooking.

"What's this?"

I swallowed, suddenly shy. "It's something I had made for you."

He picked it up, frowning slightly as he pulled aside the tissue paper. Inside was a flat display box with a glass lid. He stared at it for a long moment.

"It's an empty box. Uh, thank you, princess," he said.

I smiled. "I was thinking…I noticed you don't wear your mother's medal anymore."

He shook his head, eyes clouding.

"I was thinking you might want a nice place to display it and keep it safe," I said, biting my lip. "You could put it in your office, on the shelf over your desk."

His throat bobbed and there was a long silence. I sat perfectly still, hoping I'd done the right thing.

"That's very sweet, Iris," he said with difficulty.

"I also really don't mind if you want to wear it," I said.

He shook his head, lifting the lid. Running his fingertips over the soft velvet. "I think I'm moving on. She wouldn't have wanted me to wear my grief around my neck."

He was opening up, letting me in. I held my breath, grateful for this fragile gift.

"It's okay too if you don't want to use the box," I said. "Or if you want to put it away. I don't want you to have to look at something that makes you sad."

He stared down at the box for a long time. Then he shut it and laid it aside.

"I don't feel sad, princess," he said. "I feel free."

If our food hadn't arrived right then, I probably would have cried my mascara down my cheeks. But determined not to ruin our meal, I pushed my feelings down and we ate and talked about happier things. It was our honeymoon after all.

I didn't tell him that I'd gone to the graveyard on one of those days when Duran was at the office with Lucien. I stopped at the florist and bought a dozen roses and drove to her grave by St. Mark's Chapel. Feeling a little foolish, I'd cleaned the grass and dust from her headstone and laid the flowers on the base in a vase.

I'd probably never tell Duran that I'd thanked her for giving me everything.

Or that I was sorry she wasn't here to see how happy he was.

But maybe someday I'd tell him that before I left, the thick cloud cover parted and sun shone through. That a light breeze moved the trees and rustled the roses on her headstone.

But he wasn't ready now. Healing took a long time and we'd only just started.

EPILOGUE

DURAN

A Few Months Later

"Can I ask you a really serious question?"

Lucien paused, flicking his eyes up. We stood at the edge of the river and it was cold as fuck. In the distance, the lights of the cargo ship carrying our guns moved, but not fast enough. I knew Iris was in our bed right now, all warm and sexy and probably naked. I was dying to get back.

"What?"

I cleared my throat. "Did you let me win at Monopoly?"

His jaw twitched. "Why? Who wants to know?"

"I do."

He sighed, leaning back. He put his cigarette up and breathed out, the smoke filling the air.

"Yes, I let you win," he said.

"Fuck you," I said.

He glanced over. "Does that actually bother you?"

I shrugged. "I guess not, I just thought I had one thing on you."

He inhaled and straightened. When he faced me fully, I detected a hint of vulnerability, somewhere beyond his ice cold front.

"You have so much on me," he said. "You have a wife who loves you and that counts for everything."

"Fuck, I didn't mean it like that," I said. "I was mostly joking."

"I know," he said.

There was a long silence, but I felt him internally struggling. Finally, he rubbed out his cigarette on the sole of his boot. He shoved his hands deep in his pockets.

"I'm proud of you," he said flatly. "Now, that's all your getting. So don't even start."

I kept my mouth shut, knowing he was done. But inside I glowed. I rocked on my heels and stared out at the silvery black water. Watching the ripples grow as the ship grew closer to the harbor.

It was past midnight when we finally unloaded the shipment and locked up the warehouses. Lucien dropped me off outside our townhouse. Some nights Iris stayed at the Esposito mansion because it helped Olivia feel more at ease. They'd grown a lot closer over the last several months. But tonight, she was asleep in our house and I was glad to have her all to myself.

I let myself in. The hall light was on, but the rest of the house was dark. I went through the kitchen and up the stairs to find our bedroom light still on. I frowned, knowing she usually went to bed around eleven.

She was sitting up in bed, wearing one of my t-shirts. Since she'd given up her social media accounts, she'd been working a part time job at a fashion magazine. She'd gotten the position on her own experience and she took it seriously, sometimes staying up late tapping away on her laptop.

I slipped into the bedroom and she looked up, offering that sweet smile I couldn't live without. I bent to kiss her and began getting undressed.

"Shouldn't you be sleeping, princess?" I asked. "It's a bit late for work."

She chewed her lip. Her hair was up in a sloppy bun on her head, little bits tickling her neck. My ring glittered on her finger. It all made the most perfect picture to come home to.

"I was looking over some wedding stuff for Olivia," she said. "Just last minute ribbons for the flowers."

"I thought they had a planner."

"They do, but I think Olivia is just...too timid to push back," she said. "So I told her I'd look at the ribbons and talk to the planner tomorrow."

"It's nice what you're doing for her," I said.

She chewed her lip, her brows furrowing. "She's really fucked up, Duran," she said. "I hope Lucien gets her some therapy because she really needs it."

I mulled this over as I finished undressing and showered quickly. When I returned, she'd taken her rings off and braided her hair down her back. She'd also taken my t-shirt off and her bare shoulders peeked up over the comforter.

I went hard and her eyes slid down my naked body and rested on my obvious arousal. Her brow arced.

"What's got you so hot and bothered?" she teased.

I knelt, shifting to my hands and knees and crawling over her. Her eyes widened, the blanket pulling down. Baring her soft breasts and flushed nipples. Her lips parted as I lowered myself to kiss her, parting her mouth and dipping my tongue in for a taste.

We both moaned. I had the comforter out from between us in seconds and her thighs apart. She whimpered and her ocean eyes went hazy, her hips lifting. Begging me silently to fill her tight, little pussy.

I spat into my hand and worked the wetness over her entrance. Our eyes locked as I reached down and we both shuddered as the head of my cock slipped over her entrance and inside just an inch.

Her soft inner muscles wrapped around my most sensitive point and my vision flashed.

"I want it," she panted.

"What do you want, princess?" I gripped my cock by the base and worked it in slow circles. Caressing the soft entrance of her sex as she pulsed, trying to pull me the rest of the way inside.

"I want all of you," she breathed.

I pulled out, letting her feel the emptiness. The little whine that spilled from her lips was so perfect.

"Beg for it properly," I ordered.

"Fuck you," she moaned, lashes fluttering.

"Beg and I'll do just that." I traced her opening with the dripping head of my cock. Slowly as she wriggled, trying to push up and onto my length.

She chewed her trembling lips.

"Please," she whispered. "Please fuck me like I'm your little slut."

My hips slammed into her, burying my cock deep in her wet pussy. Her arms shot around my body and her nails latched into the flesh on my back. My spine bent, the pain bringing my senses to life. Of their own accord, my hips began pumping. Taking her the way I craved.

"Oh, God," she gasped. "That...that's so fucking good."

I forced myself to slow, not willing to finish into her so soon. Still thrusting, I shifted back onto my heels and took her lower body with me. Her eyes rolled back in her head as I gripped both ankles tightly and brought her legs together, keeping her steady while I pumped.

Wetness stained the bed beneath us. I let my fingers drift down, feeling the place where we joined. The delicate muscles of her sex contracted around my cock and a deep hunger to feel her pleasure filled me.

"I want you to come on your husband's cock," I ordered.

Her lids fluttered. She'd finally moved past the point where shame joined us in our bed. Now it was just us and all the dirty, sweet things we did to each other between the sheets.

"Yes." The word was barely a whisper.

I slapped her thigh gently. "That's my girl," I praised.

She nodded and I shifted closer, angling my cock to hit her G-spot. With one hand on her ankle, I slid the other between us and found her clit. A shudder of need moved through me as her inner muscles tensed and worked my cock in slow pulses.

Her eyes rolled back and I couldn't bit back my smirk.

"Feel good, princess?"

She nodded hard, her pretty breasts heaving. I kept my hips pumping and my thumb moving over her slick clit with a steady rhythm. A shiver moved down her stomach and wetness spilled out around my cock.

Fuck, she was getting close.

Her fingers fisted the sheets and her cheeks went pink. I forced myself to keep thrusting gently, up against her G-spot, instead of burying my cock in her as deep as I could and spilling all my cum. No, that could wait until she was done.

I glanced down, taking in the sight of my cock stretching her perfect pussy open. Fuck me, she was so tight and I was using every inch of space. Our arousal was a thick slickness where our bodies met.

"Oh...Duran," she gasped.

Her thighs locked and for a second nothing happened. Then her hips began throbbing and her inner muscles exploded. Pumping me so hard my orgasm shot down my spine and I fell over her, coming so hard my vision flashed.

Her nails raked down my back.

I gathered her wrists and pinned them above her head. Then I fucked her so hard she screamed and I was glad we were at the townhouse tonight.

When I pulled from her, my cum and hers spilled out onto the bed. I rolled off her and ran my fingers through her sex. Gathering our arousal and lifting it to her lips.

"Taste what you do to me, princess," I panted.

She hesitated, unsure if she wanted to do something so dirty. But then her lips parted and she sucked my fingers into her mouth. Lapping them clean and moaning around them.

"You dirty, little thing," I marveled.

She smiled, shyly. "I like being that for you," she admitted.

I kissed her neck. "You did so good tonight," I praised. "You should be proud."

She smiled, hair wild and face flushed with satisfaction. "I am."

We cleaned up and she fell asleep right away. Curled up with her soft ass pushed against me. I stayed awake for a while, stroking down her arm and cradling the soft curves of her hip. Silently marveling that somehow the series of fuck ups I'd had over the last year had led to this woman in my bed.

I hadn't known what I was doing when I'd taken her from the resort. But every day I thanked myself for that stupid, impulsive decision.

Because it had brought me home.

I rolled over and she mumbled, cracking an eye. "Why are you still awake?"

"You were right," I sighed.

"About what?" She closed her eyes again, burrowing into the pillow.

"That motherfucker did let me win."

There was a short silence and her lids fluttered, her confused gaze fixing on me. "Are you talking about Monopoly right now?"

"Nope," I said, flipping back over and pulling her naked warm body against mine. "Never mind. Get some sleep, princess. I've got you."

THE END

If you enjoyed Iris & Duran's story, please leave a review!

Want to read Lucien & Olivia's story next? Captured Light, the first book in their trilogy and the second book of the Captured Standalones, can be found on Amazon KU and paperback.

OTHER BOOKS BY RAYA MORRIS EDWARDS
All on Amazon KU

THE WELSH KINGS TRILOGY
Paradise Descent, Book 1 in The Welsh Kings Trilogy
Prince of Ink & Scars, Book 2 in The Welsh Kings Trilogy (out April 2024)

KING OF ICE & STEEL TRILOGY READING ORDER
Captured Light
Devil I Need
Ice & Steel

CAPTURED STANDALONES READING ORDER
Captured Desire - Iris & Duran
Captured Light - Lucien & Olivia
Captured Solace - Viktor & Sienna
Captured Fantasy - Cosimo & Lorenza
Captured Ecstasy - Peregrine & Rosalia

Sovereign: A Dark BDSM Cowboy Romance (out January 9th 2024)

Printed in Great Britain
by Amazon